If No One Speaks

A Shor'

Sa

abuddhapress@yahoo.com

Alien Buddha Press 2022

®™©

Sam Szanto 2022

ISBN: 9798839376687

The stories in this collection are works of fiction. Any similarities to actual people, places, or events, unless deliberately expressed otherwise by the author are completely coincidental.

This book is dedicated to my parents,

Clare and Gregory; my brother, Dominic;

my children, Rufus and Iris;

and my husband, Martin.

Table of Contents

If No One Speaks	Page 1
Quiet Love	Page 18
125	Page 27
Letting Go	Page 35
The Thought of Death Sits Easy on the Man	Page 40
Mikey	Page 51
John	Page 63
A Good Boy	Page 71
The Yellow Circle	Page 82
My Sister the Murderer	Page 93
Palimpsest	Page 116
Making Memories	Page 128
Someone Just Like Me	Page 140
If I Tell You My Name, Will You Tell Me What It Tastes Of?	Page 149
The Stranger in my Living Room	Page 157
Phil in Real Life	Page 160
Well, we are in Spain	Page 165
Don't Refuse Me	Page 173
The Noises	Page 180
First Love	Page 192
Everyone Loved Romy	Page 216
Apple Crumble Baked by a Ghost	Page 237
Inaccrochable	Page 256
The Cleaner	Page 273
The Second Therapy Session	Page 277
They Sang	Page 282

If No One Speaks

When they threw my kitten into the furnace, I thought: how in God's name can I survive this? But what else can I do? Sometimes I think of slitting my wrists, but picture Masha's face when she hears she will never see her mother again. Those words would be knives dragged over her skin for the rest of her life. I will survive but, I tell you, this is hell.

'Welcome to hell' was how Natalya had been greeted on her first day at IP-15 Penitentiary in Moravia. It was a freezing hell; Dante's seventh circle, reserved for violent criminals. This included those who ran and worked in the prison, as well as the inmates.

Natalya was in the fourth week of her sentence. It still felt like hell. The accommodation ('the barracks', the prisoners called it) was dreadful: thirty women to each room, a toilet that couldn't be used because there was no central sewage system; in the night, they went to an outside one. The lack of rest-time was inhumane: they got to bed at half-past one, rose at six. The bathrooms were foul: special poles were used to knock on the doors so the rats would scatter. The food was disgusting: often an unfathomable grey mass.

The work was the worst. Natalya made clothing, using a sweat machine. Much of the clothes allegedly went to the family of the prison director, Officer

Krushkev, and his business associates. The job involved cutting the fabric into exactly the right size, ninety cuts made by a saw on a chalk line: if one was not on the line, all cuts were ruined. Natalya had no experience in such work, and no training was provided. She was a writer, her fingers used to tapping keys. But when she asked if she could have a job in the prison library instead, the response was laughter.

The women worked in a silence pregnant with nerves and boredom. Every so often there was a scream, as a rodent ran over a foot, and the guards chastised the noise-maker. Natalya hoarded words under her tongue. Every day she disgorged some in a letter to her husband Vladimir. One day, she planned to write a news story about life in the prison. *Novaya Gazeta* may be interested. A book deal could follow. Natalya was not an investigative journalist, she wrote for the literary magazine *Nash Sovremennik,* but her dream was to be like Elena Milashina, the prominent journalist and human rights defender who had won accolades for her extraordinary activism. In this place, dreams were necessary.

'Stop dreaming, go faster,' one of the guards shouted at her. 'You want to stand outside all night? That's what will happen if you don't make your quota.'

In a non-prison working environment, this way of speaking would be cause for complaint. But there was no worker's union Natalya could have gone to here. No-one running one would allow a director to get away with workers doing sixteen-and-a-half-hour days with one day off every eight weeks. Half of this was 'voluntary overtime'. Waivers were signed, stipulating that the prisoner would work after hours, including weekends, 'of her own volition'. Compulsory voluntary labour. As Natalya had dragged the pen across the page, scraping out her signature, she bit her tongue.

'Tell me you don't agree with how we work and live,' she said to the women on her table at lunch time. 'There must be something we can do.'

But there were only shrugs and shakes of the head.

Natalya did not want to be the sole dissenter, she wasn't stupid. But she was willing to lead a complaint. She had visions of the women rising up, rebelling. *The Shawshank Redemption* had taken five years to reach Russia, but it had. She watched the DVD five times, for every year she hadn't been able to see it.

A prison rebellion in IP-15 was unlikely. A successful one was even more unlikely. Women did protest, but many felt it to be futile; they were rarely listened to in prison. Although it was a woman's penitentiary, many of the guards were men. Most of them, when performing punishments such as handcuffing women to beds for hours, or beating whole groups of workers with clubs, ankle boots and bars if one person failed to miss a production target, as well as threatening to take away the right to bathe and wash their clothes, of having visitors and letters, did it with no rage or anger on their faces. Brutality was apparently normal and necessary to them. The more frightened the women: the more silent they were. The more silent, the more the light slipped out of them.

Natalya believed in the illuminating and transformative power of speech. In her first days in prison, she asked women for their stories whenever she had a chance. She whispered enquiries in the queues for toilets and showers, at exercise time, during meals. She imagined she was interviewing. Some women refused to tell her anything; some merely told her the years of their sentences, as if that defined them; as if they were the courts' judgements. Natalya became aware that although they all wore the same dark-green dresses and white headscarves, and followed the same rules, the connection ended there.

'You need to do what you are told in here, girl,' Yulia, who slept on the bunk above Natalya, and had her coveted job in the prison library, said. She took another mouthful of grey mush and continued: 'You want to get out of here, see your daughter? Do anything to stress out the fucks here, you can forget about parole. And worse. Just keep quiet.'

Natalya thought of the poem, 'The Balloon of the Mind' by Yeats, which she had studied on her Russian and Comparative Literature degree: '… do what you're bid / Bring the balloon of the mind / That bellies and drags in the wind / Into its narrow shed.' She couldn't drag her balloon-mind into the barracks; it slipped from her hands and rose into the sky.

'Okay, so when we get out of here, then we say something,' Natalya said. 'Then, they can be taken down.'

'Oh, they can be taken down? How many gangster films have you seen?' mocked 'Knitting Irina', so-called because she knitted items for the prisoners for small amounts of cash. The consensus was that Irina was scarred, physically and mentally, by twenty years in prison. When she walked, her body swayed and nodded. When she slept, in the bunk next to Natalya and Yulia, she screamed.

'Even Tolokonnikova didn't manage to change anything,' Yulia stated.

Nadezhda Tolokonnikova, from Pussy Riot, had been incarcerated in Moravia six years before. She had written an open letter condemning the penal system and prison life. People read it; journalists wrote about it, Pussy Riot's international fame and Tolokonnikova's good looks selling and spreading the story. A widespread investigation into injustices in the system had been launched. But had anything changed? It hadn't, but Natalya believed it had knocked a few bricks off the wall of oppression; had weakened it.

'I have to believe things will change,' she said. 'They won't if we accept the status quo.'

Yulia dragged her pale hands through her tangled hair. 'You want to be listened to? So tell us your story. You've asked all of us: your turn.'

Natalya took a breath and began. She had been walking Masha home from after-school club. It was a woundingly cold winter day, dark early, few people around. The only sound was the crunching of their feet through thick snow and Masha's excited chatter, which Natalya had tuned out of in a consideration of what to make for dinner. Later she regretted that, the not-listening to her daughter, when it was their last moment of normality. Suddenly, a man sprang from behind a car, wielding a knife. 'Give me your bag,' he shouted. Masha screamed. Without thinking, Natalya grabbed the knife. There was a tussle, the knife was in her hands, and then it was not. Her hands, her whole body, were shaking. The man was on the floor, a shocking amount of blood around him, the knife jammed in his chest. There was more blood on Natalya's skin and clothes. Masha had stopped screaming. She was staring at her mother, the rainbows of her eyebrows raised. 'Mama?' she asked, again and again, like a stuck piece of music. Natalya's mouth was a torn-apart nest. She stared at the knife, the man, the blood. People spilled out of houses and shops, wailing angels arrived, the blue of the sirens bright on the snow. Masha was taken to her father's office; Natalya to the police station. She had to tell her story, over and over, the words soaked with sorrow.

The justice system flowed like a contagion, like the blood that had spilled out of the man's body. He was nineteen, a known thief with a record of petty crime. His name was Aleksandr Ivashov. Natalya couldn't stop thinking of Alexandr being named; of what an important task it was to bestow a name, something carried through life and engraved on stone with death. Alexandr was the name of the poet, Pushkin, whose 'Drowned Man' described the 'awful chaos / All night through stirred in his brain' when a father ignored the drowned man on the beach shown to him by his children. Awful chaos had stirred in Natalya's mind from the second the knife was in her hands, and had not left her. She could barely speak to family and friends from the day of Alexandr's death to the day of her sentencing. Vladimir found her a lawyer, a man. The lawyer spoke passionately of Natalya acting in self-defence; he spoke of her previous good character; he spoke of her young child who needed her. When Natalya talked, words were unstable in her mouth, she stammered when she answered questions. The mostly male jury found her guilty of murder that exceeded reasonable levels of self-defence; she was sentenced to two years in prison. There was a write-up in the local paper; it was not a big enough story for the nationals.

Yulia and Irina nodded as Natalya clawed out the tale. So unique to her, so all-consuming, the story was no more or less interesting to them than anyone else's. It was clouds moving across the sky; to Natalya, it was the sky.

That evening Natalya wrote, as usual, to Vladimir. Since meeting at university, aged eighteen, they had rarely stopped talking and listening to each other. In their year apart, when Natalya worked for a paper in Spain, they wrote and spoke on the phone every day. Since Masha was born, much of their talk had been about her. Now Vlad was at home with their daughter, and Natalya was here. Sometimes she wondered if he was horrified by her crime. He had not condemned her as some of her friends had; as his parents had. Although he was obviously shocked by what she had done, he had been supportive, his face desperately sad when she was sentenced. She knew he suffered too, suddenly being a single parent, facing the local gossip about his murderess wife. Whatever his pain, he would still write to her, she was sure. The letters were one of the few things that made prison bearable. His to her; hers to him. She imagined that knowing what it was like here might motivate Vlad to speak up for her, maybe to write a letter about the way women were treated in the State prisons. Perhaps he could, to paraphrase Marina Tsvetaeva, take the droplets from the fountain, and the sparks from the rocket of her words, and elicit change from them. When she made the most of the lurid details of her life it was to tacitly, passively, inspire this.

Lev, my lion, I miss you so much, Natalya wrote. *I am exhausted. I thought that would be the case in prison, but imagined becoming used to it. After six weeks, nothing has changed except that it is colder, the radiators having stopped working. The noise, even in the depths of night, is unimaginable: snores, grunts, cries, screams, masturbations. Time is silent, though, as my watch was stolen. When the bell stabs the air in the morning, I often feel I have just slipped into sleep. I'm so tired the concrete wobbles as I walk across the yard, under a sky groaning with clouds, from the barracks. The memory of our soft double bed keeps me going. Your warm body beside mine, Masha climbing in beside us, snuggling against me, all three of us dreaming together. Peace. Quiet.*

I have sent you a watch. I wish I could send you some peace at night, Koshechka, my kitten. It is not quiet here, but quieter than where you are I guess. Masha does climb in beside me every night, and she is not silent. She screams and cries, wets the bed. Masha and I are seeing a psychiatrist together. She is fearful, he says, that she will not have you back. Traumatised, too, because of what she witnessed. I'm sorry. I do not know if I should tell you this, I don't like to upset you when everything is so difficult. But I know you don't like things to be withheld from you. You like things to be spoken about.

My poor Masha, Natalya wrote feverishly. *My varobushek. I can't bear to think of her suffering. Does the psychiatrist think she will ever get over it? Give her a thousand hugs from me, hold her whenever you can, promise me. Help her face to light open like a sunflower, as it used to. Tell her no-one will hurt her. Tell her I love her, over and over, and then again. The mightiest word is love.*

Natalya was distraught that she had not considered how scarred Masha would be. Had she become so obsessed with her own situation, her own feelings, that she had neglected her only child's? Children were resilient, her mother always said, and Natalya had tried to believe this. But how many five-year-olds had seen someone die in front of them; their mother taken away by the police? How could Masha talk about that in school? Was she worried that a man would jump out from behind a car every time she crunched through the snow? Was she worried about her mother's safety, in a place she had never been, far from her home? Did she dream of screams, of red blood and blue light on white snow? Natalya had those dreams, in her rare moments of sleep. Then she lay awake and thought about whether she could have behaved differently. Aleksandr had behaved as he had because he was desperate, she had found out in court: the product of neglect, of a prostitute mother barely at home. Natalya had behaved thoughtlessly, instinctively. Her lawyer said she had been protecting her little girl, but if she had handed over the bag would Alexandr not have gone on his way? Would Natalya have stabbed him even if she had been alone? Would Masha forgive her? So many fears, and she could not speak of any of them in prison.

They were ruled by fear in IP-15, a place meant to keep them safe and to keep the world safe from them. Certainly, Natalya was not safe: no-one was. She had not been beaten by the guards herself but heard stories of those who had been. They lopped branches off the silver birches that grew around the prison and used them to hit the prisoners. Women were sometimes made to walk through the corridors bent over like commas, to show their disgrace. Guards also regularly asked for sexual favours, in exchange for contraband such as vodka. An annual beauty pageant was organised, the winner rewarded with blini. Any woman refusing to take part was beaten on the legs and soles of their feet. Or, sometimes, the violence was mental: women set against women, fights ensuing. Natalya recorded details of the brutality in her letters. When she was free, she would use them for her news article. She knew this was dangerous, but refused to silence herself.

Yesterday in the sweat room, a woman made a mistake. The saw ran over her finger and it was cut off. She went to hospital and was back on her machine today. Of course, she couldn't go as fast as before. The guard said, 'That means everyone else must work for an hour longer to make up for your laziness.' After we left, the woman was spat at by a co-worker. Thank God, I have my day off from work today, but what can I do once this letter is finished? There is little to do here but wait, and try to stay sane. Perhaps one day you will be able to visit, when it is Masha's school holiday. How could have they sent me two thousand miles from my family?

After writing to Vlad, Natalya penned a short and light-hearted note to Masha. She tried very hard to say the right things, the most loving things, struggling to find the words that would build a shield around Masha's pain. After the letter was finished, she lay exhausted on her bed. As she was drifting off to sleep, she heard a sound. A ginger cat had slunk in and was meowing. The cat's tummy was swollen and distended. Her meows were startlingly loud, and she was staring at Natalya in an angrily beseeching manner. Natalya had never had a cat, was not a cat person, but she put out a hand to it. The animal sniffed it then jumped onto the bed beside her. Its fur was mangy and threadworn, but stroking it felt wonderful. They slept together, and Natalya did not have a bad dream.

The next day, at exercise-time in the yard, the cat was on the wall. Watching. Slowly, Natalya moved closer and put out a tentative hand. The cat lurched to her feet, unsteady because of her enormous belly. With her rough tongue, she licked Natalya's wrist. Pleasure climbed inside her as if she were a window.

As I was stroking the cat, I felt a bang on my head. The guard had hit me. He said I was breaking a rule and would be punished. I thought being hit was my punishment, but I was deprived of dinner. I'm sorry if I sound self-absorbed. I know you have your pain, and Masha has hers. Mine is no worse.

A week later, the cat was on Natalya's bed when she came in at night-time. She had given birth. Ten kittens were snuffling and mewling, blind faces screwed up. The cat cleaned one after another and the babies snuggled into her body. The prisoners crowded around and cooed. Voices usually sharp as knives became soft as fur, spiky words became smooth.

I stayed awake all night, making sure the cat – I call her Petra – and the kittens were alright. In the morning, Yulia got a cardboard box from the library and we hid them under the bed. I did not expect them to be there when we came back that night, but they were, all sleeping. The kittens are ginger and white, except for one black and white one. I call the black and white one Manya, after Mother. I whisper her name to her like a love song. She lets me hold her for as long as I like. Manya is the best thing to have happened since I was sentenced; now I just have to protect her, and her brothers and sisters. Somehow.

While giving birth, Petra had bled on Natalya's bed. This was bad, for every week when the women took the sheets to the prison launderette they were inspected for soiling. Those who stained them were punished. Natalya blamed the blood on her period, but it did no good.

I was made to stand in the 'spot' after work. It was minus-twenty degrees. I would have cried but the tears would have turned to ice. I stared up at the trees, fellow living things, scratching at the sky as if they too want to get out of here. Ah ah, cried the crows as they circled. I wasn't sure if they were mocking or sympathising. A murder of crows for a murderer. We think we are the free ones, but what freedom to be a bird. When I bent my head back and stared up, the barbed wire above the fence was like scars on the sky. I wonder if I am going mad, whether there would be some relief in that. What are you thinking as you read this, Lev? Are you reading this? I have only had one short letter in the past week. I need you, please write. It doesn't matter what you say; I just need lines on a page.

While Natalya was standing on the spot, Manya the kitten was mewing in the barracks, missing her. Her mother Petra and the other prisoners tried to comfort her, but she wouldn't stop. After hours of this, one woman – Natalya didn't find out who it was – fetched a guard. The kittens were bundled into boxes and taken away. Petra scratched the guard, and was taken away too. The cat and kittens were to be burned in the furnace.

Yulia and Irina told Natalya the story at dinner, their words running over each other. Natalya could bear the pain only as long as they were talking.

'They deserve to be thrown in the fire themselves,' Natalya ranted when they had finished, tears rolling down her cheeks. 'I'm going to Officer Krushkev. It can't be legal, what they did. Is there no protection for the innocent in this country?'

'Many of us in here are innocent,' Yulia says, 'fitted up by the State. You know what happened to me, right? You remember I said I am here on terrorism charges? They were waiting when I came out of my office, a twenty-year-old working for an insurance agency. Two policemen leaning on a car. They took me to the police station, put explosive devices in my handbag and never let me out. I was accused of taking part in the Chechen Wars; it was crazy, almost laughable, sometimes I still think I am dreaming it. In the first war, I was nine; in the second, I was twelve. I protested my innocence, but you think anyone spoke up for me? Even my fiancée was too scared. I did nothing wrong apart from being Chechnya.'

Irina took over. 'You know how it works, Natalya. Don't say anything. You don't want to be in Solitary. You think it's bad now? It's even worse there; believe me.'

Most people had left the dining room. Into the quiet came the crows' deranged song.

'If no-one speaks,' Natalya says, 'nothing gets better.'

'Listen to me then,' Irina said, 'listen to me. I am speaking, and I am telling you to stay quiet. I was in Solitary once. You know why we call it *shiza*?'

Shiza: schizophrenia. Natalya could guess why they called it that, but said nothing. This wasn't her story.

'I was in there forty days,' Irina said, 'forty days and forty nights. They handcuffed me to a bed and they didn't let me go. They treated me like an animal: or worse, because at least the cats' pain would only have lasted minutes. I could have nothing: not even hot water. There was no toilet; I could go once a day when they opened the cell; often, I soiled myself. I dreamed of having TB, so I could be in hospital. When they let me out, I spoke. I went to Officer Krushkev. I said: this is inhumane. I told him he was allowing his staff to torture people. You know what his reply was; spoken through a mouthful of the chocolate he was eating in his warm office? "Jesus survived in the desert for forty days and forty nights, do you think he had luxuries and home comforts? You think you are better than Jesus, lady? I know you have a mental illness, but I didn't realise it was that severe." This is the first time I have spoken about that.'

Natalya opened her mouth, choked. Irina patted her on the back.

'I wish I were as strong as you, Irina. You have survived in here for so long,' Natalya said.

Yulia spoke. 'You are strong, you just need other ways to survive, and that means thinking differently. Do you like to visit cemeteries?'

'What? On the anniversaries of my grandparents' deaths; no other time,' Natalya said.

'You don't think they are as lovely as Gorky Park? As your own garden with the roses you have nurtured with your fingers? But by the end of the summer, your garden will be full of dead things. I think a cemetery is as lovely as any place I have ever visited, because it is the garden of everyone in it, everyone who has been loved. Most people do not think this, because most people try to think the same way as everyone else. They think it keeps them safe.'

They stared at each other, the three women, and then laughter bubbled up like a spring. Natalya thanked Yulia for the metaphor, and asked Irina if she could pay her to knit a hat for Masha for her birthday. Irina said she would, and make one for Natalya too.

Still no letter, Vlad. Perhaps mine are not getting through, censored due to my complaints. Or perhaps yours are not, as my punishment. Or maybe you don't want to write. I will carry on, because what else can I do? I have to believe you are still waiting, still loving. I read all the letters you have written since I have come here, again and again. I clench the words like pebbles held in a fist. Although I am writing, I have no real news, but I need to do it.

Today is Sunday, so in the morning we went to mass as usual. I know I rarely went at home, but when I am released I think I will. The chapel here is a special place, colourful silk flowers hanging from the corners of the ceiling; rich-hued pictures of a sorrowful but calm Jesus on the walls. Today, I stood and prayed for the souls of the cat and her kittens; and for all of us in here and all of you out there, especially you and Masha. The priest read from the book of Isaiah: 'Zion says, "The Lord has forsaken me, my Lord has forgotten me." Can a woman forget her baby, or disown the child of her womb? Though she might forget, I never could forget you.' Please tell Masha that she is always with me. Tell her, please, that I sang her name before she was born; I'm singing it in my head right now, like a hymn. Tell her I see her every time I look in the mirror, her name written in the lines of my face. Tell her. Speak of me. Don't let her grow up in silence.

Quiet Love

You became a nun because you were in love with Jesus. I became a nun because I was in love with quiet.

I've told you how I always wanted a quiet life. A hackneyed phrase, but I mean it fervently. You seemed surprised when I mentioned my noise-sensitivity, but it has dominated my life. As a young child, I saw and felt loudness like a rash, so often, even in our suppressed suburb. The shrieking in the playground, the scorching sounds of the school disco made me crouch in a corner, hands over ears. I would tell my parents to turn the TV down in the evenings and if they had friends over, to avoid the drill of their frivolity, stayed with grandparents. I refused birthday parties: going to or having. My parents, worried and exasperated, took me to a child psychologist; she said I was fine, 'just' an introvert. My schoolmates and my brother said I was boring.

As an adult, I was offered a lucrative job in London – yet, it being the big city, the only decent place I could afford was a flat above a salon. Despite the slugs of foam pushed into my ears at night, the noise was relentless. From ten in the evening, drunken shrieks invaded my skull; sirens sliced the folds of my brain. Each sound was inside me, like a crazy heartbeat. Stark awake, I'd read until it was time for the clatter and bang of dawn deliveries; the bleeping sensors and the thud-thump of rubbish collectors.

So.

You know the story of how I came here. One day, wandering backstreets at sunrise, my favourite time of day, I came to a church. Strangely, it was unlocked. I sat, soaking in the solitude. A few elderly people filed in for an early service and I stayed. Brought up Catholic, I enjoyed the familiar ritual. I started to speak softly to Jesus. Soon I was going to the church every morning. The hush embraced me; people weren't offended if I sometimes walked off without speaking, holding the God-given quiet inside me.

And then, someone in the congregation told me about a community of modern nuns in Surrey who wore what they liked and didn't change their names.

You laughed when I told you what my family said. 'You're in for a gruelling life of gruel': Dad. 'What a waste of a good accountancy degree': Mum. 'Weirdo': Brother. 'I'm not joining the circus,' I said. But to them, I might as well have been.

They accepted it, over time. When I want something, I want it. My mum liked the idea of me still being able to work, albeit at a smaller accountancy firm 'in the sticks', as it normalised the idea of me being a nun. My commute would be by bicycle rather than tube so there would be no hearing other people's music or rumbling stomachs.

A few months later, my father drove me here. I didn't bring much: my bicycle, pictures for the wall, some clothes; books and books and books. I couldn't wait to read undisturbed, for words on a page to be the only things I heard.

When Dad left with a loud farewell, I breathed in the quiet: the smell and taste of it. Peace slipped inside my body. I stood in the entrance hall, waiting for someone to show me where my room was, absorbing everything. There's nothing garish in our hallway, is there? There's peace in that highly polished dark parquet, the threadbare cream rugs; the white walls, the votive images and crucifixes. I felt like I was finally in the right place.

You moved towards me over that smooth wood like a lullaby. I took in the sight of a young woman with plaited auburn hair; a heart-shaped face; a fog-coloured top and blue jeans; a silver cross. A detailed description that does nothing to describe you.

'Jenny?' you asked. Your smile lit up your whole face, as if there were candles under your skin. 'I'm Sister Agatha Harrison – Taggie. I've come to take you to your room. It's next to mine, in the attic.'

You picked up a couple of my bags, not flinching at their heaviness. I thanked you and took as much stuff as I could carry. The rest could wait.

'Have you got any questions about life in the community, Jenny?' you enquired, as we climbed two steep flights of stairs.

I had thought I knew what to expect. After all, I had come to the convent for an interview, to see if I would be a good fit and vice versa; this was followed by a long telephone chat. But I wanted to hear you talk, so I asked what a typical day was like. What I really wanted to know was what your own life was like; had been like. What brought you here? It was too soon for those questions, though.

You said that eight nuns, including us, lived here. There was lots of group time: communal dinner every night, shared cooking duties; meetings and discussions in the lounge; services at the chapel. I wondered if she thought I would get lonely; whether I wanted to know there would be other people around a lot of the time.

'We have solitary prayer time, too, of course. You'll find it quiet,' she said. 'I guess you were expecting that... but we have fun.'

I hadn't considered fun.

You went on. In the daytimes, most of the women went out to do paid jobs; you taught Latin part-time at a private school. The community did voluntary work; you helped at a food bank on Saturday mornings. And there were jobs to do at the convent: you were the gardener. When I said that I was an accountant, you enthused about how useful it would be if I could do the community's books.

'Sister Mary Howatch used to do them, but she's gone back into the world. Hence the free room next to mine. Nice lady, she'll be missed, but she was terrible at doing the books, always making mistakes.'

She let out a snort of laughter. It was loud, but I didn't flinch as I usually would have done. It was the sound of joy.

'Are you really a nun?' I asked abruptly. 'You're not what I imagined. Sorry, that sounded so rude.'

You burst out laughing again. I laughed too.

'I really am a nun,' you said, 'we're not indoor penguins here.'

We laughed yet again.

Afterwards, we reminisced about my clumsy manner of speaking on that first day. Still, I was right when I said that; you didn't seem, or look nun-ish. Aside for the cross around your neck, if I had seen you on the street, I wouldn't even have guessed you were religious. But I would have wanted to get to know you.

As we ascended into the attic, the peaceful feeling slipped out of me as quickly as it had arrived. It left a heaving sensation, as if I were floundering in water.

*

You're approaching on your bike. Your wavy hair is unruly as always; a sea-coloured dress floats around you; it's hard to discern your shape beneath it.

As you push through the flower-scented air, the breeze dances. I watch you, my feet on the moist mossy earth and my head in the clouds. Not with Jesus, where it should be. Where it always was before I met you.

'Taggie,' you call.

My hand spider-dances in a wave.

'Off to do my good works,' you say. 'Going to the shops on the way back, my turn to cook – do you like rabbit pie?'

I have never had rabbit pie: but why not? Before you came, we ate the kind of food my grandparents would have cooked. I couldn't believe it when you told me people had called you boring. You seem so adventurous; so full of life.

'Rabbit pie sounds great.'

You smile and sail out of the gates. My heart is jumping in my chest. It is nice and unpleasant at the same time: it is the feeling of change. I am uneasy at experiencing such a human connection when for so many years I only felt connected to a higher, unseen presence. Even when we are apart, Jenny, I feel as close to you as the two words of a name. So soon, you have come to know me. But in the crucial way, we do not know each other at all and to do so would irrevocably change both of our worlds.

You have heard the fact-file of my life over the past twenty-nine years. I've told you about my family: Catholic, not very tolerant of anyone who isn't. I fitted in. Even before hitting puberty, I had found my true love: Christ. I didn't want another. When I put on my frilly white dress and patent shoes for my First Holy Communion, I thought I really was marrying him. It didn't matter that there were girls in the exact same dresses, the same shoes. Jesus and I knew how to share. I loved going to church even when most of my Holy Communion chums had stopped, preferring to lie in after nights out. I went on nights out too, but I didn't like drinking, and came home early. My classmates wouldn't have been surprised that I became a nun, I expect; I eschew social media so I don't know. I was called boring too. Even a teacher called me old before my time. I do like old people, old things. I trained as an archaeologist and spent years doing the academic work, including learning Latin. But it all started to feel meaningless. The dead things were so dead. It was only at church, when I stared at Jesus hanging on the cross in his loincloth, or as a baby in Mary's arms, that I felt connected and in the right place. I stared at that beautiful, sad face and felt a stirring. He was dead, but he was alive too: faith brought him alive. Like you, I started attending church every day, at home I read the New Testament over and over. Usually alone. I had found a house-share, in an attempt at a social life, but my housemates clearly felt uneasy with my religiosity. They didn't invite me out much.

    I wanted to believe that I could fit in, somewhere. I wanted to find my people on earth as well as in heaven. So I joined the community here. As soon as I arrived, I felt content; I got on well with the older people; enjoyed listening to their stories and learning from them. There was a lot of warmth and laughter; the evenings were a tender-grey. When I wanted to be alone, I went into my attic room and read, or prayed, or worked. I gardened, bare-foot, cracked and brown soles absorbing what the earth wanted to give. Worked at the school; the girls I taught were generally studious and friendly. Life felt rewarding and calm.

    And then you came.

    Wow.

    You don't do boundaries, do you? You're porous; you touch when you talk, you hug. You come in. I have always kept my bedroom door shut; we all do. No one enters unless they have a message. Downstairs is for meeting and talking. But from your second day here, you've been in and out. The attic is our space. We sit on my bed in PJs and talk, as if we are girls having a midnight feast. I don't draw my curtains, somehow it seems safer. Occasionally, in the light of a half ring of gold, we read poetry. We move back and forth with the rhythms like rowers moving oars through water. I like the epics: Ovid, *The Odyssey*; you enjoy Neruda, Machado, Rumi. When you read, your voice is so quiet it can be hard to hear the words, and I move closer.

You respect my boundaries. If I am praying or meditating, you return later. If I'm getting dressed, you wait outside until I'm decent. I try to keep the barrier in place because I am fearful of the flood if the dam is breached. Compared to you, I am reserved. You are open, disclosing comes so easily. When you explained about your extreme sensitivity to noise, I was startled; I would never have guessed your yearning for quiet. I could see it was a painful subject and longed to hold your hand.

Yesterday, you came in while I was Skyping with a student who had been ill. I motioned for you to sit on the bed, the lesson was nearly over. I shouldn't have; it wasn't professional. As your naked feet kissed the floor, my voice started to tremble. When you lay on my bed like a love letter, I lost the thread of what I was saying entirely. Trying to concentrate on Ovid, I couldn't stop staring at the lines on your soles. Each line with a meaning, if only I could dig to the root of it.

'Will I get questions on the poet's feelings in the exam?' the student, young and enthusiastic as I should have been, asked. 'Miss, Miss... can you hear me?'

I said something vague. I could only consider my own feelings at that moment. My own are savage and destructive as the sea, life-giving and protective as womb-water. When I met you, my brain was baptised in salt water; scrubbed with it. The night you arrived, I stood in my almost bare bedroom and listened through the wall to your susurrations. Of course you asked if I really was a nun, I wasn't behaving like one.

But I am a nun, and so are you. Nothing can or will happen that is beyond the bounds of friendship. I push myself back to the present. You have disappeared, off on your bike to do your good works. I bend to my gardening; my own good work. I kneel, ready to yank up carrots by the roots. We'll have them with the rabbit pie.

*

That night, I don't pray or meditate. I read an anthology of Neruda poems. When I come to the words 'a flower climbs up to your lips to seek me', I touch the black words on the white page, follow their curves.

There is a knock on my door.

'Come in, Taggie,' I say.

Feet stroking the floor, you move into my room. You sit on my bed, head below the rosary on the wall. How long, I wonder, will we do this for? Will our quiet times become a whisper, then silence? Or will our bodies become boats that we sail somewhere we can't be heard?

I look at you, and I know.

125

124 was spiteful. He hit me so hard I thought my cheekbone had broken. He said it was my fault, I hadn't smiled enough. 'You're here to please me, girl,' he said. I stared at the wall, at the pink and green mildewed concrete, as I said sorry. Sorry – a flimsy word, falling apart in my mouth. On my first day here, I was told to apologise if I offended anyone; if I did not, they may not come back. None of them has said sorry to me. As 124 was leaving I smiled and said goodbye, while blinking back tears of pain.

'Why give them numbers, Shabrina?' Naomi waves my notebook at me. 'Why write about them? Why do you not want to forget all about them, as I do?'

'Why do the police give criminals numbers, Naomi?' Answer a question you don't want to answer with a question. I snatch my book. Now I'll need a new hiding place, and there are few in this tiny shared room.

'I don't know, Shabrina.' As she frowns, her thick eyebrows pull together. 'Why do they? And what do we have to do with the police?'

'Do you really just forget about these men, Naomi?'

'If you can't forget, you won't survive,' she says.

Naomi has been here for five years; she is practised at survival. I consider her a friend, but don't trust her: I don't trust anyone. I don't like her knowing about my book; I like to have secrets to close myself around. So much of me is open, for sale; I need things that aren't. It's my survival.

I ask Naomi why she was hunting through my things and she says: 'Why would you mind if you have nothing to hide, Shabrina?'

Answer a question with a question. I imagine she was looking for money. That doesn't make her a bad person: every girl here would like the money to escape.

Naomi doesn't push it, about the numbers. The truth is that I don't know why I do it. Sometimes allotting numbers and recording facts makes me feel as though I'm filing a police report, getting these men locked up, even though paying for sex isn't illegal here; sometimes I feel as though I'm writing a story. I have always wanted to be a writer, not that anyone would want to buy my words, just my body.

When Naomi has gone, to sit in the corridor or walk around outside, I hide my book in my clothes. Then I rub pale concealer into the bruise 124 gave me yesterday, the shape of a damaged flower. They don't like to see pain, these men.

As there are five minutes before 125 is due, I flick through the channels on the TV in the corner, find Groovetrap, dance around my small patch of land. Dancing is another secret thing I do. If I were to be seen, there would be a punishment.

There is a knock on the door. Usually, they barge in. I've seen them in the corridors, after they've paid the madams, elbowing each other out of the way in their desperation to get to us, to get into us; they are usually equally desperate to get away from us. His knocking gives me a chance to be seated demurely on my bed, looking at the floor.

125 is a man who buries himself into me. I lie beneath him on my faded turquoise bedspread, red dress rucked up, passively accommodating as a grave. Normally they leave as soon as they have wiped themselves down, go back out into the corridor that smells of spices and sweat, heading for work or their families. Few say goodbye, or even make eye contact. That's fine. But 125 is different. He doesn't roll off as soon as he has finished, he lies next to me and gently squeezes my arms and thighs. They like us fat, we are given drugs to help us put on weight; cow steroids, Naomi says.

So that he knows he needs to go, as the next customer will be here soon, I sit up on the bed and pull down my dress. But his eyes are on me like heat. What does he want?

'What's your name, girl?' It's the first time he has spoken: his voice is quiet.

We are not meant to tell them our names. We are not meant to have any kind of relationship: they are customers; this is a business. The madams don't want anyone getting freebies, or taking us away from here. But we're meant to be polite so the men come back. A difficult balance.

'What's your name?' I ask him, smiling so he doesn't think I'm being rude. I don't want to get hit.

'I asked you first.' He puts on his trousers, the pockets flopping out. I have an urge to tuck them in.

'My name is Naomi,' I say, because why does it matter? Let him think he has power, and let me have my secrets.

He nods. 'Mine is Dayita.'

Dayita looks as if he wants to say something else; there is a moment when the air between us is soft. He moves to the door, then turns.

'Thank you, Naomi. Would you like betel?'

I nod, and he puts some in my hands.

125 wasn't like the others. 125 was called Dayita. He was not handsome, but he was kind. He was generous, giving me betel. On his fourth finger was a wedding ring; his wife is lucky. I hope he comes back one day.

126 had been drinking at the brothel bar, his breath reeked of beer. He asked my age before we started. I said eighteen; eighteen is legal. They like us younger than them but old enough that we know what we are doing. He struggled into me, and the act lasted for ages. Afterwards, he burnt my back with a cigarette. I didn't cry until he'd left, which he did calmly, as though he had put out all his anger with his violence.

Naomi bathes my back, soothing its fire. I share the betel that Dayita gave me. I say one of my customers left it by accident; that it fell out of a pocket. I don't want to tell her about Dayita: she would be jealous. Yesterday, someone hit her in the mouth and loosened a tooth. Even if I did tell her about Dayita, it's not much of a story. He wasn't the first to be nice. He wasn't even the first to give me betel. But he was the first to look as if he saw my true worth.

His thighs were sweaty and stuck to my skin, I write about 127. *As he did it to me, I stared at the torn curtains: a change from staring at the wall. The curtains are olive green with red swirls. I wondered who sewed them, whether they had liked the pattern or if they were forced to follow it. When 127 finished, he asked if I had enjoyed it. What could I say? I said yes.*

I have a dream about Dayita. He comes to my room, takes my hand and leads me through the corridors and alleyways of this giant brothel, until we are out in clean fresh air. Then the dream fades. It's the first time that I haven't had a nightmare since I've got here. Every other night, I have dreamed of the man who raped me when I was fourteen; the man who sold me to the brothel owners: my husband.

One evening, Naomi says, whilst combing her hair, 'A man asked for me today, by name. But when he turned up, I didn't recognise him. He didn't recognise me either.'

My heart beats faster. She looks at me with her eyes narrowed.

'That's funny,' I say, as calmly as I can. 'I guess there are other Naomis here.'

'You don't know anything about it, do you Shabrina? He wasn't number one hundred and forty, was he?' Naomi's plastic comb has snagged on a tangle; she swears as she attacks it.

'Of course I don't know anything,' I say. 'Did he say what the other Naomi looked like? Was he violent?'

'Why would I ask? He had to make do with me, anyway. He wasn't violent.'

I want to ask more, about what he had looked like, but don't want to arouse her suspicions any further. If he had given her betel, she didn't share it.

Weeks pass. I see at least fifteen customers a day; the madams tell them I am a former child-bride and they like that. None of the customers is Dayita. He was probably from a different city; many men pass through here for work. I hope, every day, to see him again. Hope cannot fix a heart, but it can let the light in.

Whenever I am alone in the room, I dance, my lungi swaying freely, and I write, my thoughts flowing freely.

And then, there is a knock on the door and it is him. Dayita is wearing a brown shirt that is almost the colour of his skin, the top two buttons undone. He smiles at me.

'How did you find me?' I ask, looking at the floor.

'I remembered the location of the room. Why did you lie about your name? You're not called Naomi, are you?'

I shake my head. He is smiling, but I know how quickly smiles can slip off a face. Does he want to punish me for lying?

'I see why you need to have secrets, living in a place like this,' he says.

I sit on the bed and he gently pushes my red dress up. Again, he buries into me as if he doesn't want to leave. As he is reaching his climax, he throws his head back. The act isn't enjoyable for me, it could never be that after what I have experienced, but it is not unpleasant.

I expect Dayita to bid me goodbye as soon as he is done, perhaps after offering more betel, but he doesn't move from the bed. He asks how long we have until my next customer comes.

'We probably have ten minutes,' I say.

I lie close enough to hear his breath. He runs his fingers along my skin, touching the cigarette-burn scar. I trace his spine, the string of bones thin as a river.

'So if your name is not Naomi,' he says into my pillow, 'do you trust me enough to tell me what it is? So I know whom to ask for, next time?'

I tell him it is Shabrina. He says that is beautiful.

'I am glad to know your true name. Names are important, in this world. Do you know the meaning of mine?' Dayita asks.

'I don't. Tell me, please.' I do know the meaning, but I want to hear that lovely word in his mouth, the vowels lazy and snug.

'Beloved. I was always ashamed to have such a girly name.'

'I guess your parents must have really loved you, to give you that name. I cannot imagine love like that.'

Dayita leans towards me, presses his lips to my cheek. Lift me up, I think, take me away from here; I can make myself small enough to travel in the palm of your hand.

'I hope you find someone to love you as you deserve, Shabrina,' Dayita says.

I think I have, but how could I tell him that? He is married, he is a customer, there's no way we could be together. But I can write our story with any ending I like. In my book, 125 can change into Beloved.

Letting Go

Amelia's crying wakes me. The red eyes of the clock say 12.45. For a couple of minutes, I ignore her in the hope she'll go back to sleep. She turns up the volume.

'Don't you know I have to be up for work in six hours?' I mutter, dragging myself along our skinny corridor.

There is an unfamiliar, plastic-y smell. I want to investigate, but Amelia's cries are growing louder. The neighbours have never complained before but it would bug me to be woken by someone else's bawling baby: my own is bad enough.

'When's this going to stop? I need to get you off the breast; you're sixteen months… shush, sweetheart, shush….'

Amelia stops crying when she sees me and staggers to her sleeping-bagged feet, beaming with pride at her prowess, arms outstretched. I pick her up and press her soft warm cheek to mine. Motherhood is this: a tug of war between scratchy annoyance and oozy love. We sit together on the futon by her cot. Her new teeth bite my nipple and I say, 'Ow, let go,' and as if she understands she adjusts her mouth. I smooth her sparse blonde hair.

The plastic-y smell is stronger.

'What's that smell?' I ask Amelia, in a sing-song voice, as she sucks.

And then I know.

'Help me.' The cry comes from somewhere in this fourteen-storey towerblock. Then there are more voices, the words overlapping but the tone the same. And then there is an alarm.

Me getting to my feet detaches Amelia; she mewls before reattaching. Out of the window, flames the colour of a sunset. A knock on my front door.

'Fire,' an unfamiliar voice shouts.

'Have you called the fire brigade?' I call. 'Is it your flat?'

No answer. They will be knocking on other doors, I guess.

I ring nine nine nine, my heart hitting the walls of my chest as if it's trying to escape. Cradling Amelia's head, feeling her gentle tug at my breast, I ask for the fire service. I tell the operator who answers what I have seen and heard. I tell her I have a baby.

'You're safer staying inside,' the operator says in an East London accent. 'I'll let the crews know about you.'

We wait. Shouts baffle the air, but the fire brigade do not come.

I peer through the front door's spyhole. There is smoke in the hall. Tentatively, I open the door. It is very hot. The thick acrid smoke floods my face. Blind, choking, I shut the door. I want to scream but I'm dumbstruck, don't know what to do. There is no-one to ask. I drink a large glass of water as quickly as I can.

Somehow Amelia is still breastfeeding. It makes me laugh, big chaotic chuckles. I sit on my bed, my baby sewn to me.

Amelia comes off the breast asleep. Holding her with one arm, I go to the cupboard and take out towels, soak them in the bath then wedge them under the front door. Walk around the flat. My bedroom window gives a view of burning cladding dropping like plastic rain.

An hour passes and we are still here.

Mum answers her mobile with fear in her voice. It will never be good news at this hour. She asks if Amelia is okay. Her great love for me has transferred itself to Amelia, and I am glad.

'Amelia's okay; she's asleep. The tower is on fire,' I say through a coughing fit.

'I can't hear you.' Her voice is on the edge of dread. 'What's happened?'

'Fire,' I say, 'it's on fire.'

'What? Say it slowly, darling.' And the third time, she understands. 'Have you called the fire brigade? You must call them. We'll call them.'

'I've called the fire brigade.'

'Where is the fire? It's in your flat? The one next door?'

'I don't know where. Somewhere in the building. Below, maybe.'

'If it's not on your floor, you'll be safe. These buildings were designed for safety. Hold on, we're coming. I'll get Dad up, he'll drive. We'll take you back here.'

They live sixty-five miles away.

'I love you, Mum.' I clutch Amelia.

'We're coming,' she says. 'Don't worry. Just keep Amelia safe until we come.'

'Tell Dad I love him.'

There is so much noise. The building's bones are breaking.

'I love you,' I repeat; three dense words; I try to pin them to her. She thinks I was calling for advice. I was calling to say goodbye.

A man flies past the window.

'Let me out.' '*Karitha.*' 'Help me.'

Thick black smoke is moving silently through the letterbox. We need to get out. I pull away the wet towels, wrap Amelia in one and put another over the lower part of my face. I step into the hallway. The smoke bullies me back. I can't do it. Dizzy, struggling to breathe, I take my daughter to the window.

Bits are flying from the tower. I think about swaddling Amelia in a duvet… jumping… we would die. She has to live. I want her to be a doctor; to save people.

Fat flames are swallowing the cladding. A firefighter on a crane is trying to put water everywhere: up, down, all around. I pick up a red cushion from the sofa, open the window and wave it.

'We're here,' I scream. 'Help me, please help me, I've got a child in here.'

The firefighter's hose is not long enough to reach the top of the tower. Water and fire, the elements we have been reduced to, fighting each other. Life is simple, at the start and the end. This can't be Amelia's start and end.

'Save us.'

There are so many fire engines, so many fire fighters. The fire is stronger than them in its brutality, its need to consume. There is another jumper. Mesmerised, I watch the plastic of the window frame melting.

There is a loud popping sound and the glass in the kitchen window smashes.

My daughter is quiet, staring at me with her large sapphire-blue eyes. She trusts me. I have to try.

A crowd has gathered on the ground, staring up at the tower. I open the window again, pain coiling itself around me, waving waving, my arms flags of desperation. I lean out as far as possible and scream, knowing they won't hear the words but hoping to catch their attention. Someone points. It's a man I have passed walking in and out of the building; we have smiled at each other but never spoken; how I wish we had spoken; do we even share a language?

I show Amelia. 'Hold out your arms.'

My voice is a thread to the people on the ground; they take it; they are ready, arms out. So many people.

I kiss Amelia, my daughter, my known and unknown love. I press my skin to hers, imprinting myself on her. I pray to God, over the wailing of the sirens, to keep her safe.

I can't do it, and then I can. I let go.

The Thought of Death Sits Easy on the Man

At five in the morning, the mountain is silent. At first it seems as if the moon, its tongue filed down to almost nothing, will be her sole companion.

But then, through the window, Evie sees someone else. A man in a yellow bobble hat, climbing the brown paths. It irritates her; she had got up this early to be alone.

You don't own the mountain, Evie, her dad says. *I'm saving to buy it for you, though.*

Evie hoists her heavier than usual rucksack onto her back, adjusting the straps. She locks up her father's house.

The jagged non-narrative of the highest mountain in England rises before her. Only the clouds, scudding similes, are higher. This is the sublime. Her dad liked to quote Wordsworth, delivering the words in a portentous tone to make her giggle. She wished she'd written down what he said. One she did remember, because it came from a poem she studied for A-level, was: *The Power which these / Acknowledge when thus moved, which Nature thus / Thrusts forth upon the senses.*

Trying to think of more Romantic quotes, Evie walks quickly forth. It is chillier than usual for early October, dew furring the rocks and grass. The ground is mossy and mulchy. The cold bites Evie's face, her nose especially. Her dad joked there was a gap in the market for a hiker's nose-warmer; he'd invent it and make a mint. He never did. Evie's dad was a dreamer; a weaver of tales and fantasies. Her daughter, four-year-old Vivi, doted on by her grandad, has inherited this ability.

Evie walks on and up. It is strange being companionless. 'Lonely as a cloud,' she says aloud. Cloud-lonely was the way she'd wanted it on her first and last time on her own up here. All the other times, Evie's dad was there, climbing with her; slightly ahead when she was little – slightly behind, when they were both older. They helped each other when they needed it.

In the quiet, memories flood in. The first time she came to the Lakes, Evie was eleven. It was the summer holidays; her parents had split up two months' before and her dad had moved out, to live in the Lakes. Her mum drove Evie to his new cottage, the almost-silent journey taking hours, waiting in the car until Evie's dad came out, turning the car around straight away. Evie barely registered her mum leaving. She was staring up at the mountain, speechless. The next morning, her dad asked what she wanted to do, and she pointed through the living room window and said: 'That; climb that.' Her dad laughed and said there was no McDonald's at the top, just views. 'I want to climb it,' she said. So they had. It got tough on the way up, particularly when it rained and Evie's fingers stung with cold; her dad blew on them for warmth. But it was worth it at the end. They had sat, almost at the top, backs against the stone, watching hordes of people ascending and descending; the young and the old; the proper hikers with their walking poles and boots; a couple of teenage girls in flip flops. They had a picnic: she remembered the intense sweetness of the Kendal Mint Cake.

After that, Evie and her dad climbed every time she visited. Sometimes they did it on a fine day, England, Scotland and Wales laid out as their prize, other times fog would descend and they could only see about thirty yards. Evie loved it in all weathers; all seasons. They didn't always talk as they walked and climbed, and that was fine. When she stumbled over a rock or skidded in the mud on a descent, he was there, fingers stretched out for hers. He taught her the hand-over-hand scrambling technique; cheerleaded when she was on her last legs. 'Worth it at the top,' he'd say, and it was. They always ate Kendal Mint Cake, and she wished she'd brought a bar.

The last time they climbed together was two years' ago, before the pandemic. Evie's last sight of her dad was his smile frozen on her phone screen. Even on that call, he made jokes; quoted poets. He talked of the hike they would do when they saw each other again.

And now, Evie's face is frozen, she is not smiling, her dad is not here. She wonders whether he would have approved of her doing this alone. She could have brought her husband, George. 'You need to stay with Vivi; she's too small to climb. Anyway,' Evie told him, 'I know the mountain.'

What an arrogant thing to say. Who could know a mountain? Even her dad had not known Scafell; he loved it, but love was not the same as knowledge. Mountains were as unknowable and mighty, as dangerous and beautiful, as God.

Danger aside, Evie is here and will climb. She moves on and up. She hasn't gone far when the drizzle begins. Then the rain. The water drips down her nose; inveigles itself into her anorak. The trees hiss. Evie thinks again about going back, but has psyched herself up for this day for a long time.

You can do it, Evie.

Of course she can: she's done it so many times. Not just Scafell Pike; Helvellyn, Skiddaw and Great Gable, others she can't remember the names of now.

Then, suddenly, a shaft of sunlight glazes the crags in iridescence, tints the clouds lemon-yellow. She sees the man in the bobble hat; he has stopped, is rooting in his backpack. Evie slows. Even a simple hello feels beyond her. Also, she is a woman, he is a man. It seems an odd way to find a victim, climbing a mountain in the early morning, but you never know.

Oh, Evie; you should trust people.

She is naturally a faster walker than the man; it's difficult not to catch up. She could wait for him to move forward, but that brief flash of sunlight has gone and it is drizzling again. She doesn't want to plod along. Nor does she want to be frightened; not here, not today.

'Morning,' she says, over her shoulder, as she passes the man. In her brief glance she sees wiry black hair poking out from the bobble hat, a slight frame in a dark anorak. He is wearing trainers rather than walking boots, so probably not a regular climber.

He catches her up.

'Morning. I was told I'd have the best experience if I got up at the crack of dawn. You're the first person I've seen up here today: live round here?'

He has a Southern accent. If he was a local, he would know that it's not done to chat to strangers when climbing. She wonders if he's chatting her up, although can't believe he is. She's a forty-two-year-old woman permanently pale from sleepless nights; unmade-up, hair unbrushed.

'My dad – has a house around here.'

She looks at a flock of sheep, doing their sheepy things, so as not to look at the man. She thinks of a shepherd or shepherdess, another person up early, transporting them to their field. There is no one else around though.

'I've just bought a house up here,' the man enthuses. 'Hope I get to meet your dad soon. I don't know anyone yet; my friends thought I was mad to come.'

He's lonely, Evie. You can spare a few minutes.

'Where did you move from?' she asks.

Teddington, South West London, he says. Evie laughs, explaining that she is originally from Isleworth, just a few miles away from Teddington: her mum still lives there. Evie now lives in Wimbledon, also close by. More interested now, she asks what brought him to the Lake District. He has recently split up with his wife; they have a girl and a boy, twelve and ten, he says. Evie guesses from the strained sound of his voice that he is fighting back tears. She hopes he isn't climbing with the intention of doing something stupid.

'I'm sorry,' Evie says. 'My dad moved up here when he divorced my mum. He was very happy here. It's a wonderful place to live, it really is.'

Evie looks up the mountain, wreathed in mist. There is a long way to go. It's not Evie's job to cheer up this stranger, she has her own pain pulling at her limbs like a wilful toddler, but her dad would have tried to do so. He'd have found a way to make him laugh, probably by telling some ridiculous story. Evie can't think of anything else to say. They climb in silence, the man slightly behind her.

Gradually, the flower of morning opens up. Evie has zigzagged up the Cumbrian Way, it is now time for the unremitting climb to Angle Tarn. There are more people appearing, packs on backs.

'Are you going as far as Esk Hause?' The man, still close behind Evie, is starting to pant.

'I was hoping to go further.'

The first time Evie climbed with her dad, they had made it to Esk Hause, but the next time she had been keen to continue on. She felt no fear, when she was young, and had always been fit. By the time she was eighteen, they were scrambling up to Ill Crag, Broad Crag and finally Scafell itself.

Surely this man will not be with her all the way. She doesn't want an audience for what she is going to do when she reaches the top.

It might help you, Evie.

'My name's Robin,' the man says, 'what's yours?'

She tells him, walking faster to preclude any further conversational overtures.

As the altitude increases, the wind wallops her body. For a minute, she feels nervous. What if the weather is against her? She can't bear the thought of coming back to do this on another day.

'Wow,' says Robin, and Evie slows to see what he is looking at. She had almost forgotten the tumbling waterfall at Rossett Gill.

'"Stones and boulders are not portrayed … They number millions,"' Robin proclaims, a little self-consciously she thinks.

'Is that Wordsworth?' Evie looks at him in surprise. He doesn't have the look of a poet; maybe he is an English teacher.

'Alfred Wainwright. Goodness, is that a golden eagle?' Robin exclaims.

The dark brown bird, a golden plumage at its nape, is balanced balletically on a rock. Evie doesn't know if it's a golden eagle; has never seen one. Her dad would have been thrilled: he loved birds. He had pointed out buzzards and kestrels, but never a golden eagle.

Evie feels sadness eat away at her internal organs, nibbling her heart. The eagle drifts away.

'I've got a couple of bars of Kendal Mint Cake,' Robin says. 'Think I'll stop for one if you fancy joining me?'

This is her opportunity. She opens her mouth to say she wants to reach the summit before too much of the day is gone.

Spare some time.

They sit, backs against the rock, two metres between them although the latest lockdown has eased. Evie has grown used to distance; physical and mental.

Robin hands her the bar of chocolate. She squirts hand sanitizer on her fingers; that was something she and her dad never brought with them. She tears off the wrapper and takes a deep bite. The sweetness of the minty sugar hits her, as it does every time. They eat in silence. When they have finished, Evie takes out a pack of baby wipes and they both clean their fingers.

'Not so chilly now,' Robin remarks.

'Let's get on before the sun goes in again.'

Scrambling up a ridge across a long boulder field, under a cadmium-yellow sun, Evie realises that sweat has replaced the precipitation on her skin.

There is not far to go, and she has a sick feeling that is nothing to do with the walk or the altitude. It is the feeling that when she reaches the top, a terrible statue of Time made from the ancient rock will be waiting.

You need more sleep, love. Terrible statue of Time what?

For a long while, the whistle of the wind and the pastoral underscore of birdsong is the only thing that Evie hears. But then:

'This is tough,' Robin says. 'Don't know if I can go any further.'

He is bending over, hands on thighs. Evie has a momentary flash of concern; should she dissuade him from going on? Could he have a heart attack? He is slim, not much over forty, probably; statistically, he ought to be okay. She is not responsible for him. But then who is?

'Stop for a bit. Plenty of rest stops are good, my dad always said.'

They stand, taking in deep breaths of the fresh air.

'Why did you choose to move here, Robin?' Evie asks.

'I used to come on family holidays to the Lakes, as a kid.' He straightens up; smiles: his teeth are very white. 'They were happy times. I thought it'd be a nice place for my kids to come and visit.'

Evie looks up at the snow-white cirrus clouds in the now angelic blue sky, so that Robin won't see the tears in her eyes.

'It will be,' she agrees. 'Are you feeling okay to go on? Only, the hordes will be ascending about now. Feels like a festival without the music and booze at peak times.'

'Peak times, good one,' Robin says, although Evie hadn't meant it as a joke.

After a while, Evie's steps feel laboured. Perhaps she's no longer as fit as she was. She never gave up when she was with her dad, though; she will not now.

Almost there, sweetheart.

'We did it, Evie!'

They have reached the top of the mountain. Evie is awed as always to be at the point where heaven meets Earth. She and Robin smile at each other, not-quite strangers any more.

'My dad always quoted Wordsworth when we got to the top,' she says.

'Ah, something like: "The thought of death sits easy on the man / Who has been born and dies among the mountains?" I'm trying to get my children into Wordsworth; they're resisting me at the moment.'

'Keep trying,' Evie says. 'I hope Vivi will like poetry; she's more into fairy tales at the moment.'

'What now, Evie?' Robin asks. 'I've enough lunch for the two of us if you want to share?'

'There's something that I have to do first,' Evie says, but makes no move to do it. Robin looks at her.

Evie feels tears prick her eyes. She looks down at Wastwater, the deepest lake in England.

'Seventy-nine metres' deep,' she tells Robin, pointing.

'What's wrong, Evie?' Robin asks.

'My dad died two months ago,' she says slowly, still looking at the lake. 'He had a stroke, then he went to hospital and caught coronavirus.'

Evie thinks: if it were not for the time we are living in, Robin would touch me. She feels his sympathy as though it had left marks on her skin, however.

'I came up here to scatter his ashes. They're in my rucksack.'

She takes out the urn. It contains the man who taught her to love mountains; who taught her to climb, to move on no matter how tough it seemed.

Robin watches, saying nothing. Evie is grateful for that. She stands under the sun, swollen in the sky like a syllable, like the long vowels in 'love' and 'father'. She opens the urn's lid; pours out the ashes. Her father flies into the chainless winds.

Thank you. Goodbye for now, my love.

'Goodbye, Dad. Thank you.'

'Are you alright, Evie?' Robin asks.

'Not really, but I'm glad I did this,' she replies.

'You should come back here with your daughter one day,' he says, and she nods. One day, she will.

'What did you bring for the picnic, then?' Evie asks.

Mikey

The weather is wilder, the wide sky whiter. The fields are bottle-green and mud-brown. Within drystone walls graze sheep and cows: the quintessential Yorkshire Dales. In about an hour, they will be home.

In one way, Rebecca can't wait to be out of the car: she's been driving most of the day. In another, she hopes the trip never ends.

Rebecca flicks her eyes left. Her sister Paula is scrolling through her phone and sipping a takeaway mocha.

'Have you heard from Mum?' Rebecca asks.

'I'm texting Ricky.'

Ricky, an actor with a small part in a TV drama, is Paula's on-off boyfriend. Not very on if he isn't going to be with Paula tomorrow, perhaps.

'Could you text Mum?' Rebecca tries to sound patient. 'She might be worrying. We're late.'

They are late because Paula had wanted to look at the shops in the service station. She bought presents for their nieces and nephews, chocolate and wine for herself.

'We're only later than the time you estimated for our arrival. We're not late for anything.'

'Late is late, Paula.'

'Mum will have too much to do for tomorrow to worry about us.'

'Please, Paula, text her.' Rebecca makes an effort to speak slowly.

Paula gives a gaudy sigh. 'Fine, I'll do it in a bit.'

For God's sake, Rebecca thinks. Can you just do something I ask when I ask it? But she says nothing more. Paula's emotions are birdlike, they wheel and dive.

Driving over a moor, Rebecca sees that it's snowing. At first, she is pleased; snow is always exciting, even when you're thirty. Then she remembers that this is the North West; snow can be a force to be reckoned with.

Paula chirps with excitement, rolling down her window to take photos, letting in a blast of cold air.

The snowflakes are kindly at first then come down with a sudden anger, like a charming person revealed as a psychopath. There had been no warning of snow on that morning's weather report. Rebecca would have chosen the motorway rather than the prettier B roads for this last part of the journey, if there had been. Maybe she was subconsciously trying to delay their getting home: home that was not home.

Paula's pinions swoop when Rebecca suggests stopping. 'We can't. You said yourself: Mum will worry.'

But snow is spawning snow. The car is battered along the road. Rebecca slows, tries to remember whether she should be in a higher or lower gear for driving in this type of weather. Although originally from Cumbria, she has lived in the

South for twelve years. When she has come back to the North West, she has taken the train, her dad driving her around for the duration of her visit. He loved driving; insisted on chauffeuring his daughters. 'I live to serve, girls,' he would say, tipping an imaginary cap.

High gear, says a voice in Rebecca's head.

They are alone on the road. No cars, no people; just nature. The trees hold the snow with easy acceptance, comfortable in its transience, like a child holding a parent's hand to cross a street.

The snow falls harder and harder and harder; it is difficult to see the road. Flurries move horizontally in bursts across the windshield. It is now a blizzard.

'We'll have to wait for this to pass.' Rebecca tries to sound assertive. She is the older sister, and the driver. She should make the decision. 'It's not safe, Paula.'

'Are we going to be stuck here all night?' Paula's voice seems to have less substance, as though her lung power has diminished.

'Of course not,' Rebecca says. 'We'll wait here for a bit then we'll go on. Worst case scenario, someone will rescue us.'

Dad would have rescued us, Rebecca thinks; whatever the weather. Dad in his yellow Land Rover: the boot always contained an umbrella, a raincoat and a cowboy hat.

Rebecca pulls over, remembering a long-ago tip to straighten her wheels in snow. At least she had learned to drive up here; she only needed fourteen lessons, because her dad was keen to take her out to practice; enthusiastically slapping L plates onto the Land Rover. Paula learned too, and passed her test, but hadn't driven much since. She lived in London; there was little need for a car.

'I should call the AA,' Rebecca says.

'But we haven't broken down,' Paula protests.

'We can't get anywhere in this car in these conditions,' Rebecca snaps, 'and it may not start again when it is safe to move it. It's a Ford Fiesta, not a four-by-four.'

'I should have got the train,' Paula whispers.

Rebecca takes her mobile from her coat; the reception is tentative. She googles 'AA + snow'.

'I'm so cold.' Paula's teeth are chattering. 'It's like a Russian novel.'

Rebecca turns the key in the ignition and puts on the heater. On the AA website, she reads advice that is already inapplicable, given the suddenness and severity of the blizzard. Towards the bottom of the page is a box with a 0800 number to phone in an emergency. She does so; listens to hold music for ten minutes before her call is answered.

'We need to know you're stuck before we can come out,' a woman says. 'Can you move your car? Put it in second gear; edge forwards and backwards.'

The car refuses to move.

'You should have carried on driving,' Paula shouts.

Rebecca is on hold again. After another ten minutes, she is informed that there are many people stuck in the snow in North Yorkshire. Her case has been logged. A breakdown vehicle will be sent out as soon as possible; Rebecca will receive an update call. Goodbye now.

Rebecca turns the heater off in case they get poisoned. Paula texts Aunt Clem, their father's sister, who is coming up from Cornwall with her family. She warns her about the snow. Rebecca calls their mother, as Paula has not yet texted her. There is no reply – she'll be preparing for the next day, as Paula surmised. The wake will be at the family house; a catering company has been booked, but their mother will be flapping around, will have found herself tasks. Rebecca leaves a message.

An hour later, and the AA has not arrived. An update has not been given. Rebecca's phone battery is forty percent. Panic is pleating and folding and knotting inside her mind. The snow is stripping away her normal calm. Or maybe it is the funeral. Is there any chance they will be stuck out here all night, and miss it?

Rebecca and Paula shiver in their thin jackets and trousers. It's March; it shouldn't be this cold. The Beast from the East, Paula says. The vapour of their breath is visible. Cold weather puts added strain on the heart, Rebecca knows. Her father's heart, his kind heart, killed him. Nothing to do with cold weather, presumably: too much excess and too little exercise. Mikey Dean believed in living for the moment; and the moment was meant to be fun.

A rustling. Paula is taking a newspaper from her handbag. It is the *Guardian*. Rebecca is surprised; her sister works in media sales for the *Evening Standard*, she assumed that was the paper she read. Their father had been a *Guardian*-reader; he bought a copy every day, even when it became available to read online for free. When he retired, he went out every morning to get it from the town: 'Keeps me out of the way of your mother,' he laughed.

Paula is pulling out sections of the newspaper; she hands a sheaf to Rebecca.

'Help me put these over the windscreen. It'll keep the warmth in a bit.'

A good idea; Rebecca wishes she'd thought of it. What else can they do? Their suitcases in the boot contain additional layers they could put on. She is worried about going out in the blizzard to fetch them, though. Surely this will soon pass. It's hard to believe that this morning in Kent, at lunchtime in London when she picked up Paula, the sky was azure.

Despite the cold, Rebecca feels sleepy. She leans her head against the rest. The wind and snow buffeting the car is a two-part harmony, pulling her....

'Don't fall asleep, Beck.' Paula pushes her shoulder. 'It's not safe.'

'Talk to me, then.' Rebecca's speech is slower than normal, as if she is a clockwork toy that needs winding-up.

'What do you think about angels?' Paula asks. 'Do you think they're real?'

'Angels?'

'We have guardian angels,' Paula asserts. 'Ricky's seen his. When he was a child and had a terrible fever, an angel sat in his room all night and by morning the fever was gone.'

'You believe that? His Mum probably gave him an overdose of Paracetamol, or whatever it is you give kids.'

'Of course I believe him. If you'd heard him talk about it, you would too.'

'No offence, sis, but he's an actor – it's his job to make people believe stuff.'

Paula shakes her head: dismissing her sister's scepticism. 'I'm trying to visualise my angel, asking her to help us.'

'If you see her, ask if she can get hold of a heavenly snow plough.'

'I should have known you wouldn't take it seriously; you've never had a spiritual bone in your body. Dad would have believed me. And it's in the Bible, so Mum would too.'

'In the Bible, a man turns water into wine, I don't take that seriously either: although that would be a good skill to have at parties.'

Paula tuts.

Half an hour passes. The light is dimming, soon it will be dark.

The car feels even colder. Rebecca knows she will have to get the warm clothes. Her sister agrees; does not offer to help. She's on her phone again.

Rebecca opens the driver's door. The cold is needles entering her skin, the wind so strong she thinks it might pick her up and smash her into a tree. There is so much snow, high around the car. The wheels are cradled by ice and snow. She takes uncertain steps, bullied by the chill air.

Brushing snow off the boot-release button makes Rebecca yelp with pain. She pulls her suitcase out. Paula's is heavier; lifting it destabilises Rebecca. Her feet slip beneath her, and she crashes to her knees. She stays where she is, as if praying to the snow. Tears spill down her face. She hasn't cried since the evening that her mum phoned her with the news. She couldn't. Now they have arrived, the tears are warm and long as a good life. She has melted.

Through her tears, Rebecca sees a light: a bright green orb in the sky. For a second, she thinks it is the AA. But the light is static as the sun. Rebecca stares, wondering. The back of her head tingles. Her tears stop, and she feels a moment of inexplicable joy. And then the light is gone. She is kneeling on the fearfully cold ground, snow soaking her jeans.

Rebecca clambers up; shoves the cases into the car. She unzips them and roots around for jumpers. In her suitcase, there is a scarf too.

'Paula, are you okay?'

Her sister has her head in her hands. She appears to be gripping her mind, holding tight as if frightened of losing it.

'I'm not okay.' Paula's voice is muffled.

Of course she's not okay; nor is Rebecca. There is this situation, and there is the far worse one they will face tomorrow, then every day for the rest of their lives. The loss of their father.

What should I do, Dad? Rebecca asks silently.

There is something near the gear stick: a feather. Rebecca picks it up and strokes it. Has it travelled from Kent too? It has no snow on it. She wonders which bird it came from, as it is pure white, not streaked with grey like pigeon feathers, the ones she normally sees.

'Where did you get that?' Paula asks.

Rebecca shrugs.

'White feathers are a sign that an angel's present.'

'They're a sign that a bird's been present,' Rebecca replies. 'Here's your jumper.'

They both put on the jumpers. Rebecca adds her scarf, tucking it into her coat.

'You were so clever to bring that,' Paula says.

Rebecca looks down at her hot-pink cashmere scarf. She packed it not for the warmth, but because she felt her father would like her to wear something cheerful to his funeral, even if it did shock some members of the congregation. He loved bright outfits; in his twenties and thirties, while setting up his handyman business, he sang in clubs and at weddings. He was known locally as 'Mikey the Rhinestone Cowboy' because he belted out Glen Campbell songs, wearing patterned shirts and cowboy hats. Hence the cowboy hat in the Land Rover: he'd never quite left that part of his life behind. Whenever he drove, he listened to country hits.

Rebecca takes the scarf off. She winds it around her sister's neck.

'Don't you want it, Becks?'

'It's alright.' Her dad had always told her to be kind to her little sister.

Rebecca looks out of the window; the snow is blank as amnesia. It is falling more lightly now; weeping down. No bright lights. She doesn't want to tell her sister about what she saw; she is the rational one. She has always been the rational one.

'Where's the AA?' Paula asks.

Averting her eyes from the phone's battery level, Rebecca calls the 0800 number again. After eight minutes on hold, a different bored-sounding person answers. Someone's on their way; assuming they can get through.

Rebecca gives Paula the news. Her sister looks pained and confused, as if she is falling through herself, a feather spiralling to the ground.

'Assuming they can get through? What if they can't get through? We're stuck here all night?'

'The police will get us if the AA can't, surely. They have helicopters. Paula, please don't cry, I promise it'll be okay.'

'It's not just that. I don't want tomorrow to happen, Beck. I can't bear it.'

'I can't bear it either,' Rebecca says. 'But Dad will be there with us. Remember how he always said he wouldn't stay away from his own funeral?'

Paula gives a choked laugh. In an attempt to lighten the atmosphere, Rebecca turns on the radio. Music skips into the car.

'I'm gonna be where the lights are shinin' on me—'

'Oh my God,' Rebecca breathes. And then she and Paula are singing along.

'Like a rhinestone cowboy / Riding out on a horse in a star-spangled rodeo / Like a rhinestone cowboy / Well, I really don't mind the rain / And the smile can hide all the pain.'

'Thanks Dad,' Rebecca says, at the end. 'Bet you were singing along, too.'

'You know what?' Paula is reaching into her bag. 'I've just remembered that chocolate I bought from the service station. Food keeps you warm too, right?'

Paula takes a large bar of salted-caramel milk chocolate from her handbag and splits it in half. Rebecca lets a piece dissolve in her mouth. It is bliss.

'Do you really think Dad will be with us tomorrow?' Paula says with her mouth full.

'Mikey Dean loved a show,' Rebecca says. 'He's not going to want to miss this one.'

They sit in silence, sucking on the chocolate.

'I wonder if we'll see any other signs of guardian angels. Surely hearing that song was one. And there's the white feather.' Paula indicates it, lying by the gearstick, between them.

Might as well indulge her, Rebecca thinks.

'What else are signs of visiting angels, Paula?'

'Bright lights are another one,' Paula says.

'Really?' Rebecca thinks of the green orb.

'Why? Have you seen any recently?'

Paula had always been into 'spiritual stuff', as their mum called it. She had regular tarot readings, attended medium events and psychic fairs. She had met on-off Ricky at a medium event; his grandmother had come through and told him he needed a girlfriend: Paula had been sitting next to him. Their dad had been spiritual, too, had his birth chart done and was interested in Buddhism. Their mum, a Sunday churchgoer, mocked him. Rebecca did too. Now she wished she hadn't.

'Why the sudden interest in angels?' Paula asks.

Rebecca is about to reply when a noise makes her look out of the window. A yellow lorry is driving slowly down the road.

Paula squeals, and the sisters hug. How much warmer we would have been if we'd held each other before, Rebecca realises.

The vehicle draws up alongside them, and a man and woman climb out. They stride over to Rebecca's car, as if the snow is a theatrical illusion.

'I'm from the AA,' says the man, when Rebecca has rolled down her window. On his coat is a name badge that reads 'Mikey'.

John

'One, two, three,' yells a paramedic, hefting the gurney. 'Sarah, stay with us, okay?'

'Who did this, Sarah?' Luna cries.

I switch on the radio as a distraction from my thoughts. Singing along to 'Wichita Lineman', I try not to let the ballad take me to a place of tears. Despite the wreckage of my personal life, I've been looking forward to seeing my sister Luna. Tonight, we'll have a takeaway, a bottle of wine, a chill and a chat. Tomorrow, I will drive back to Bristol, finish packing, get on a plane and fly to Tokyo: new job; new home; new life. One day, maybe a new relationship.

Through a scalding sunset, I draw up in front of the tower block. Luna's new flat, the first she's owned, is on the ninth of the twelve floors. I look up and up. There's something awe-inspiring about so much concrete Brutalism. Brilliant views, Luna says.

I find a spot in the car park and turn off the engine, exhaling in relief that the two-and-a-half-hour journey is over. I open the door and get out. The cold air is zested with rubbish and damp grass.

As I am walking to the boot for my overnight bag and laptop, I notice a woman getting out of a black car. She is staring at me. I smile; she does not. The stereotype of unfriendly Londoners seems to be true.

The woman walks quickly over. She could be in her late twenties or early thirties, with long dark hair all over her face, wearing high-waist jeans ripped at the knees and a baby-blue fur coat with a hood. She is gripping a leather bag.

'Why did you do it?' she shouts, in what people used to call an Estuary accent.

My heart stammers. Is this about the car park? Am I in the wrong spot? I didn't think there was designated parking. Then again, Luna doesn't drive, so may not know about it, and if she did may well not have thought to inform me.

'Sorry, do you want me to move my car?' I ask.

She's running her hands over her bag. 'This isn't about your car, you skank. Just leave him alone, will you?'

'I don't know what you're talking about.'

When she speaks next, she sounds on the verge of tears. 'We've got a kid; did you know that? She's four; needs her daddy. Leave him alone.'

'Who?' I respond.

'My boyfriend; you've been shagging my boyfriend.'

I snort with laughter; it's how I respond to stressful situations, but it's the wrong thing to do. Her face contorts.

'You bitch,' she says.

I look up at Luna's apartment, wondering if she can hear this. There's no sign of her. She might be at the back of the flat, if she's home. I gave her an ETA, but I'm fifteen minutes' early, and her timekeeping isn't good.

The woman is so close that, underneath the pink suffusing her cheeks, I see freckles.

Neither of us speaks again. I sense that she hasn't rehearsed this: that all her thought went into finding me. Her anger feels like a language foreign to both of us: I don't understand it; she can't translate it into action. Her fury needs something to do, but she's not sure yet what that is. Anger is only ever the start of something.

'I need to go,' I say. 'I'm visiting someone. And I'm not the person you want to speak to; you need to talk to your boyfriend again.'

I move, but she blocks my path. 'I've talked to him; that's why I'm here. You're not going until you admit it too.'

A man with dreads, walking a small eager dog, passes near us on his way to one of the other blocks. I think of calling for help.

'I'm from Bristol,' I tell her. 'It's really unlikely I know your boyfriend, and even if I do, I'm not sleeping with anyone. Nor would I ever sleep with someone else's boyfriend. Now please can you get out of my way?'

'He showed me a photo,' the woman yells, 'on his phone. So don't lie to me, yeah?'

I walk towards the block. In one of the lower flats, someone is looking out of the window.

'My boyfriend's name is John,' says the woman, to my retreating back. 'Still claiming not to know him?'

I turn.

'John?'

My ex's name is John. My ex, who is still officially my husband. The man who, a month ago, told me that he is gay; that he has a boyfriend who he wants to be with. Now he has a girlfriend too? A girlfriend with a four-year-old child: his child? 'My' John is forty, a university professor. Is this woman a postgrad? But how would she know who I am and where I was? John didn't know I was going to see Luna; what I do is none of his business any more. Has she followed me to London from Bristol? In which case, why not confront me at my house? Or at the service station I stopped at?

'How do you know John?' I ask.

Her smile is not a smile. 'Now you're admitting it.'

'No, I asked how you know John. I'm not admitting anything.'

'John's my boyfriend, as I said – my boyfriend, who you've been fucking. Our little girl's called Esme, if you're interested.'

So as not to have to look into her rage-filled face, I glance up at the sky, at the illegible stars and bobbing moon. I breathe deeply.

'Listen, I'm sorry you've been messed around by your boyfriend. No one deserves that. But my John is not your John. My John has just told me that he's gay.'

'What are you talking about?' She is clutching her leather bag tightly, as if it contains her anger. 'John's not gay. You're lying.'

I turn again, striding to the tower block.

'Don't you walk off,' the woman shouts. 'I'm not finished. I'm not going until you promise to leave him alone.'

The block is only a few paces away.

Heavy footsteps: behind me. I know they are hers.

At first, I feel as though I've been poked with a pencil. The feeling comes again and again. A warm, slimy liquid runs down my back. Has the woman poured something onto me; a bottle of water? But water is not slimy.

The feet are running; car tyres are screaming.

Breathing is difficult. Standing is difficult. I drop my laptop; my overnight bag slips from my shoulder. The pain arrives: I feel it, and then I become it.

'Jesus, have you been stabbed?' It's a man's voice, heavily accented: Spanish or Mexican.

It is as though I am being poked a thousand times, and each time the pain ramps up. My vision has narrowed – it's a black circle closing in.

'I'm calling an ambulance,' the man says.

My legs are noodles; they won't hold me up.

'Sarah!' Luna's voice. 'Oh my God, there's blood everywhere. What happened? Help her, help her.'

My ribs feel charred; breathing through them is the hardest work I've ever done.

Luna is on the ground, one hand on my shoulder. The man is there too. They talk to each other. Something is tied tightly around my back. Luna has blood all over her clothes. For a second, I think the woman has stabbed her too.

'The ambulance is coming,' Luna says. 'Keep your eyes open. Please, Sarah.'

My breaths are shorter, shorter, short. A polyglot of accents echoes in my ears, and overlaying them is the screeching of sirens.

I try to take a breath, but my body doesn't let it in.

'Keep your eyes open.' Luna is crying. I want to comfort her; can't.

As though I am underwater, my hearing fades.

There is a ringing in my ears... and that is it – the pain is gone, replaced by peace. Sorry, Luna, my eyes won't stay open. I need to sleep.

Time has passed, I taste its sourness. I'm now lying, outside of myself, on something hard: a gurney. I remember the paramedics putting me into an ambulance, Luna flickering around like a frightened firefly. Medical words are ping-ponging around the ambulance.

Imprinted red on my eyelids is that woman's face: angry, yet empty. Where is she now?

'Sarah, do you remember what happened?' Luna asks gently.

'John.' I force out the word. John is the name of the woman's boyfriend: John is the name of my ex-boyfriend. There has to be a link.

'You want John?' Luna frowns.

'Does she have a next of kin?' a paramedic asks. 'It'd be a good idea to call them.'

'I'll call John,' Luna says.

Later, I find out there was a crowd waiting for me at the hospital. They talked quickly and loudly, taking ownership. I was searched – for more stab wounds, I think. My clothes were cut off. Four pints of strangers' blood poured into me. Such a difference from the violence inflicted – the woman stabbing me with a knife probably taken from her kitchen, she might have chopped coriander with it the night before – and the consequences of that violence, an almost-murder.

Jigsawed back together, I am in a bed with IV drips in my arms. Luna sits beside me.

'The police are looking for the woman, Sarah,' my sister says. 'Someone filmed what happened on their phone, from the flats, so there's a chance they'll catch her.'

Did someone film me being stabbed rather than call an ambulance? Have I gone viral?

'Why would she have done it?' Luna is asking. 'It's not the nicest block to look at, but I feel safe there, nothing like that has happened before as far as I know. I can't believe you almost died outside my home, when I was inside and could have saved you....'

She goes on and on, and I say nothing. My throat seems silenced, as if my vocal cords have had a knife through them too.

'I phoned John,' Luna says. 'Well, tried to. He was in a lecture, so I left a message.'

In my head, I hear the lyrics to 'Wichita Lineman', which I heard in the car, that couplet silvering the air: 'And I need you more than want you / And I want you for all time.' How much did that young woman need or want this John? Or was he an excuse to vent fury on a stranger? Perhaps he doesn't exist.

Two nurses come in; one takes my blood pressure, the other hands me a menu card. I'm not sure which meal it will be.

'This is the best hospital,' Luna says, smiling at the nurses. 'You're in such good hands. My new boyfriend's a paediatric nurse here – did I tell you? I met him at a party a couple of weeks ago.'

'What's his name?' I croak.

'John,' says my twin.

A Good Boy

There was nothing exceptional about me until I had the operation. However, the day that I was born – 10th January 1946 – was special. Not because of my birth, which didn't affect many people, even my parents: they already had five kids. But thousands of miles away, while my mother was labouring to get me out of her body in Leeds General Infirmary, the US Army was bouncing a radar signal off the Moon from Fort Monmouth, New Jersey. On the same day in London, the UN General Assembly was meeting for the first time. So, there was potency to that day.

You're interested in my birth? It wasn't particularly traumatic, as far as I know. People didn't talk about that type of thing in those days. I know Mam was in hospital for ten days; that was the norm then. I wish I could remember when I was the most important thing in her life. I imagine her smiling down at me, tired but happy. While the US Army Signal Corps was trying its best to probe another celestial body and fifty-one nations were stuffing themselves into the Methodist Central Hall in London, all Mary West was interested in was the beauty of her sixth-born child. Maybe. There are no photos from that time.

And then, once those possibly blissful ten days were over, the reality. Mam and I went home. To my father, who I'll tell you about later. To my siblings: ten, eight, seven, five and three years old; Susan, Mickey, Jennifer, Bill and Evie: only Jennifer is alive now. I wasn't the last child my parents had: two years' after me,

Albie came along. We squashed into a flat on the seventh storey of a block in Quarry Hill; destroyed now. Mam spent most of her time cooking and cleaning. The older kids played with the younger ones, helped them with getting dressed and all the rest of it. I got a rudimentary education: it wasn't compulsory for parents to send kids to school until 1948, so my four eldest siblings had less schooling than me. I was clever, so found school okay. I especially enjoyed the teachers reading to us and singing songs. At break-times there was milk, although on cold days their ice-collars made it difficult to stuff the straws in. In the summer, the liquid curdled before the teachers got the bottles into the classroom. But in the spring and autumn, the milk was good.

You want to know about my father, of course. He worked as a smith, and drank most of his wages away. Same as so many men who'd survived the war. In the late nineteen forties, there weren't SSRIs or talking therapies. There was alcohol. It chased away the memories, I suppose.

Was he scary? He came home slurring, and his slurs struck the night. Sometimes we kids would run out of the back door. We'd come home a few hours later, hungry and cold. Evie once told a teacher about Dad hitting Mam, but she was told not to tell wicked lies or would go to hell.

As I got older, Mam got a broken arm and severe concussion. At the hospital, she said she slipped. I began to worry that he would kill her. Mam was a skinny woman and no more than five feet tall. Dad was six foot. Not right, is it, someone like that picking on a little woman like Mam, who had never done anything but protect him?

Some people think violence is hereditary, don't they? As a boy, I'd never hurt anyone beyond the normal rough play, but what Dad did to Mam made me so furious I wanted to smash my fist against his face, throw him out of our high window. But I wasn't strong enough, and he would kill me. I had to devise a plan to get rid of him.

My first idea was poisoning, and an idea quickly formed for how I could do it. My father hated flies so much that he kept fly-killer paper in the house. To my mind, my father was more dangerous than a little insect, and deserved to die more than one.

When he was at the pub, I got hold of his special Queen's Coronation mug and unearthed the fly paper. I would make my father a very special cuppa. The fly paper had a strong scent, and the fumes started to overwhelm me as I scraped the adhesive into the mug. Albie found me sleeping. He clipped me around the ear for my foolishness, even though he was younger than me.

'I've got a better idea, Stan,' he said.

Albie's idea was to loosen the carpet on the staircase, so that Dad tripped and broke his neck. He said he would do it but I told him it was my duty, as the elder brother.

Dad caught me in the act. And that was where it all started.

'You used to be a good boy – what happened? Get out and don't come back.'

'Please no, Fred,' Mum said. 'He still is a good boy. It was one silly prank, wasn't it, Stan? You didn't want to seriously hurt anyone, did you?'

'Wake up, Mary, he was trying to kill me.'

'If you want someone to be angry at, Fred, be angry at me.'

'Be angry at me,' Albie shrieked. 'It wasn't Stan's idea, it was mine.' My father raised his eyebrows, thick and heavy like slabs of meat. Then he raised his fist. I assume the only reason he didn't hit anyone was that he couldn't decide which of the three of us to whack.

'I'm going,' I said.

My mother and brother took it in turns to hug me. The hallway glittered, as if washed in tears.

I spent my sixteenth birthday walking the streets, the open throat of the sky above me. Two months were spent sleeping in parks and shop doorways. I was spat at and pissed on, although sometimes drunks gave me the rest of their bottle or put a shilling in my hand.

I stole food to survive. Yes, that was how I ended up in Borstal. Was it awful? At least it was warm. We did sports, had lessons. Bit like school, the difference being that the pupils and teachers were terrifying, and we were locked in our cells on what felt like a whim. And there was no milk. My mum, weeping, came to visit, as did my siblings. Often Mum would have a black eye or a cut on her face.

I started getting headaches. They were hands squeezing my skull, as lights burst like stars behind my eyes. The air trembled. The doctor was fetched after I'd been shouting with pain for hours. I was put in a van and taken to hospital. Not a normal hospital; a psychiatric hospital. Yes, that one.

'I'm not mad,' I shouted when I found out where I was.

The next day I met Doctor Johns, the psychiatrist in charge of my case. You've done research on him, I know. Was he a monster? He didn't look like one, with his round-rimmed glasses and dapper suit, his permanent smile. His moustache made me think of the school milk, the competitions after drinking it to see who had the whitest top lip.

'We believe you have severe mental problems, Stanley.' Doctor Johns had an excited look on his face. 'Your father says you're very aggressive: you tried to kill him.'

'He's been trying to kill my mother for years,' I said.

'Don't worry, Stanley, all of this is treatable. We have wonderful medicines and therapies these days. You're in safe hands.'

Yes, he really said that.

The wonderful medicines were psychotropic drugs and electroconvulsive therapy sessions. The ECTs were like a hammer smashing against my skull, again and again. It made the headaches I had in Borstal feel like nothing.

Doctor Johns sat by my bed, smoothing the knees of his suit trousers. Smiling as always.

'Excellent news, Stanley,' he said.

'I can go home?' I was barely able to push out the words through the drug-fuzz. Did I have a home anymore? Had I stretched the bridge of my life so far that I could no longer cross it? Even being murdered by my father seemed a better alternative to the ECTs. I had had eight by then, and felt I knew what it was to be hit by a wrecking ball in the blind dark. When I could open my eyes afterwards, the bright light bit my retinas.

Doctor Johns frowned briefly before pasting on his smile again. 'Home? Oh no, Stanley. Your father is adamant that you can't return until you've been properly cured. He just wants you to be a good boy; it's all parents want for their children, isn't it? And I have a brilliant idea for what could enable that to happen. There is a little operation which I fervently – fervently, Stanley – believe would seriously alter your innate levels of aggression. Remove them entirely, perhaps.'

'No thanks,' I said, dribbling.

Doctor Johns' moustache drooped a little. 'The problem is, Stan – can I call you that? we're friends now – is that aggression gets worse if untreated. Imagine you get married – handsome boy like you, you'll have your pick – then you'll want children, won't you?'

I thought of my large family. All of us in the flat when Dad was down the pub, playing card games and laughing. Even Mum. I thought of Albie and I restoring a bike we'd found, polishing it and getting spare parts from the scrap yard; Jennifer teaching me chess; Mickey letting me go on his paper round and buying me sweets at the end.

'You wouldn't want to harm your own children, would you? We believe this operation will stop that happening. You'll have a peaceful, easy life.'

Bells rang in my head.

'The procedure will mean pulling back the skin on your forehead before we drill two small holes into your skull,' Doctor Johns said cheerily. 'After that, a nylon ball will be inserted into each hole. It'll be over before you know it. It's an easy operation, no different from slicing through a block of cheese really – easier than curing toothache.'

'I don't want it,' I said. 'I'm not going to hurt my kids.'

'Your father has given permission,' Doctor Johns said, as if I hadn't spoken. Perhaps I hadn't. I was so woozy, it was hard to know what was happening. 'He clearly wants the best for his son. You're lucky; I couldn't stand my dad, ha ha.'

'What if I say no to the operation?'

'You're lucky to be in a position to have it. Special – the chosen one. Not many people have been cured the way you will be. Once it's over you won't go back to Borstal; you'll have your freedom.'

My mother had taught us to respect doctors. Perhaps I was aggressive. I had been in Borstal; and was the only one of my siblings to have been thrown out of the family home. I had tried to kill my father, twice.

'Good boy,' Doctor Johns said, touching my shoulder through the hospital gown.

One more smile, and he was gone. I watched the moon shine onto my bed. The stars, though, they sank down. And then it was dark, and I was left staring at the windows' empty eyes.

At four minutes past one in the afternoon, I was wheeled into an operating theatre.

I woke with swollen eyes, feeling bruised and nauseous. My face was wet with sweat. Sitting up, I was immediately sick on the bed clothes, to the disgust of the nurse who had to clean it up. There was a pain in my head that I can only liken to having a broom handle inserted repeatedly into my skull. My skin was burning. The feeling of my hospital gown where it touched my flesh was torture.

'It's going splendidly so far, Stanley.' Doctor Johns was the happiest I'd seen him. 'Your family won't recognise you.'

I could say nothing.

'You're in illustrious company, did you know that? Lenin and Einstein both had their brains scrutinised. Einstein's was kept in mayonnaise jars and given to friends by his pathologist. Can you imagine that?'

Can *you* imagine that?

'We should see a complete difference after the next stage,' Doctor Johns said. 'You'll be put under your old angry self, then when we wake you up – new Stanley. Like turning a coin over: bad boy on one side, good boy on the other.'

The second stage lasted for nearly nine hours; a long time to turn a coin over. I was awake, strapped down, the doctors watching as my pupils dilated.

The surgery involved electrodes being placed into my hypothalamus, then they shot volts through the electrodes into my brain.

Want to have a break? Well, if you're sure, I'll carry on. Visiting time is limited.

So, back to the op. I screamed and screamed throughout. I have had flashbacks of that surgery every day for the past fifty-six years; nightmares every night.

It was all good from Doctor Johns' point of view.

'Calm down, son,' he said, smiling as always as I screamed. 'Thought Borstal kids were tougher than this.'

I emerged from the operation in a stupor, incontinent and unaware of who I was or what had happened to me. I was an empty country, the other inhabitants having fled when the looters and pillagers arrived.

My mother and siblings visited. Mam took my hand and said something, but I didn't understand. Words swallowed themselves on my lips, time after time. They sizzled like the wings of moths. I lay back on my pillows and closed my eyes. I felt my hands being gently squeezed, heard whispered goodbyes.

Eight days later, I was told I could go, the plastic balls still sticking out of my forehead. As they thought I had been cured of my natural aggressive tendencies I was permitted to go home, although I didn't know how I would get there. My family were all at work or school. Even Mam had a job now, in a clothing factory, Dad having been laid off. He was trying to borrow a friend's car to pick me up, was the message I received from Mam. But on the day of my discharge, I didn't know if he had been successful, and resigned myself to taking two buses.

I walked out of the hospital into a mid-winter city which was virtually silent. My legs were like cotton wool and my head screamed with pain. I carried my bag on my back, and even though I had little inside it, it felt as though I were carrying my coffin.

I made my slow way to the bus stop. There were a few old people waiting, all of whom stared in horror as I approached. I touched the plastic balls on my forehead and lowered my head. Gazed at the few cars prowling past.

In a blaze of light, a bus arrived. I waited for the old people to make their way onto it; none of them thanked me, all avoided meeting my eye. As I effortfully climbed the step, I realised I had no money for a fare. I tried to explain to the bus driver that I'd just come out of hospital, had no money, would I be able to have one free ride? I'll get the money to the bus company afterwards, I said. He shook his head. Everyone on the bus was watching me.

I got off the bus without arguing and sat at the stop, leaning my head against the cool plastic. I was so tired my eyes began to close.

When I woke, it was dark. There was no one at the bus stop. I got up and saw that the road and house tops had an icy sheen. I didn't feel cold, which seemed strange. I didn't realise then that the operation had affected my ability to feel temperatures appropriately.

Suddenly a car was heading down the road towards me, travelling too fast. In an almost balletic movement, it glided off the road. Skidded on a patch of ice, I suppose. It narrowly avoided crashing into the bus shelter.

Dad got out of the car and walked towards me, seemingly unharmed by the crash. Of course he was; nothing touched him.

As he got closer, his smile froze.

I don't get many visitors in here, and I was worried when you approached me. I trust so few people these days, especially those I don't know. Few people have had my experience, so I don't expect understanding; just an audience.

The Yellow Circle

I introduced Anthony to Eau Sauvage on his birthday. Wearing it would perfect him; make him elegant, smooth his edges. He could wear it with a suit. In my dreams, it would make him speak with a French accent.

On the day, I took Anthony for dinner at Le Salon Privè. He suggested a drink at a pub afterwards, but we had to go straight home for the present-giving, I said. He obviously thought his luck was in, kissing my neck in the Uber.

We sat side by side, and I took out the gift-wrapped present. I had to force myself to hand it over, like a child playing Pass the Parcel. He unwrapped it, had a cursory glance, thanked me and laid it on the bed.

'Put it on now, please,' I said. 'Sauvage Parfum is the latest version of Eau Sauvage, and that was my… it's just such a special scent.'

For two years, I had mulled over whether Anthony was ready to receive a bottle of Sauvage from me. It wasn't just a scent. Sauvage was transporting, exalting. It was a yellow circle into which I could step and it would close around me, protectively.

Anthony twisted off the magnetic cap; pressed the atomiser against his wrist. The citrus notes, the spicy lavender and the woody base made me shiver.

'It's nice,' he said: still in his Estuary accent.

'Nice?'

'Very nice,' he clarified, stroking my cheek.

Anthony put the bottle of Sauvage on the bedside table. I stroked the label to reassure it of its importance.

'So, want to give me another birthday present?' My boyfriend moved closer.

'I've got my period.'

We got ready for bed in silence. Anthony was soon snoring. I put my head under the duvet and sniffed his wrist. He stirred and moved away.

Deep in the night I opened the window, a smell of oil and metal coming in on the wind. The Sauvage on the dresser caught my eye. I sprayed it into the air, inhaling deeply. Then I lay with it on the bed and ran my fingers along the ribbed pattern on the bottle until I felt soothed enough to sink into a light sleep. I woke holding it.

In May, Anthony got the PhD for which he had spent the past five years working. Recently, he had been spending so much time on it, I had hardly seen him. I said we should go on holiday to celebrate. He said he needed to focus on getting a job; he didn't have the money to go away. I'll pay, I said. I suggested Calabria, in Italy. It was where the bergamot that went into the Sauvage Parfum was picked. Due to recurrent earthquakes, it wasn't too touristy; it was somewhat wild, but with beautiful beaches and landscapes.

We spent a week there and on one of the heady days of extravagant drunkenness, under an ozone blue sky, the warm Ioanian Sea whispering words of love, the smell of bergamot drifting over, we got engaged. The next day, we were both so hungover we couldn't get out of bed but a fiancée was a fiancée. I changed my Facebook status to 'Engaged' and waited for my mother to see it.

Back home, we didn't make plans for a wedding. But my mother asked to meet him, and she and Anthony were as unimpressed by each other as I had expected. 'Are you sure about this, Katie? You don't seem besotted with each other,' she muttered as we washed up the meal I'd cooked; Anthony was on his laptop in the next room, applying for jobs. When she'd gone, he said: 'She didn't ask a single question.'

Things went on as they were. And then summer came to England with a green brilliance. At first going outside was a warm hug; then the heat was pressing and exhausting. It stayed and stayed. The smells of suntan lotion, barbeques and Lynx Africa were omnipresent. My small terraced house, which trapped the heat, had a stale odour even when the windows were open. When Anthony was out, as he was increasingly often, I sprayed Sauvage until I used up the bottle, and he didn't comment. I replaced it with another bottle, and he didn't comment.

Our relationship died with the autumn leaves that came early because of the hot weather. There had been more and more pointless, unresolved arguments: as if we were flies trapped in a room, banging against the windows. Yet I didn't expect it when he said he couldn't take this – take me – anymore. I asked what the problem was, and he looked at me as if I were dense.

'You're obsessive,' he said.

'What?'

'You know what I mean. What is with you and smells, Katie?' he demanded.

'You're dumping me because I'd like you to wear aftershave?'

'I've done research. You may have pica, or a mineral deficiency. You should get referred for therapy.'

'I thought pica is when people want to eat coins and soil,' I said, but he wasn't listening.

'I'm not surprised you've got issues, considering your relationship with your mother, and what happened with your dad, but I can't help you anymore. It's over, Katie, I'm sorry.'

I told him to pack, right now, and left the house, which belonged to me, while he did. I skulked round a corner until he came out with two suitcases and a rucksack, head down. A few minutes later, he texted: *Call if you want to talk, I didn't want us to end like this x*. I blocked his number.

Anthony left the Sauvage behind. A parting gift, I supposed. I sprayed the scent in every room, the way someone else may have listened to a love song on repeat. The next day, I went to buy another bottle. I dressed in a faux-fur coat, stuck on feathery eyelashes, painted my lips a deep red. The woman behind the counter at Boots asked if the Sauvage was for my boyfriend.

'It's for my fiancée,' I said. 'He can't get enough of it. It's so important, scent, don't you think? Did you know that in ancient Greece, adulterers were punished by having their noses amputated?'

On the way home, my hands shook with the desire to be alone with the bottle. Perhaps Anthony was right about my smell obsession, but I had never told him why Sauvage meant so much to me. It was the aftershave my dad had worn. After he had gone, the bottle stayed on his dresser for a year. Then I took it into my room and sprayed it on the pillow, put the bottle in the wardrobe. One day it was gone; my mother must have thrown it away.

A month after splitting up with Anthony, I told Mum. She said she was sorry, but not surprised, and had I considered Tinder? She had met a lovely man on there.

One day at work, I saw an unfamiliar man. He was walking down the corridor carrying a plate of sandwiches. He was olive-skinned, with dark curls that cuddled-up at his neck. I stared as he walked closer closer closer, mouth twitching in a smile that got wider wider wider. As he passed, I caught the smell of bergamot. He wore Sauvage.

I rushed to my desk, searched on the Intranet for new starters. I found a photo. He was Jean Sentir. Jean – my dad's name was Johnny.

Before I could work out a way to introduce myself to this heaven-scented man, my boss asked for a meeting. Her office was a fug of coffee. She sent for more coffee, leaned back in her big chair and asked if I wanted to talk about anything. No, I said. But she did. She was concerned about me: I was frequently late, missing deadlines, irritable with colleagues.

'If you want time off to see your GP, to get a referral, that's fine.'

I replied that I had recently ended an engagement, so wasn't feeling myself; I would look into private counselling. That's good, she said, and it seemed like the best idea to put me on desk duties while I was sorting myself out.

I couldn't find a therapist I liked the look of online, so tried to seem perky and conscientious at work in order that my boss wouldn't find a sneaky way to fire me. It wasn't a problem socially, as I wasn't socialising. Mum phoned every other Sunday, and we spoke for as short a time as possible. A few other friends WhatsApp'd sporadically, but for the past two years I had been mainly going out with Anthony's friends. They were still Anthony's friends.

With the coming of winter, things worsened. The season was always bad but having Anthony had helped. Alone, I spiralled. At home I noticed a sulphurous odour, and spent hours cleaning then spraying with Sauvage until the air vibrated and it was necessary to go outside to stop coughing. I vacuumed every inch of carpet and soft furnishing, washed bed linen at ninety degrees, took out the bins daily, poured bleach on every surface. Still the stink remained, insidious as an unspoken grievance. The smell was worst in the hallway, so that my skin felt as if it were popping, and I scratched incessantly. I stopped cooking, food tasted cold and dead, and spent evenings in the bath.

In the small hours, I stared out of the window at the sky lightening and the clouds racing. Sometimes, when the smells and thoughts got too much, the dark too narrow, I roamed in the bitter white wind.

I hadn't seen Jean, who was in another department at work, again, and he had glided out of my daydreams. But on Christmas Eve I saw him with a colleague on the high street. His hair curled insouciantly. I got close, brain misting at his smell. I was gulping in his odour like an asthmatic using an inhaler when he spun around. His colleague turned too.

Jean said, in a glossy French accent: 'Are you alright?'

Lines barred his forehead, but his look was of compassion.

'Do I know you?' he persisted.

I shook my head; walked away. I found myself in Boots. Even given my mental state, as I said in the interview, what happened next was out of character.

Over to the scent counter I went, and there was Anthony. A girl with frothy blonde curls and shiny ballet pumps was with him. She wasn't close enough to smell, but I suspected she would use Marc Jacobs' Daisy. My stomach clenched.

I moved to the shelves nearest the scent counter, picked up a shampoo bottle and bent over as if I were studying it, willing them to leave. I was low on money, but the woman behind the counter would let me have a spray of Sauvage. If I did that in every pharmacy in town, I would feel better by the end of the day.

'I love that Eau Sauvage,' the girl was saying loudly.

Oh savidge, she pronounced it; I gave her a mark as black as soot.

'I'll get you that for Christmas, shall I?' she asked Anthony; I almost laughed. Almost.

'Oh, that's a gorgeous smell,' the woman behind the counter, who I saw so often she felt like a friend, said. 'We've had one lady buying a bottle at least once a week. She must have a swimming pool-full. This is the last one; hope she doesn't come in!'

She laughed gaily, and the girl joined in; Anthony didn't.

'You know what,' he said, 'there are loads of other nice aftershaves, this one reminds me of the ex....'

'The psycho ex?' the girl asked disdainfully. 'This is such a lovely smell; let me buy it for you, sweetie.'

She handed over banknotes and was given the Sauvage, my Sauvage, in return. She slung the box into her bag. Then she walked off, holding Anthony's hand.

I was practised at following people. I moved behind Anthony and his girlfriend. They paused before a café window. Anthony said something that made the girl turn to him. They kissed, and she put down her shoulder bag in order to loop her arms around his neck.

I grabbed her bag and ran. There was shouting. I ran on. I was fit, had to be for my job when not on desk duties, so it was easy to run until the shouting had stopped. I slipped into a park. It had a public toilet, and I locked myself in. Then I opened the bag, ripped the cellophane from the box, tore the cardboard and took big gulping breaths. Sauvage: my love.

But the scent wouldn't stick in the air, dissipating like a dream. It disappeared like the memories of my dad's face.

It was twilight when I left the park. The shops and cafes glowed with decorations; a row of mini-Christmas trees protruding above them. Merrymakers were congregating.

I had taken the Sauvage home but left the bag, containing a purse and phone and travel-card, in the toilet. I could have tried to get it back to the girl, who I now knew was called Collette, apologising profusely, appealing to Anthony, but I didn't want to. On some level, I wanted this to be the act that changed things. I wasn't sure why. Possibly it was that Christmas Eve was the anniversary of my dad's death. I had found him hanging in the hallway. I'd phoned for an ambulance, and held his hand until it came, breathing in all that was left of him: the smell of Sauvage. Strange to put on aftershave when you're about to kill yourself. Maybe it was a hallucination. Or had he put on the aftershave for Mum, out at her Christmas party while he was putting the sheet around his neck and moving the chair from the dining room? I'd gone with him in the ambulance. My mother arrived at the hospital three hours' later: she hadn't looked at her phone. By the time she wobbled over in her heels, smelling of booze, her mascara and lipstick smudged, I was in a private room holding a coffee that a nurse had brought me. I'd only had one sip, the astringency gripping the sides of my tongue, but kept holding it.

Fourteen years' later, I crept along the streets like a secret. I looked into lit windows that made me think of aquariums, families beached on sofas staring at screens. One man was on a treadmill, going nowhere fast as I was going nowhere slowly, and that made me laugh a high laugh. I walked until the curtains closed, until the dew came. Then I went home, gait clumsy from tiredness.

The stench had gone; the house just smelled tired. I lay and stared at the pale ceiling. Maybe this was how Dad felt, unable to fit into his life, like a tiny sticker lost inside a big envelope with no one willing to reach in and pull it out. Who knew? He hadn't left a note.

I went to bed, abandoned myself to exhaustion. In my dreams, I heard the church bells that had rung during Dad's funeral. I woke and the doorbell was ringing. Then the knocking began. I had done the same, numerous times. I thought about not letting them in but the hall light was on. Besides, they would come back.

It was him: that was a surprise. Jean Sentir. His dark eyes had a sorrowful expression, or it may have been embarrassment now he knew who I was. We never like nabbing our own.

'Police Sergeant Katherine Miris?' he said, for form's sake, and I assented to make his life easier. He explained why he was there and what would happen next, the familiar words whirling thickly like snow. As he gently led me away, I breathed in his smell and the yellow circle closed around me.

My Sister the Murderer

Roseanne

In Fifth Grade, we learnt about the Salem witch trials. The principal fact that stayed with me was that women were judged to be witches if their breasts were pointed rather than round. My class laughed lasciviously at the soft, bun-like sound of the word 'breasts' in Ms Gormley's mouth. That semester, when I walked in on my twelve-year-old sister Courtney naked in the bathroom, I saw she had small triangular breasts. She was touching them, pressing the nipples, staring at herself in the mirror. When she spotted me behind her in the glass, she screamed.

'You're a witch, Courtney.' I wasn't trying to be mean; I just had a habit, at that age, of saying whatever was in my head.

'What?' she yelled.

'You've got pointy breasts: that means you're a witch.'

Courtney slapped me: it was so unexpected, so painful, that tears sprang to my eyes.

'Mom, Courtney hit me,' I shrieked.

'You're a liar and a pervert, Roseanne,' my sister shouted, going back into the bathroom and slamming the door.

In the kitchen, as Mom handed me a bag of frozen peas wrapped in a dishtowel, she said: 'You'll understand why your sister needs privacy when you're twelve, Rosie. Be kinder to her.'

Two years later, when my breasts were developing – round not pointed, thankfully – I went to my best friend Karin's house and as we drank hot chocolate with marshmallows, her older sister Nerissa showed us how to insert a tampon and put a condom on a banana. Nerissa was my heroine. If I could have swapped her for angry, miserable Courtney, somehow the light of our parents' lives, I would have done so like a shot.

Courtney

Roseanne was the clever one. At Harvard, she majored in English Language and Literature. She was the pretty one, too: limbs that stayed skinny no matter how much she ate, poker-straight golden hair and cartoon-huge blue eyes.

I took Social Sciences at Northeastern, had only to look at a Krispy Kreme to pile on the pounds, while my hair was a mousy frizz. The mousiness came from Mom, the frizz from Dad. No one knew who Roseanne looked like.

I tried to get on with my sister. During my college days, I invited her up a few times. She visited me just once, when she was in Boston for an interview for a newspaper's summer internship program. On the Friday night, after her interview, I gave her the bed in my room and scrunched-up like a ball of paper on the floor. On the Saturday, I took her out with a group of friends which included a boy called Jon

I was crushing on; he was from Pennsylvania, like us. One look from Roseanne and Jon was hers. She came up every other weekend to visit him; I saw her in passing.

Roseanne got a place on the internship program and after college was given a job writing for the *Pittsburgh Post-Gazette*, quickly moving to the *Philadelphia Daily News*; I sent congratulations cards for both positions. She married Jon when she was twenty-four and was pregnant at the wedding. She chose her best friend Karin as her bridesmaid; I did a reading wearing a dress the color of a new bruise.

Roseanne and Jon bought a house in Philly, a ten-minute car journey from Mom and Dad's house where I still lived. My postgraduate qualification in social work didn't pay. Eight years' later, I had a job as a children's social worker but was unable to afford a rental. It was fine being at home, though. Unlike Roseanne, I always got on well with our parents. She griped that I was their favorite; it did seem to be true, but if one child was pleasant and helpful at home and the other argumentative and unhelpful, how else could they feel? Also, they knew she needed them less: the world loved my little sister, and it didn't love me.

After Roseanne's daughter Liberty (Libby for short) was born, Dana followed two years' later. I was surprised by the choice to have a second child so quickly, given how much Roseanne moaned about motherhood. She returned to work full-time four months after Dana's birth, and the girls spent their early years in daycare. It wasn't the childhood we'd had: Mom was there after school, cookies and milk on the table, until fourth grade when she started working again part-time.

I assumed that once the girls passed the baby stage, Roseanne's whining about motherhood – the sleep-deprivation; the rudeness of the mothers at the baby and toddler classes who mistook her for the au pair due to her youth; the difficulties of combining a career with motherhood, etc. – would lessen, but there was always something to complain about. Her attitude infuriated me. I loved children but aged thirty-two was diagnosed with primary ovarian insufficiency and told I wouldn't be able to have my own. The news sucker-punched me; I went to bed for a whole weekend and cried. Mom and Dad were great, offering support without condescension. I didn't tell Roseanne; she would have said something like 'You don't know how lucky you are, you can live how you want to', and I couldn't have controlled my temper.

The one area in life in which I thought I was doing better than Roseanne was relationships, after I met a fellow social worker, Tim, who seemed to adore me. My sister said not to get married as that was when it turned sour, although I knew it would be different when I married Tim. Roseanne said Jon worked too much; did too little around the house; most of the childcare was left to her; etc. They often spoke to each other through the girls.

After Jon's parents moved to New York for work, his sixteen-year-old sister Monica came to live with Roseanne and Jon so her senior year wouldn't be disrupted. The little girls had to share a room so Monica could have her own. Roseanne and I would have killed each other if we'd had to do that, I reflected.

Roseanne

On the day that Monica died, the sky was the color of tin. It was one of those days that never gets warm. I was in the office, wearing my scarf as the heating had failed, when my phone rang. It was Jon's mom, Hannah. She asked if I knew where Monica was. Hannah had driven over from New York for lunch with her, but Monica hadn't showed; Hannah couldn't contact her. My stomach constricted: Monica was usually thoughtful and reliable. Later, Hannah said I sounded nervous on the phone.

'I saw her this morning, but haven't heard from her since,' I told her. 'Go on over to the house, Hannah. I'll take a lunch hour.'

I couldn't afford to take time out, we were covering the senate elections, but Hannah had sounded worried and Monica was officially in my care. As I walked out the building, I called Monica's mobile, which went to voicemail; I left a message asking her to call me.

Hannah was on the stoop when I drove up, dressed in a white coat with a feathery collar and a tweed skirt. Her arms were wrapped around herself.

'It's not like Monica,' she said. 'Is it, Rosie? I haven't seen her for six weeks; I'm only in town for the day, I thought she'd like to be taken out for lunch. I had a reservation for tapas, you know it's her favorite.'

'It's not like her, but I'm sure she's fine.'

I wondered if I should tell Hannah that Monica had been quieter than usual recently. I'd remarked on it to Jon and he'd said: 'Teenagers'.

'How are my grand-daughters?' Hannah asked, as I fumbled for my key. It was at the bottom of my bag, and as I tipped it sideways, bits of tissue confettied out.

'Libby's doing great at school, top at Math and English. Dana can't wait to be six next month,' I said with a smile. 'I've got a soft play party organized. It'll be hell, but she'll love it.'

Hannah repeated just those words, 'It'll be hell', to the police. It aided the prosecution's case that I disliked motherhood so much I couldn't stand to have a third young person in the house.

Hannah and I shouted Monica's name in the hallway. No reply. The house seemed empty as a lung after a long exhale.

Monica's bedroom door was shut; I knocked then entered. Nothing obviously wrong, just typical teenage clutter: make-up on every surface; chocolate wrappers on top of clothes on top of school books.

I called Jon and told him that his little sister was missing.

'Rosie, it's auditing season, I can't just take off home. If she's not back by six, I'll leave. Get Dad over to help look if Mom's panicking, but Monica will be at a friend's house.'

'Hannah's called Angel, her best friend,' I said. 'Monica was meant to go to her house to study for a test after seeing your mom. She can't get hold of her either.'

But I was speaking to dead air.

The school said Monica hadn't been in all day. They said it wasn't like her to skip classes. She was a straight-A student; conscientious and hard-working; set to go to Yale if she got the grades.

Monica wasn't back by six, and Jon and his dad Mike arrived at the house separately. Mike was tight-lipped. I collected my girls from their after-school clubs and cooked them supper, then stayed home with them while Jon drove his parents all over town. They visited every store and eatery that Monica might have gone into. They showed photos of her on their phones. No one had seen her.

The police were unconcerned, teenagers having a habit of going missing temporarily: 'She'll be back when she gets hungry,' the desk officer laughed.

At bedtime, the girls asked where Monica was. I said she was with a friend, and they would see her tomorrow. Then I sat in the family room, in the dark, staring at the TV without knowing what I was watching. I reacted to every sound, every light that swept into the room from a passing car. I rang Monica's phone, again and again; each time, it went to voicemail.

The defense team used records of all these calls in court, substantiating their argument that I was worried about my sister-in-law. The prosecution called me a good actress.

As I waited for news, my mind raced through possibilities. Had Monica run away? Was there boy or school trouble? I couldn't imagine either. My sister-in-law had been the easiest houseguest. However, she had been slightly strange over the last couple of weeks: polite as usual, but with a kind of anxious excitement, and she seemed not to want to look me in the eye. Hormonal, perhaps. I had been edgy the last few days myself for the same reason. Monica's and my periods had coalesced as women's often do when they live together. That would probably have been a sign of us being witches centuries ago.

At ten o'clock, Jon messaged. They were coming home. Could I have supper ready? I prepared scrambled eggs, easy food to eat. The three of them were tired and quiet. Hannah and Mike pushed food around their plates then went up to sleep in Monica's room. In the morning, I called my editor and explained I couldn't come to work. I joined another fruitless search. The police took an interest once Monica had been gone twenty-four hours; they searched too. Her disappearance was on the local news.

The knock on the door came two days' later, and the officers asked us to sit while they spoke to us. Monica's body had been pulled from the Delaware River. My sister Courtney had confessed to her murder.

Courtney

I opened the door and two police officers stood there, bathed in the light of a violent sunset. It was just routine questioning of everyone with a link to Monica, however tenuous. But when I saw the guns on their hips, I crumbled: down on my knees, on the scratchy hall carpet.

'What's the matter, ma'am?' one policeman inquired, 'get up, please. If you have something to say, we can go into a sitting room.'

'What's wrong, Courtney?' Mom asked.

Still kneeling, I stretched out my hands to the officers. 'It was me,' I announced. 'I killed Monica.'

'No, you didn't,' Mom implored. 'Courtney's a social worker,' she told the police.

At the station, I was strip-searched and put into an orange jumpsuit that smelled of body odor. The room I was questioned in was claggy. The water in the small plastic cup was cloudy. Tears dribbled down my face.

'Why did you kill Miss Monica Andrews?' a detective asked.

I stared at the table, which was grey like a bad history. Already, I was regretting my confession. The idea of prison was terrifying.

As I spoke, the detectives listened attentively, like the birds listen to the air; alert for what they wanted a murderer to say. I did my best to sound convincing without telling the truth. If I did that, I would implicate my boyfriend, Tim. He loved me. And yet, he had been sleeping with Monica, a girl fourteen years' younger than him and almost family.

I hadn't suspected an affair. Tim had been behaving oddly, but I'd thought he was worried about money: we were getting together a deposit for our first house. One night over pizza in our favorite Italian, I asked Tim if he was okay: he was barely eating or talking. He broke down and told me everything. He had met Monica at a club when he was on a bachelor night party. He was sorry, but didn't want to stop seeing her. He was in love with her.

'But you love me,' I said.

Tim had been considering proposing, I knew. How could he have changed his mind so fast? Perhaps my inability to bear children was an issue. Monica, a child herself, would be able to push a baby out easily.

I pleaded with Tim to choose me, prostrated myself, but he just told me I'd meet someone 'more worthy of me'. He seemed relieved the secret was out.

The next morning, I went to Roseanne's. Monica left for school at nine, I knew, because Roseanne had moaned that even though her sister-in-law was the last to leave the house, she never washed-up breakfast. At eight forty, I rang the bell. I hadn't planned what to say, I just wanted to appeal to her: female to female. I wasn't intending to hurt her. I was a children's social worker, a good person: I'd never been in a physical fight apart from with my sister, which didn't count as all siblings fought.

Monica looked scared when she saw me standing on the doorstep.

'Can I come in?' I asked.

'I'm about to go to school,' she said.

'A quick coffee and a chat are all I want.'

I followed her into the kitchen: past the flashy coffee maker, the Nutri bullet, the best of the children's artwork. Monica reached into a cupboard for mugs and her robe slipped to reveal creamy, smooth skin. I thought of Tim touching that young flesh.

'Stop having sex with my boyfriend, Monica. Please.'

Monica turned from the coffee machine and slowly put the mugs onto the breakfast bar.

'I'm really sorry,' she said, her face young and fresh as a spring garden, 'that you're hurt. We never wanted that.'

'We': that stabbed me. But perhaps if she'd left it at that, it could have been different. I wasn't there to harm her; just to talk. I could have gone home and bided my time. They probably would have split up within a month with the excitement of the sneaking-around gone. Tim would have come back.

But she said: 'I love him.'

'You hardly know him.'

'Tim and I have something special. I want you to know that I wouldn't be with him if it wasn't serious. I'm really sorry, Courtney. It's so awkward that you're Roseanne's sister.'

'You're not having him,' I spat.

Monica ran her hands over her face. 'You're angry with the wrong person.'

I picked up the closest thing – a saucepan – and hit Monica.

The coroner found that she had unusually thin skin; most people wouldn't have died from a hit like that. It was just bad luck, really.

It took me a while to realize she was dead. I shook her, slapped her. She didn't respond. I knelt beside her body for half an hour, then carried her out to my car. This was an area where most people were out in the day; no one saw. I waited until night, rolled Monica's body up and put it in the river.

I hoped everyone, including Tim, would think Monica had run away. I wasn't planning on confessing, but then the police came: I wasn't strong enough to lie outright.

During the long hours of questioning, I stated that I went to Roseanne's house to see her. She was having a hard time and I wanted to share the burden, as sisters do. She wasn't there and instead I got into an argument with Monica. My sister had wanted Monica to leave the house, it wasn't big enough for all of them, I said; I was backing Roseanne up. When confronted, to my amazement, Monica started hitting and clawing me; I smacked her with the pan in self-defense.

'I am so sorry for what I've done,' I said through my tears.

Roseanne

The papers lapped-up the story of a woman killing a young girl. Far more was made of it than if a man had committed the murder, I suspected. Most of the stories and op-eds were by women. The popular papers cited potential lesbian motivations; *The New York Times* wrote about the third wave of feminism, how women had stopped pitting themselves against men and started to fight each other. The witch trials were brought up.

The newspapers all stated, as if it were fact, Courtney's untrue claim that I hated Monica; resented having her in my house. I couldn't imagine why my sister said this. Couldn't imagine why she would have killed Monica. Both things, the hatred Courtney seemed to feel for me, and the fact of Monica's death, were devastating.

The publicity nearly finished my parents, who wouldn't believe Courtney had done it. What happened splintered Jon and I, too; we couldn't talk to each other about it. Hannah and Mike wouldn't speak to me. I was asked not to go to Monica's funeral.

'It'd be best if you stay home with the girls, Rosie.' Jon looked at me under the ridge of his forehead. 'They're too young to come.'

I felt that eight-year-old Libby, at least, may have benefitted from the chance to say goodbye. She worshipped her aunt. I, too, wanted to say goodbye. I had cared for Monica, and her killing tore a hole in me. But I had no voice in all of this. So I said nothing, and this became a habit. Words could perhaps have broken up the pain a little, but they were kept inside.

And then there was another knock on the door. Two detectives. They asked if I would accompany them to the station for a polygraph test.

'Of course,' I said, assuming this request was to do with Courtney's case.

It was suspicious that I didn't ask why I should take such a test, I was told later. But my sister had confessed to Monica's murder, and as far as I knew was guilty. I felt my own innocence shining white as an x-rayed bone.

At the station, I heard that Courtney had taken back her testimony. She was now saying that, believing I killed Monica, she confessed to stop my two children losing their mother.

I failed the polygraph test; Courtney passed. I was arrested.

'I didn't do it,' I said, 'why would I have?'

'We have proof that you did.'

They told me and told me things about myself, that day and the next, and I felt myself unwind like a bandage, ready to be wrapped again into the murderess they wanted me to be.

They told me: there were two sets of fingerprints on the murder weapon, a saucepan that was part of my wedding set. I had used it hundreds of times. With it, I made porridge the morning Monica was killed, and didn't wash it up. Courtney's DNA was explained by her dropping round Dana's birthday gift the day before. She claimed to have picked up the saucepan then; she often tidied up a little in my home, apparently.

They told me: Tim had testified to being with Courtney when Monica was killed. When the truth eventually came out, I wondered why. Maybe he felt guilty for his part in it. Maybe he thought suspicion would fall on him. He wouldn't want people knowing that he, a children's social worker, had been sleeping with a sixteen-year-old; he probably imagined being fired. Also, Tim's parents were evangelical Christians, he may have expected them to disown him.

The police told me: a precise time of death for Monica couldn't be established beyond a few hours. Later, it was found that mistakes were made with forensics.

I told them: I was not guilty, there was no reason for me to kill Monica, I was fond of my sister-in-law. I said this over and over until the words were like sleep, until I had melted down to the size of the small facts.

When I was not being told things, I was in a cell. For three days, the longest time I have been away from my daughters, I walked around the walls in shock; numb and cold.

I called Jon when I was allowed, but the phone rang out. I kept trying, desperate to speak to Libby and Dana. The only visitor was my friend Karin, who held my hand and said the idea of my killing someone was crazy. She found me a defense attorney, who told me I had a good case. The motive wasn't there, he said.

And yet, at the preliminary hearing, the court found probable cause that I had murdered Monica and the case was bound over to trial court.

Because of the widespread pre-trial publicity, my trial took place in Erie County, six months after my voluntary trip to the police station for the polygraph. There I listened, shackled, to the prosecution lawyer stating that I killed Monica because she refused to leave my house. My defense attorney protested that no one apart from my sister, who couldn't be considered reliable owing to her lies to the police, witnessed me saying I wanted Monica to leave the house. Jon stated that he hadn't noticed ill-feeling between Monica and me, but he was at work much of the time so may not have realized 'what was going on'. He didn't look at me while he testified. Love, with all its gestures, all its memories, all its allegiances, seemed to have slipped away.

I sat in the courtroom, trapped between known and unknown, past and future, listening. When the trial finished each day, I wrote to my girls although I was unsure if Jon passed the letters on. Libby and Dana didn't come to the courthouse, of course. I thought of them at school, wondering if they were being bullied by their classmates for what I had been accused of. Would Jon let them think their mother was a murderer? I wondered how well he was taking care of them. Were they attending their ballet and swimming classes? Did Jon remember Libby's pecan and walnut allergies?

The case wore on, much of it dull. But then it was Courtney's time to testify, and the courtroom was full of reporters. Some of them I recognized. They made so much noise the judge threatened to throw out anyone not directly involved with the case.

I stared at my sister, a familiar stranger, her hand on the Bible.

'Ms Oliver, why did you voluntarily confess to killing Miss Andrews?' was my defense attorney's initial question.

'I panicked.'

'You panicked?'

'I retracted my testimony when I realized my little sister needed to accept responsibility for her actions,' Courtney said. She didn't look at me either. 'What message does it send to her two daughters otherwise?'

I was sentenced to life imprisonment for the murder of Monica Paige Andrews.

The press loved the story. As a tribute, my paper only wrote a short article, but the *Inquirer* splashed it over their cover for days. The case made the news in over thirty countries. The articles focused on me, Courtney, and Monica, with many comparisons made between our appearances – in the pictures, I looked either shabby and harassed ('The Mom Child-Killer') or dead-eyed and heartless ('The Face of Evil'), and my body shape was picked over: I was both a 'Wisp of a Woman' and a 'Base Barbie Doll', with several commentators musing on whether I suffered from anorexia. Courtney was photoshopped to look glamorous, a reversal of how it was when she was in the frame for the crime: as was Monica. Our three ages were given in every article; Tim's and John's were not. In the pencil sketches of our lives, in the drama and pathos-packed 800-worders, there were no mentions of college degrees or careers. There were many elucidations of the hidden hatred between women. Many articles focused on motherhood, and how some women rejected their role: 'Monica Murdered by the Mom who should have Mothered her' screamed one headline: confusing and clunky subbing, I thought. The press defined me through my role as a mother while considering me a she-devil who hated children. On social media, tens of thousands of strangers bayed for my blood.

Courtney

I didn't read any of the publicity after the verdict; it was too painful, even though some of the photos of me I glanced at were so nice I would have liked to cut out and keep them. Roseanne looked dreadful, for once.

I had, undeniably, ruined my sister's life. I didn't mean to. Roseanne's conviction was a shock; I had assumed her lack of any real motive would get the case thrown out. Jon's testimony didn't help her.

Prison was terrible. But I rationalized that if either of us was going to survive there, it was Roseanne. She would get out, of course she would. Somehow, she would make sure of that. The police could then fit up some poor homeless person for the murder: could prison be much worse than the streets? Prison was warm, at least, and had a library.

And yet Roseanne's luck seemed to have run out. Now what could I do? How could I let her children suffer without their mother, believing her to be a murderer?

Roseanne

I wintered in jail, striving to become sheer air, a ghost. Like a ghost, I was condemned to wait.

Sometimes when I woke, before opening my eyes, I forgot. It had happened when I was pregnant, too: I would lie there in bed, feeling relaxed and myself, before moving and feeling the heaviness. The weight now was a mental one, my brain densely packed with thoughts. What had I done to be so terribly punished by my sister? was what I thought most often. Courtney and I didn't get on as kids, she maybe secretly disliked me as an adult, but why had that corroded into hatred? Why were our parents so partial, so blinkered? Had my sister killed Monica and if so, why? If not, then who had? These questions were like fog pressed against a windowpane; I couldn't see past them to the answers.

My isolation and misery were exacerbated when Jon told me he was moving to New York. 'My parents need me,' he said, and he needed to get away. He found new schools for Libby and Dana; he would commute to Philadelphia while looking for a job in New York.

Neither of us considered it suitable for the girls to visit me in prison; it would be traumatic for them. The trial over, I received letters and pictures from them; they wrote that they missed me. They also told me of their new friends, their new school, their new apartment, skating in Central Park, how good a cook their grandmother was, and about the chihuahua they had been promised. I wrote that I missed them, so much, and loved them, so much. I said I wouldn't be in prison forever and was appealing the conviction.

I tried to feel positive, a new attorney having taken over my case. Naomi Adams was a high-profile woman based in New Jersey, working pro bono in exchange for the publicity. She was slick and charmless, but I didn't care about her personality if she could free me. She said the fact that I had no clear motivation to kill Monica was to my advantage. I had no past criminal history, no history of violence or mental health issues, either. And polygraphs were not always conclusive.

While I waited and hoped, I asked Mom and Dad to visit. Only Mom came. Dad wasn't too well, apparently. Wearing an orange ski jacket that clashed with my prison jumpsuit, Mom sat across from me with a thin smile, vague pain on her face. Silences hung like missed beats in an unrehearsed piece of music.

'You look well, Rosie; prison can't be too bad,' she said. Her tone made me think of an old wrapped sweet found coated in dust in a handbag, eaten purely to remove the flavor of a meal. A mistake as soon as it was felt, soft and wrong tasting in the mouth.

'I want you to know I'm innocent, Mom,' I said. 'My new attorney says I have a good chance of having my conviction overturned.'

'Well, that's good to hear,' she replied. 'But if you didn't do it, Roseanne, who did? I know Courtney didn't.'

'I don't want to talk about Courtney.' My voice was louder than I meant it to be. 'I'm the one in prison; could you think about me?'

'Is it my fault you girls don't get along? I've always wanted you to.'

I had known that she would say things like this. Things that were about her and Courtney, and not me.

We made more pale conversation and she walked away.

Courtney

Dear Roseanne,

I have confessed again to the murder. I hope it ensures your freedom.

Changing my story wasn't something I did to hurt you. It was just the easiest thing to do. I'd thought I deserved to be punished, but then realized I had been. I'd lost the man I loved. Tim was sleeping with Monica. When I found out, all I could think was that I couldn't lose him. I couldn't ever have children, and that was only bearable if I could have him. He'd just had his head turned by a silly, pretty girl. I asked Monica to leave him alone. She refused. I lost my temper, and she died by accident.

You probably think I've always hated you. In fact, I always wanted to be you. That may seem strange, as we both know I was Mom and Dad's favorite. Conventionally, parents favor the golden child. That was you, with your Harvard education, your beauty, your children. I was medium-clever, not that pretty, and barren. Mom and Dad saw all that and wanted to look after me. I guess they thought no one else would.

Rosie, I'd like to tell you that I'm doing this because I feel so bad for you, my little sister; or even that I feel so bad for Libby and Dana. I do feel bad. I also know I can't get away with this forever. Your new attorney's good, she'll work it out. And Tim is crumbling; he can't live with himself. He suspects I killed her.

I know what prison's like: I'm not going there again.

When you're free, live a good life. Make it count. Love your girls and appreciate them. Don't let them compete.

I'm sorry.

Courtney.

Roseanne

After I had been in prison for three months, I was called to the governor's office. She told me that I was to be released from prison. Courtney had committed suicide; was found by our mother hanging in her childhood bedroom. She left a letter for the police admitting to Monica's murder, and a note for me. The polygraph test I took was found to be invalid.

The next day, my best friend Karin was waiting outside the jailhouse, tears running down her cheeks. I ran to her, and we held each for a long time, before she took my arm and led me to her car. I would be staying with her for a while. Jon had rented out our home: I couldn't go back until the contract's expiration date. He had been trying to sell it but, as a murder was committed there, vendors had shown little interest; renters weren't so choosy. Nor could I afford to be. For now, I had my oldest friend. Karin and I sat up all night talking, drinking hot chocolate with marshmallows as we did when we were children.

At the weekend, Jon drove the girls over to Karin's. She had gone to stay with her sister Nerissa for the weekend; I was so grateful to have the space for my girls and me to hopefully reconnect. I was also so nervous about seeing them. What must they think? What may the trauma of their mother having been in prison, of the two deaths, have done to them?

When their dad had gone, Libby and Dana edged toward me like shy foals. I knelt, as I used to when they were smaller. Then they were in my arms, and I was bent low in the embrace. We all wept. So much water had flowed from my eyes recently; it had proved to be thicker than blood, in most cases; but not all.

The three of us ate dinner and watched TV. I had planned for them to sleep in Karin's spare room while I took her bed. Libby, though, asked if she could sleep with me, and so of course Dana did too. The bed was too small for us all but who cared. I held their restless bodies until dawn, arms and heart aching.

On the Saturday, the girls were talkative. They asked if I was sad that Auntie Courtney was dead. I said yes. Courtney was a deeply troubled person, but I didn't want hatred to consume me as it had her. Hatred was a distortion of love, and I could have done more to make Courtney love me; to make her see she had advantages; to have made her a bigger part of what she regarded as my charmed life. I remembered the time I saw her touching her breasts in the bathroom mirror; I saw her, she saw me, but we couldn't see the two of us together. We never could. I longed for a moment with my sister, just to talk, but she had walked into the unspoken.

The next morning, I managed not to cry until the girls had gone, holding hands as they scampered to their father's car. He gave me a small wave and I waved back, because he was their father, and because together we had created sisters who held each other's hands.

Palimpsest

In primary school, there were not sports days but 'junior challenges'. No winner in any event, no awards, everyone part of a team. Parents came to watch, though my mum was rarely there because as a doctor she couldn't get time off. At Waldemoor School for Girls, however, where I was finishing Year Seven, sports day was its traditional competitive self. It was that type of school, Ofsted Outstanding and 'fiercely achieving', as the poster spread across the fence declared, making me think of lions fighting for the largest piece of carcass.

When I woke on the day itself, July 7th, sunlight was piercing the curtains' thin skin. I hoped it would be hot enough to warrant a cancellation. I knew there was a chance of that because I'd overheard a conversation between the head of PE, Miss O'Connor, and the deputy head, Mrs Milleen, about whether the school would be in trouble if girls got sunstroke.

'If it's over thirty degrees, we'll cancel,' Mrs Milleen had murmured. 'Organise letters home reminding the girls to wear suncream and hats, and to bring extra water, Maria.'

As I dragged myself out of bed, sweat clinging to my body, I checked the weather report. The day's high would be twenty-nine degrees, the weather person slinked.

'Good luck for sports day, Sofia,' Mum said, when I came down to breakfast; she was already on her second piece of toast. 'Don't run too fast and get heat stroke.'

'There's no chance of me running too fast.'

'Wish I could be there to watch you,' she said while brushing toast crumbs from her shirt and rising from her chair.

This year, I wouldn't be the only one with a mother in non-attendance; the parents of us predators were not invited for sports day, just assemblies and plays. I didn't know why sports day was different; it made it seem insular and disturbing, as though it could have happened in *The Secret History*, a book I had just devoured even though Mum said it was too old for me.

'Are you alright, Sofia?' Dad slid a piece of toast onto my plate. 'You're looking pale.'

I considered leaping on this idea – feigning sickness or a migraine – but my parents wouldn't let me stay at home alone, and if they were with me, I would have to languish in bed all day like Beth in *Little Women*.

The changing room was nearly full. I found a peg at the end of a row, took off my clothes and folded my skirt neatly before placing it into my gym bag, wishing I could fold myself away too.

'Where's Rachel Bentley?' I heard Keeley Waters ask, and someone replied that she was off sick. There was a Greek chorus of disbelief: Rachel Bentley was the Year Seven sports star. She was always first in cross-country but a good sprinter too; great at the long-jump and high-jump; a marvel at the discus, shot-put and javelin.

'Probably skiving because she was scared she might lose a race,' Carrie Simmonds sniggered, and Keeley smiled.

Miss O'Connor, skin tarnished brown like an old tree, strutted in with a clipboard. She noticed Rachel Bentley's absence immediately, and was displeased by it. Rachel had been due to take part in all the activities. Miss O'Connor bustled around nominating people to undertake these events instead of her star. I was asked to throw the javelin. I felt pleased; running made me wheeze, but I wasn't bad at the javelin. It could mean a pinch of praise for minimal effort.

'The javelin's the second event,' added Miss O'Connor. 'Keeley and Carrie, can you mark the distances, please? I'll show you what to do.'

Keeley nodded; Carrie pouted. The two were best friends. Carrie was eerily beautiful, a living doll with silky blonde hair and Mangaesque ice-blue eyes. She was a cross between Jessica Wakefield in *Sweet Valley High* and Rebecca in *Rebecca*. At school, she could do and say as she liked and no one told her to shut up or slapped her porcelain cheek. Keeley was smiley and jokey; on her own, she could be nice to me. Carrie was always mean. She once came up and asked, voice snaking into my ears, if she could have a private word; thrilled that she might be willing to be my friend, I trotted after her. She murmured that I had lice, she had seen one hopping on my hair. I fought back tears of mortification. Carrie then told everyone in the class not to sit next to me, or they would catch lice. That night Mum checked my hair and said there was nothing there. No one sat next to me for days, and Carrie smirked whenever she saw me, nudging Keeley to make her laugh.

We trooped outside. Miss O'Connor's whistle shrilled. The first event was the eight-hundred metres, which seemed to take forever to start and forever to run.

And then, the javelin throwing. Carrie and Keeley were holding tape measures to mark the distances. I stood in line, second to throw, aertex top sticking to my back.

Marina West was first. When she threw, Carrie and Keeley were chatting, and Miss O'Connor had to shout to them to pay attention. Carrie sashayed over to mark with her tape measure. It was a good throw: sixteen metres. I had done seventeen in an athletics lesson, and people had clapped. Even Rachel Bentley had clapped.

'Sofia Carter,' called Miss O'Connor, and I was given the javelin.

It could have been different if Anaya Regan in Year Nine hadn't fainted. She had just won the eight-hundred metres; maybe not having Rachel Bentley to beat spurred her on to strive fiercely for greatness, as she set a new school record. She also collapsed ten minutes after the race and Miss O'Connor, the only first-aid-trained adult nearby, ran to help.

'Do I throw?' I asked Marina, who shrugged.

'Get on with it, Sofa,' Carrie called.

She called me Sofa because, like a sofa, I was fat and squashy. Keeley laughed, as if Carrie had pressed a button on her back to make her do so. I had a doll like that when I was little, except she cried rather than laughed.

I picked up the javelin, cold and smooth beneath my hot fingers, its point a pencil with which I could write *I'm not a loser, bitches*. I held it along the length of my palm and gripped the back of the cord with my thumb, the first two joints of my index finger behind the cord.

Carrie and Keeley resumed their chat. Were they talking about me?

I pulled my arm back as far as I could, arching my body, legs scissoring. Power flowed into and through me. I took the run-up and hurled the javelin.

It flew; it would be my best throw ever.

And then, the javelin went the wrong way. It should have gone left but veered to the right.

I could see what was going to happen, and screamed her name. Everyone else must have seen it too; they screamed her name. She ducked and I thought, thank God, it'll miss her.

But it didn't miss her.

The javelin struck Keeley above her eye. She stumbled and fell. There was so much blood.

The screaming went on and on.

I wanted to help, to do something for Keeley, but couldn't put my body in the right place. Mrs Milleen appeared at my side.

'Come on, Sofia,' she said, 'let's take you inside and sit you down.'

Mrs Milleen and I crossed the field as the ambulances were coming down the school's long driveway. I looked at Keeley's prone body then flicked a glance at Carrie, whose hands were covering her face.

People made space for Mrs Milleen and me to pass. Only once, when I played the Tin Man in my primary school's production of *The Wizard of Oz* had so many people looked at me.

Mrs Milleen took me into the staff room. It was empty and smelled of old food. I sat on the edge of a scratchy green chair, as Mrs Milleen used a machine to make tea. I had never drunk tea before. It scalded my mouth, but it was good to have something to hold.

'She'll be okay, Sofia,' said Mrs Milleen, sitting opposite me. 'She's in the best hands. It was an accident; you mustn't blame yourself.'

She couldn't say Keeley's name, I realised. I couldn't speak, I just held the tea. My head felt as if it were full of the thick padding my parents laid in the loft.

And then Mum was there. As she wrapped her arms around me, the tears came.

Keeley died in hospital three days' later. I hadn't gone back to school in that time, and knew I wouldn't return before the summer holidays. Mum hadn't been to work, although Dad had, which wasn't the natural order of things. I sat in my room and Mum made hushed phone calls. She brought up all my favourite foods, including the doughnuts and chocolate I was rarely allowed, but I couldn't force much down my throat.

I tried to read – I was on *Lord of the Flies* – but the words wouldn't stick in my mind. I thought about Keeley, all the time, thoughts that were rainbow-quick, faint as a heart. I remembered the time we had to give speeches about our holidays and she talked about a family trip to Greece; her younger brother would only eat chips (everyone laughed at that) but she loved halloumi cheese and taramasalata, and I wanted to ask what those fantastic foods were, but thought Carrie would mock me if I did; also the time she came to school on her birthday wearing scarlet lipstick, which made her look prettier and older, and was told to remove it by a teacher; I wished there were more memories.

I also thought of Keeley's family, who I had never seen, so my thoughts were just fantasies: I imagined her nameless brother and their parents, who must surely be crying non-stop, stopping all the clocks, cutting off the telephone, preventing the dog from barking with a juicy bone. I thought of how Carrie must hate me, even more than she did already, and what she would do when she saw me.

Mum assured me that Keeley's family didn't blame me; she had talked to them on the phone. They had suggested I go to the funeral, but I couldn't bear to. Mum said we could visit the gravesite together afterwards; lay flowers.

Just before the funeral, I was told the police needed to talk to me about what had happened; it was just procedure. Everything was 'just' something, and given the enormity of what had happened, that seemed paradoxical.

'How do they know what happened?' I asked. Mum looked blank. 'I mean, they weren't there.'

'They were told by the witnesses. There's nothing to worry about, Sofia.'

'Nothing to worry about.' I laughed: she didn't.

The police came that evening, two women, and Mum brought in tea and biscuits she had made herself, and sat beside me, holding my hand. The officers had quiet, kind voices, but I couldn't look at them, as if they were shining spotlights into my eyes.

They asked me to tell them what had happened on sports day, then they asked if Keeley and I had ever argued at school.

'Sofia has never argued with anyone in her class,' Mum said, and I wanted to ask how she knew. I had never told her about what Carrie had done to me, with Keeley looking on. I also wondered how the police would have reacted if I'd said that I had argued with Keeley.

'Keeley was very smiley,' I said, realising it sounded like a crap rhyming poem, and burst into tears. Mum passed me a tissue. I tried to say more, as if this were Keeley's funeral and I was delivering the eulogy, but thoughts skimmed the top of my mind with a bird's wing and didn't land.

The police officers got up to leave soon after that. They talked to Mum at the front door.

'They're satisfied it was an accident. You look tired, Sofia,' Mum said, 'go to bed and I'll bring you up warm milk.'

The milk didn't help. I lay under thoughts of Keeley, as if they were a heap of photographs of her, compressing me with their flat weight.

In September, I walked into the Year Eight classroom for registration and the first person I saw was Carrie. There was an empty chair next to her. I sat as far away from her as possible and took out my pencil case, pretending to search for something in it. Girls came into the classroom, some talking, some in groups, some alone. No one took the chair beside Carrie. There was an empty one beside me, too, but then I felt a hovering presence. For a second, I had a crazy thought that it was Keeley. I saw her everywhere. When I walked, she walked with me; we were two pieces of a broken line.

'Can I sit here, Sofia?' Rachel Bentley asked.

She had changed her hair over the summer, cut it short; she looked older. I had grown a fringe, but didn't think it made me look any different. I had also lost weight; now I was more of a fainting chair than a squashy sofa.

'How was your summer, Sofia?' Rachel asked. 'Did you go anywhere?'

I couldn't believe she was asking such a normal question. Did she not know about Keeley?

'I went to Greece,' I said. 'Larnaca.'

I had made my parents book a week's holiday in Greece, because of Keeley. It didn't help my grief: thoughts of her still filled every part of space and time, were present in every grain of sand on the beach and every droplet of sea water that touched my skin. For her, I had eaten halloumi and taramasalata as often as I could, though I hadn't liked either.

'That sounds amazing,' said Rachel. 'I'd love to go to Greece. My parents made me go to running camp. I'd much rather have been lazing on a beach.'

'I thought you loved running,' I said.

'It's what I'm good at, so....' She shrugged.

I didn't say anything else. I had settled into my misery as if it were an old coat, and wasn't used to having normal conversations. Rachel smiled, not seeming to mind.

Every desk was taken now, except the one beside Carrie. She was staring straight ahead. Our new teacher came in and the chatter faded. My chest constricted, expecting that the teacher would say something about Keeley, but she didn't. For the whole day, no one did. In every class that I had with Carrie, there was an empty chair beside her. She didn't make eye contact with me, and I tried not to look at her. I wondered what she would say if she knew that I had written letters to Keeley all through the summer holidays. My therapist had suggested it: I liked writing the letters more than the therapy sessions.

At lunchtime Rachel asked if she could sit with me, and Marina West joined the table too. Marina talked about her holiday in Cornwall and I talked again about Greece.

After lunch, we had PE with a new teacher. At the inquest into Keeley's death, the school had been criticised for the way sports day had been run: there should have been more trained first aiders; Year Seven girls should not have been left to do a javelin event unsupervised. Mum had told me that Miss O'Connor had been sacked ('And quite right too,' she added vengefully). The new teacher, a woman whose name I forgot as soon as she said it, made us do netball. I was wing attack, WA emblazoned on the back of my purple bib: I pretended they were the initials of my new name, Wilhelmina Angel or Wanda Amazing. Rachel Bentley was centre: when she passed the ball to me and I managed to get it into the net, she high-fived me.

Carrie was goal keeper; she didn't move from the goal circle. Keeley had always been goal defence in Year Seven; she played in matches on the A squad. Carrie and Keeley always made sure the other got the ball. Marina West was made goal defence and she was good, too, catching the ball every time it went into the defensive third. She and Carrie didn't interact, as if the goal circle that Carrie stood in was a country as far away as Greece.

By the time the bell rang for the end of school, no one had mentioned Keeley. Had I erased her when I killed her? I thought of the word I had learned in the summer, from *The Handmaid's Tale*: palimpsest. Had Keeley's life been a manuscript page erased so that mine could be written on it? It didn't seem fair, given what I had done; but then life was not.

Making Memories

Present

There are at least two hundred women in the cell. Nicky and I are the only Western ones. We are all in uniforms: dark trousers and tunics the colour of illness.

The warden indicates two thin, dirty mattresses at the end of a row. We sit. The warden leaves. The cell has a hopeless, stale smell.

The other women stare, laughing and muttering. One winks. I look away at black writing on stone walls, the words like code.

There is a layer of fuzziness as though my senses have been anaesthetised, although every now and then terror streams before my eyes. An ant runs over my leg, then another, there seems no point brushing them away.

Nicky is crying. I move my hand towards hers but can't touch her.

Past

'Cheers, Aoife! To our freedom!'

Glasses raised, Nicky and I squeeze our faces together. She presses the button on her phone a couple of times. It's not good enough; she takes another. This one, along with the five we took earlier, and the ten we'll take later, will be filtered then posted with taglines like # Making Memories #Airport Adventures # Girls on

Tour # Best Friends Forever # So excited!!! # Living our best lives! She'll get around 200 likes, including from me.

'Another bottle?' Nicky is already standing.

It's when she's at the bar that I see him, crossing the room to the toilets. Very blond hair, sparse darker facial hair, tanned skin. Very good-looking. He looks over as if he's felt my stare and our eyes meet; he smiles.

I see him again eleven hours later, at New Bangkok International Airport. The alcohol and the turbulence have misshapen me. Nicky looks fresh, having drooled on my shoulder for the eight hours of the flight.

'Photo in front of the airport,' Nicky commands. 'An old-fashioned one.'

And there he is, walking towards the smooth mouth of the airport, carrying a large backpack. I unglue my tongue and call: 'Hi there, could you take a photo?'

The man says sure, in a languourous Australian accent. His eyes are freezer-light blue. Nicky smiles widely as she hands him her phone. He seems to struggle with how it works: we don't question that, at the time. Then he takes the photo.

As we wander through the doors to the customs queue, the man introduces himself as Andy. He asks what we're doing in Thailand. We say this is a two-day stop-off on the way to Australia, where we're spending the summer before going to university travelling and working, starting with Sydney. Andy says he's from Sydney; he has also been travelling and working ('Shit zero-hour contracts') in London. He's stopping over for two days too, to check out Thailand, he's never been. He's staying in the same place as us ('No way!'): the Mandarin Oriental.

'Need to treat myself,' Andy laughs. 'Been staying in some pretty bad places in the UK. The cockroaches were some of my nicer roomies. What's your excuse, girls? Got sugar daddies?'

Nicky has a rich daddy. He insisted we stay in luxury for the first two nights of our trip. My parents have stretched themselves paying for my air fare, I couldn't ask them to stump up for anything else. I have babysat every Saturday night for the past year, while studying for A-levels, to be able to afford this trip.

'So what you guys up to in Thailand?' Andy asks, as we stand in the immigration queue, passports in hand.

'Partying,' Nicky says. 'Fancy joining?'

'Never say no to a party,' Andy says, and they smile at each other in a way that is as exclusive as our hotel.

Nicky lies on the bed, thumbs flying across the screen of her phone. I explore our suite, exclaiming as I look around. There is a sofa, two armchairs, a pouffe, shiny tables holding large vases of lilies that push out a powerful smell, pleasantly anodyne pictures on the walls, a thick gold rug on the floor. If the air of Bangkok is a soup, the suite is a sorbet. I gaze out of the window at the city, absorbing the sleek lines of the twinkling skyscrapers that are like rich men winking and the Chao Phraya River gliding along with the smoothness of money changing hands.

'Smile.'

Nicky has her phone in her hand. She takes several photos of me with Bangkok in the background, several of her, several of both of us.

'Let's dress up, go out. Andy said there are a few great bars.'

'I thought he said it was his first time here.'

'Did he… maybe he read about them. Whatevs. Come on, let's go, we're only here for two nights, let's make the most of them.'

She takes an apple from a glass fruit bowl and takes an extravagant bite.

Andy chooses a bar that is based on a theatre. It is dark apart from a few lamps and dressing-table-style bulbs around mirrors. Heavy, wine-coloured curtains surround each table with claustrophobic glamour. We sit on wide, hard leather chairs and drink cocktails. Nicky flirts with Andy; I sit almost in silence.

Nicky goes to the toilet while Andy is at the bar; he comes back with a cloudy green drink, a cucumber wound seductively around a stick inside it. He leans close as he puts down the drink, and I smell his woody aftershave. Hopefully, there's a queue for the ladies. To eradicate the silence, I ask him about the drink.

'It's like a margarita but with chili,' he says. 'They call it a Roppongi Gimlet.'

I don't like chili. I take a sip and my throat burns. I start coughing, and Andy pats me on the back, laughing. My skin shivers under his hand.

'So, Aoife, that's an Irish name, right? I visited Dublin recently, great *craic*.'

Craic sounds so ridiculous in his Australian drawl that we both laugh. I tell him that my Irish dad met my Yorkshire mum when they were students in Leeds and ended up there. Andy is interested in what they do for work, what our house is like, what we do at weekends. I don't like taking up so much airtime so try to divert the conversational channel his way, but he keeps asking questions, as if he's a TV interviewer and I'm a celebrity.

'Finish what you were saying about your dad's business, Aoife,' Andy says. 'Does he make a lot of dough as a freelance writer?'

Nicky is back, having redone her make-up. Her gaze sticks on him and then me as if we are together inside a pot of honey.

'Selfie time,' Nicky says. 'Are you on Instagram, Andy? Facebook? Snapchat? Twitter?'

'Ah no, I don't do all that social media stuff. I'll take one of you gorgeous ladies, though. Give us your phone, Nicky.'

The next morning, Nicky refuses to explore Bangkok: she's hungover and wants to be pampered. What a waste of our last full day, I think but don't bother saying.

My mind a dark city, I fetch my backpack and shut the door hard; the noise is painful in the silent corridors. The lift whispers down to the hushed lobby. It is as if someone has pressed a mute button on real life. The Thai girl at Reception bows as I pass, and I'm so embarrassed that I laugh.

I feel the difference as soon as I push through the gold-rimmed glass doors. The street is a furnace of noise, as though everyone is angry. Cars, mostly at a standstill, hoot incessantly; motorbikes on which children ride side-saddle weave around them. It's so humid my skin feels as though it's sticking to itself.

I walk to the Creative District, to the Buddhist temple of Wat Suan Plu. The temple's blue mirror tiles are calming. It is as I am staring at the carvings that a voice says my name as if it is a question. I wonder, for an instant, if he has followed me. But he looks surprised. And pleased.

We wander the shrine room, looking at the adornments and vivid gables. Andy knows all about the temple. He directs me to the Reclining Buddha, who has flowing golden limbs and a tranquil mask-like face. The kind of face that sends you to a different place.

Outside again, the midday heat wraps itself around me. Seeing people with parasols, I realise I have forgotten to bring suntan lotion. My pale skin burns easily. Andy thinks the gift shop sells it; I hope he will offer to come with me, instead he says he will look after my backpack while I go. I tell him he doesn't need to, I'm used to the weight, but he's insistent.

'Tell you what,' he says, 'I'll take our bags to the café and buy us a drink.'

When I come back with the lotion, he is sitting with glasses of iced tea. I take a sip from one then smooth the cool suntan lotion onto my arms.

'Do each other's backs?' Andy takes the bottle, splurges cream onto his hands.

I gasp when his hands touch my back, rubbing in lazy circles. My body is sloppy with want. Then his hands knead my flesh, and I groan.

The sun cream comes too late, that night my skin is burned and painful. I've tried to disguise it with make-up but the gold eyeshadow is patchy on my tired lids and the foundation doesn't conceal my red skin. Nicky is wearing even more make-up than usual, and a puff-sleeve crop top that reveals more flesh than it covers. She had a massage, a facial, a spray tan and eyelash extensions while I was burning my skin in the name of culture.

Andy is sitting in the hotel bar where he suggested we meet, chatting to a dark-haired man. He hadn't mentioned knowing anyone in Thailand so I assume they've just met although their conversation looks intense, as if they are talking about finance rather than making small talk about travel plans. They stop talking when they see us, and there are kisses and introductions. The man's name is Boon-Nam. He is polite and softly-spoken, but there is something about the way he looks at Nicky and I, as if we are slabs of meat on a self, that makes me dislike him.

Boon-Nam buys champagne. I don't think I've had much before the room starts spinning. Boon-Nam is speaking to me in his soft voice but I don't know what he is saying. Nicky and Andy are squashed together, laughing. He has his hand on her thigh.

No. I saw him first.

I stumble to my feet and crash down next to Nicky. Everyone stops talking.

'Nicky, you need to go to bed,' I slur. 'Early flight.'

'You're the one who needs to go to bed,' Nicky says, in a light voice. 'Come on, sweetie, you've had enough for one night.'

I watch my anger as though it is a flame licking up a newly lit match.

'That's what you'd like, isn't it, Nicky? Me out of the way.'

'What's wrong with you, Aoife?' she asks.

Boon Nam places his hand on my shoulder. 'Let me see you to your room,' he says, nicely but firmly.

Nicky comes back at ten am, wearing yesterday's crop top. I have showered and am putting clothes into my backpack. We don't look at each other.

The silence is heavy in the suite, in the lobby, in the airport. I buy food and water for myself, she does the same, and we sit reading our books, a chair between us. She keeps looking up, I suppose for Andy, who is meant to be on the flight. He doesn't come.

At the gate, there are police with guns and large dogs. We pass through the x-ray scanner without incident.

We are waiting to collect our backpacks when the dogs start barking and jumping. My throat starts to close. The security officers grab our bags and rifle through them. The barking of the dogs is like bites taken out of the air.

The packages, rolled-up bags of white powder, are in our tights and socks. When they are found, the noise increases. The police and the guards surround us, shouting in Thai.

'Call my dad!' Nicky shouts, over and over.

They take us into a small room and a Thai man interrogates us in English. The taste in my mouth is acid adrenalin.

'You tell us why you smuggle the drugs, we let you go,' he says.

We tell him we didn't know the drugs were in our bags. He repeats that we must tell him why we did it. Nicky says that we have been set up. She says the drugs must have put into our bags by an Australian man that we met.

'What is his name?'

'Andy....' Neither of us knows his full name: he's Andy from Sydney. But we know he was staying at the Mandarin Oriental, and I say that.

'I will check,' says the Thai man.

He is away for an hour and six minutes: I know because I have nothing to do besides look at my watch. Nicky has her head on the table. She is emitting a thin, shrill noise.

When the man comes back, he says that the hotel does not have anyone named Andy or Andrew staying with them, and no one fitting his description has stayed there recently.

'But I stayed in his room last night,' Nicky says. 'You must check again.'

'I have already checked.'

I remember Boon-Nam. Maybe it was his room. I tell the man to look for Boon-Nam, but he shakes his head.

'We have seen what is on your phone,' he says.

'What are you talking about?'

He says that there were texts on both of our phones to heroin suppliers, specifying how much of the drug we wanted and the address we would deliver it to in Sydney, Australia.

'But....' There is a pressure in my head. 'This is all lies, you're lying.'

'You were flying to Sydney today?'

'Of course we were; you've seen our flight tickets.'

'We have called the number that you texted; I spoke to men who confirmed that two young British girls were bringing them drugs to sell on. The men will be tried in their own country.'

'This is all – a fabrication. A set-up. Someone got hold of our phones—'

'You tell me why you did it,' the Thai man says, 'then maybe I help you. You need money; that is why?'

'I don't need money. My father would give me money if I needed it,' Nicky says.

'How about you?' the man asks me. 'Do you need money? Is that why you smuggle the drugs? So you can stay in nice hotels?'

Present

In prison, our job is to embroider flowers onto shirts. I spend ten hours a day doing this, alongside the other women inmates. The routine is comforting, and boring. Everything is the same, every day. We eat the same meal – pork soup and rice – every day. Every day, we walk around the grounds, seeing the same sky and the same trees. Every day, twice a day, there are prayers in Thai, and I kneel with my head touching the ground like a sad flower. Once a week, there is a Thai massage session; one week we get it, the next we receive it. These moments of hands on skin are what I live for, this feeling of connection to another human.

One day after prayers, when we have been here for five months, the guards come for Nicky. She looks back at me as she walks away, blank-faced as she never was in all those hundreds of photos. And that is the last I see of her.

My father writes to say that Nicky's father got the best human rights lawyer money could buy. He tracked Andy, really Alan Cummings, down in his native Wellington and he was arrested. He must have agreed to some kind of deal as he said Nicky had nothing to do with it. It got her off her life sentence. Life means life here: ninety-nine years. Drugs mean death, unless you plead guilty. We couldn't deny that they had found the heroin on us, and I didn't want to die. I still have my life sentence, although my parents got me a lawyer too. The lawyer and I write to each other each week. I ask him whether there is an appeal date; he says he is working on it. If it fails, I could stay here for ten years before being transferred to a British prison. The appeal could well fail now that Nicky has been released: it makes it seem as though I were the guilty one. He tells me to be realistic about the fact that when this comes to court, they will say that I was jealous of my rich friend. That I smuggled drugs because I didn't have the kind of money that bought expensive hotels. That I wanted the man who wanted Nicky: or pretended to.

Most of the time, I am on the border of despair and numbness. Occasionally I feel angry: with Nicky, with the man I thought was Andy, with me. Mostly, I am bored. Few people speak English, so I can't talk much. I stopped reading, once I had read the five books in the library written in English. I have asked for more, but they haven't come. I doubt they will. Too much knowledge is dangerous. Too much knowledge gives people the freedom to escape, at least in their minds.

Someone Just Like Me

The neighbours are friendlier than I'd expected. As I am putting the bins out, the man across the road shouts over: 'I heard someone had moved into Sisi's house, I didn't realise it was you.' He beams at me. I smile, wondering if I should know who he is.

'How are you settling in?' the man asks. 'You must let Val and I know if you need anything. And we'd love you both to come over for a glass of wine.'

'That's very kind. We're settling in well, thanks.'

I go back inside, skin fizzing with pleasure to have made a connection. I wonder how I can find out the man's name. Then I realise that he must know Matt; he'd said 'You both'.

'You didn't tell me you'd met the man across the road,' I say to Matt.

'I haven't.' Matt is staring at the oven, face papered with confusion. 'Do you know how this thing works, Anthea?'

'There'll be a manual.' I look in a drawer, find a thick file with 'Appliances' written on it and pass it to him.

'Thanks, love. You were saying something about the man across the road?'

'Yes, he asked us over for a glass of wine. I think we're going to like it here.'

The friendliness does not abate. When I walk down the street, people wave and shout hello. Before moving to Twickenham, Matt and I lived in East London for three years and, beyond reciprocal thanks for taking in Amazon deliveries, barely spoke to our neighbours. I'd imagined that here it would, at least for a while, be the same, Matt and I as alone as the hooks we've put up in the hall but not yet put our coats onto. Obviously we've found our tribe. Or I have, as more people say hello to me than to Matt. I'm not sure whether he's noticed.

On Fridays, Matt and I both work from home, and it's our tradition to go out for lunch. For our first meal in our new area, we go to the Sunshine Café at the end of the road. It has Formica tables and chairs stuck to the floor, plastic vines rambling across the ceiling and faded photos of Turkey on the walls. Having ordered at the counter from a cheery man with a Turkish-sounding accent, we find a table. On the next one, a woman is spoon-feeding a baby in a highchair. She looks over as Matt and I sit down, her face breaking into a smile.

'Ah, hello, Anna,' she says. 'How are you?'

'Hello. My name's Anthea, actually,' I say, smiling to take the sting out of the words.

'You're not Anna?'

'No, I'm not.'

'But you really look like Anna.' The woman is frowning. 'Are you her sister?'

'No.'

'Really? You look so similar.'

'Right,' I say, fighting the urge to apologise for not being the person she thinks I am. She shrugs and turns back to her baby. I turn to Matt, who is smirking. When my jacket potato with tuna mayo arrives, too much yellow butter puddled on the plate, I'm not as hungry as I'd thought.

The next day, the same thing happens: someone greets me as Anna. I feel as if I'm wearing a skin that doesn't quite fit.

'I can't wait to come face-to-face with this Anna,' Matt laughs. 'It'll be like meeting a celebrity.'

I'm on a South West Train when the meeting happens: on the way to meet my friend Debbie to see a play. As I am settling into a seat, looking forward to thirty-five minutes with my audiobook, I hear a cheery: 'Hello, Anna.'

As I am about to reply, wondering if I should get a badge saying 'I'm Anthea, not Anna', a voice from across the carriage says: 'Oh hi, Jodie.'

Jodie, standing in the queue to get off the train, calls: 'We must get together soon, Anna, honey; I'll call you.'

When she has gone, I look across and meet Anna's eyes.

'Wow,' she says, 'you look so like me.'

The resemblance is uncanny. We both have long, wavy blonde hair – hers also clearly dyed – tied in a ponytail, blue eyes and aquiline noses. We also have pale skin with freckles across our cheeks. Anna is a little thinner, but apart from that we definitely look like sisters: even twins.

Anna pats the seat next to her. I stand as though a button has been pressed on my body.

'I need to know all about you right now,' Anna says. 'I feel as though I've got a doppelganger! Don't tell me your name's Anna, that would be too much.'

'My name's Anthea. I've just moved to St Margarets with my partner, and I keep being mistaken for you.'

Anna asks exactly where I live, and when I tell her, she widens her eyes.

'We're just around the corner from Madrid Road. Russell Drive, do you know it? The houses are pretty similar to those on Madrid Road: thirties terraces.'

We talk on, and I learn that Anna is also going to the theatre with a friend. I'm not surprised to learn that it's the same show I'm seeing with Debbie. That's not the only thing that is the same, I discover. The coincidences are remorseless as the days of a heatwave, and the more excited Anna becomes the more I feel as though I am disappearing, melting into her. I keep on smiling a sunny smile, however, as we learn that we both: 1) come from Reading, although Anna went to a private school there; 2) went to Nottingham University, she to study English and me to study history, two years' apart because Anna is younger and had a gap year; 3) after graduating did a PGCE, although neither of us lasted in the teaching profession and

4) work in the civil service now; 5) have partners – hers is Mike – who work in IT and are dark-haired and bearded ('Matt looks nice,' Anna says); 6) play tennis and run (we did the Great North Run three years ago; Anna's time was faster than mine).

'This is so spooky, I love it,' Anna exclaims.

The train reaches Waterloo. Anna stands and I do too. Realising that we are the same height, I laugh a broken note of sharp amusement. She gives me an odd glance then takes my arm. We fall into step (both of us walk quickly) and move through the throng to board the Northern Line for Leicester Square. When we are on the tube, Anna puts my number into her mobile.

It is a relief to see Debbie standing outside the theatre. She comes forward for a hug. Then the arms around me freeze.

'Anna,' Debbie says with pleasure.

The knotted-tight, layered entity that is 'I' vanishes then.

'Gosh you two, don't you look alike? Are you cousins?' Debbie asks.

'We've just discovered each other; can you believe it?' Anna shrills.

Anna introduces us both to her friend, Dee, who has been unknowingly standing next to Debbie. They too look slightly alike, both with black bobs and heavy-rimmed glasses.

'Wow,' Dee says, 'I need to get a photo of you and your doppelganger, Anna.'

'How did I never notice that you look like each other?' Debbie asks. 'Are you sure you're not sisters? You look identical.'

'I'm sure we're not sisters,' I say, watching a man in a fedora walking a cat on a lead. No one remarks on this strangeness, so I don't either. It is, after all, Central London.

While Debbie is searching her bag for our tickets, I tune into Dee and Anna's conversation.

'Remember that programme I was telling you about, when we had lunch?' Dee is saying. 'I think I've found the stars of it. You two are perfect.'

Anna squeals.

'What programme?' I ask.

'I work for BBC Three,' Dee says. 'We're doing a programme about genetics, a boffin talking about face mapping techniques and that kind of thing. We were scouting for twins, but you look as alike as most of the twins I've seen. More, actually.'

'We'll be famous, Anthea,' Anna exclaims.

After the theatre trip on Friday, I stay in the house for the rest of the weekend. On the Saturday, Matt suggests a trip to the local farmers' market, but I say there's too much to do here: boxes to unpack, cleaning to be done.... But I don't unpack or clean anything. I find myself on property apps, looking at houses in other areas of London. Matt and I watch a film in the evening, but even though we are snuggled on the sofa the air feels dense and awkward with the secret of my meeting with Anna. On the Sunday, Matt suggests a picnic in Bushy Park, which we have yet to visit. It's hot, for September, it could be the last nice weather we have all year, he cajoles. Again I refuse. He says in that case he'll meet up with some mates for a drink or two, and I say that's fine. As soon as he's left, I close the curtains and go to bed.

A week passes. Anna rings me a couple of times, but I don't answer. Then the texts start. She wants to arrange a dinner date, she and Mike are dying to meet Matt, she wants to see our house; imagine if we decorate in the same way! I don't answer the texts, but still they come, her tone friendly and upbeat, as if she doesn't think I'm avoiding her. I get a voicemail, too, from Dee, about the TV show. I block her number. I still haven't told Matt about meeting Anna.

 And then, as I had known there would be, there is a ring at the doorbell.

 'Matt, don't answer it,' I call, but he doesn't hear and opens the door. I hear a woman's voice.

 'Anthea,' Matt calls, in a strained voice, after a few minutes. 'There's a lady here who says you arranged to come on a TV show? She can't get through to you on the phone?'

 They are both staring at me as I descend the stairs, clinging to the banister rail.

'Andrea,' Dee gushes, 'I hope you don't mind me coming round, Anna told me where you live. I've brought the contracts for the show. Do you mind signing them now? We're on a bit of a tight deadline with this one. The director was thrilled when I told him the Anna and Andrea story, did she tell you?'

'Anthea,' I say in a small voice. 'Not Andrea.'

The show, 'Someone Just Like Me', is a competition. A geneticist studies eight sets of twins and Anna and I, and decides which pair looks the most alike using facial mapping software. Anna and I win, scoring ninety percent. Our baby and childhood photos flash up on screen, and it transpires there has always been a marked resemblance. I scrutinise them, thinking how cold and glassy my face looks, more doll than girl.

The next stage of the competition is close scrutiny from a panel of fifty strangers. They also judge us to be the pair who looks most alike. Anna and I are the overall winners of the show. However, in case we are twins pretending not to be, we are given a DNA test. This discovers that although we're not related, our ancestral mapping closely matches.

Anna and I win a long weekend away with our partners, which the TV company will film for a follow-up show.

'I don't want to go,' I tell Matt.

'I don't think you have a choice,' he says. 'You signed the contract. Anyway, why wouldn't you want to go? It's Dubrovnik, everything paid for. It'll be great to spend time with Anna.'

'Anna and Mike.'

'Yes, of course, Anna and Mike.'

Walking into the airport, I am surrounded by twenty-somethings.

'Can we get a selfie, Anna?' they yell.

If I Tell You My Name,
Will You Tell Me What It Tastes Of?

I don't know why this café is so appealing. It's small and stuffy; rickety tables, blowsy-flower artwork. The toilet is down a flight of perilously steep steps and the hand dryer is broken. But it's quiet and calm; steam from the coffee machine rising languidly into the air. The cakes are good too, little French ones, much tastier than the bolshy big ones visibly drying up like bad-date conversation in the lit cabinets of the coffee chains. Today I am too nervous to eat cake but have given in to the temptation of hot chocolate, the Spanish type with chocolate sticks that dissolve in hot milk.

I am the last person in the café today, waiting for a date who is nearly an hour late. Gazing out of the window at a faulty streetlamp spitting white beams of light onto the pavement like strobes in a nightclub, I decide that I am being foolish and should leave. I also think: I could never go to a club now. Not even a pub.

A waitress comes over and I automatically look down at the Formica table. She is not the one who served me the hot chocolate; that one has gone without me noticing. In a tone that suggests she means the opposite, this waitress asks if she can get me anything else. I tell her, my words a trifle muffled by my sequinned facemask, that I'm fine.

To avoid eye contact with the waitress, I look at my phone again. There is only an email from my agent, which I ignore for now; nothing from my date.

Probably, he walked past, saw me and scarpered. I shouldn't be surprised, but my heart feels as though it's being squeezed.

The waitress is wiping up the chocolate I spilled on the table. She is about to move away but then looks over at me and keeps looking. Her cloth drips brown liquid onto the floor.

'You're Fabia from *The Cottage.*'

I nod, a wave of tiredness washing over me.

'I can't believe it's you. You were brilliant on the show, Fabia,' she says. 'I texted in twice for you to win, all my friends did too.'

'That was nice of you,' I say, managing to stifle an apology for the waste of money.

'It's what I want to be, famous,' she tells me. 'It must be amazing.'

'What do you want to be famous for?'

'I've got two thousand followers on Instagram; I'm hoping I can double that by the end of the month.' It doesn't seem like an answer, but I have no interest in asking her anything else. 'Do you get people coming up to talk to you all the time?'

'Not as much anymore,' I say, because humility is popular.

After leaving *The Cottage*, a TV production located on a set in Watford, as a runner-up, I was besieged. Desperate to go home after two months away, I had to stay in different hotels for self-isolation purposes. I couldn't go out and, once I'd had media coaching, spent most of the time speaking via Zoom to marketing people and journalists. My agent dealt with my social media sites. Now, my followers are decreasing (only four million on Twitter, at the last count), and the agent wants a ghost-written book to increase my popularity levels again.

'Can we do a selfie?' The waitress is still smiling, but her eyes are sharp as a tin opener. 'My followers won't believe I've met you unless they see a photo.'

She takes a phone in a gold case from her apron.

'I'd rather not, sorry. Covid, you know....' I'm double-vaccinated, but still. It's also a useful get-out clause.

'Sure. I'll take one of you on your own, then.'

I arrange my features, and the waitress takes one snap after another.

'So, is it real?' she asks, scrolling through the photos on her phone.

'Is what real?'

'Like, do you really taste and feel people's names? Or was it, you know, a thing to get you onto the show?'

'It's real,' I say.

'Well, Fabia, if I tell you my name, will you tell me what it tastes of?'

My sister Nell says I shouldn't do it; I'm not a circus act.

'It's Lorna,' she tells me, as if imparting the location of the Holy Grail.

Lorna: the rinse they give at the hygienist that tastes of bleach. I pretend it hasn't come to me, looking out of the window at a pigeon desperately searching for scraps.

'Lorna... I get delicious *petit fours*.'

'Ooh.' She is wreathed in smiles. 'I've always thought it's a lovely name, too.'

'Well, I should go—'

'I bet Mary, that's the owner, would like to meet you, Fabia. I'm not sure if she watched *The Cottage*, she's old, like forty, but we don't get celebs in here usually so she'll be excited. She's just out the back—'

'Another time that would be super. Just the bill now, thanks.'

I can't cope with meeting Mary, which is biting into a grubby orange Space Hopper. Even if I lie to her too, Mary will probably tell me her mum's name, then her gran's.

Outside the café, a carpet of colour ripples across the sky. It's cold, the air taking a nibble out of me as I stride away. I hear a familiar glissando slide: my phone ringing. At last. But it's not my date, Paul. 'Paul' conjures up wallpaper paste mixed with porridge, but his big dark eyes and white-toothed smile made me swipe right.

'Fabia, are you there?' It's my sister, Nell.

'Nell' is the tangy stench of mosquito spray. She doesn't tell people that, but she does divulge that Dad is a roll-mop herring so vinegary it stings my eyes and taste-buds and Mum is Marks & Spencer's Battenberg cake. Nell understands my condition better than most, as synaesthesia runs in families. She has sequence-space synaesthesia, where linguistic sequences have spatial dimensions in the brain (Nell says the months of the year are a horseshoe; the days of the week are an athletics track). Mum has colour-grapheme synaesthesia, seeing numbers as colours and sensing their interactions ('that sparkly ruby-red four and that suave green seven fancy each other like mad,' she said when she saw my door-number plate). Dad thinks we're all mad.

'I want to run a couple of names by you,' Nell says.

Nell is pregnant with her first child. It's not the first time a prospective parent has asked me about names, but it's the first time my sister has. I sigh inwardly. Whatever I say will be wrong, and I won't be able to lie this time.

'What do you think of Joey for a boy and Anastasia for a girl? And I'm trying to decide between two hospitals, West Middlesex and Kingston, if you can do those too.'

'Are you sure?'

Nell had been phlegmatic when I told her what I thought of her now-husband's name: 'Ewan' floods my nose with a field of sheep dung. But babies are different.

'Joey is roof tiles on a hot summer's day while Anastasia is the dandruff on a waxed jacket. For the hospitals – Kingston is a turkey wishbone hooked between two fingers about to snap it; West Middlesex is that chocolate body-paint that tastes of digestive biscuits.'

'I see.'

What did she expect? Baby powder on just-bathed skin; unicorns jumping over rainbows; stroking a My Little Pony's mane?

'I don't dislike the names, Nell; you know that. It's just what happens.'

To mollify her, I ask how she's feeling and the details of her birth plan; agree to help her transform her spare room into a nursery.

Half-listening as Nell talks on, I walk past aged trees stretching soundlessly to the sky and around half-dry puddles. The light has turned miserly. I'm nearly home by the time my sister says goodbye. I think of my plans for the date-less night now stretching ahead: putting on pyjamas and drinking too much wine in front of any TV show that is not reality sounds good.

I am at the corner of my road when I see three teenage girls standing there. They stare at me, their words grating at the edges of my hearing as I approach.

'Hey, you're Fabia,' shouts a tiny-waisted and voluptuously-bottomed girl in a jade tracksuit, when I am about to pass them. 'What do you think my name is?'

'I don't know,' I say, pulling my black faux-fur coat more tightly around me. How could I know? I have lexical-gustatory synaesthesia, not psychic abilities.

'It's Danielle,' she pouts out, and her friends giggle.

Oh no. *The Cottage* was won by a girl named Danielle. I'd tried to be friends with her. She loved yoga, so I forced my body into cat and cobra on the thin strips of electric-green AstroTurf. Our friendship detonated after I was made to participate in a reward-based task: hooked-up to a lie detector, I was asked what the name of each of the participants did to my senses; if I answered honestly, we would all receive a three-course meal. After living on meagre rations, my mouth watered at the prospect. Unfortunately, 'Danielle' evoked a road flooded with sewerage. My Instagram following did rise by three million that night, so perhaps it wasn't all bad.

'My mum was really upset,' Teenage Danielle says now. 'I was named after my aunt, and she's got breast cancer.'

'I'm sorry to hear that,' I tell her.

'Fabia, do you know Lady Gaga or Pharrell?' one of the other girls, hot-pink tracksuit and feathery soot-black eyelashes, asks. 'I read that they have your disease.'

This is a question that I have been asked many times. The singers Pharrell Williams (the metallic smell of half-dried blood) and Lady Gaga (the paint flaking off a statue of the Virgin Mary) are both reputed to have synaesthesia. A number of articles about me, and synaesthesia in general, have run alongside large photos of these two celebrities. This is despite the fact that these more famous two are always unavailable for comment and none of the writers appear to know much about their experiences of synaesthesia.

'It's a condition, actually, not a disease,' I say. 'No, I don't know them.'

Once, not long after leaving the show, when I still drank in pubs, I said as a joke that I had sung on stage with Lady Gaga. That was a mistake.

I look down at the grime-coloured pavement, waiting to see if Danielle has any more accusations, if the other tracksuited girls have the same name as a *Cottage* contestant (Patricia, orange jelly babies, wouldn't be too bad; Melanie, sports kit left unwashed for a summer, less good). When they don't, I stride away, the sound of their laughter following me like exhaust fumes. Rain is falling in a silent serenade, but I don't want to stop to search for an umbrella in my tote bag. I want to be home, curtains closed, doors triple-locked.

And then, my phone chimes with a text. *So sorry to stand you up! You won't believe this, but I fell down the stairs at work and had to go to A&E, just out with a fractured elbow and a packet of codeine. Any chance we could try again at the weekend; same place?*

I put the phone back in my pocket, and round the final corner.

Oh God.

I don't know whether they are fans or foes, journalists or synaesthetes. Whoever they are, they are mushroomed together on the grass verge. Waiting.

The Stranger in My Living Room

A stranger is sleeping on my sofa. I have no idea who he is or how he got in.

It is four in the morning. I woke up needing the toilet then wanted a drink of water; this involved passing through the living room, where the man is asleep.

As I creep closer to him, my heart knocks the walls of my chest and terror inches icily up my spine. He could be mid-thirties. Unhealthy-looking: a chalky, oddly blistered face. Smooth collar-length dark brown hair. He is dressed entirely in black, and is wearing only one shoe.

What is he doing here? This is not a hostel. This is a top-floor duplex in a purpose-built block, entry by buzzer, on a quiet East London street. My husband died two years ago; it is just me and our twin girls living here now.

The twins: I run to check on them. Jess and Lucie are in bed, still and silent. It is a warm night, their window open, very wide: I close it slightly. The gap in the billowing curtains sends moonlight splashing onto Lucie's face. Jess has her duvet over her head.

I go slowly downstairs, taking ragged breaths. The man hasn't moved. Should I grab a knife? Call the police? But what if one of the twins invited him in? At the thought of this, rage fills me.

I snap the light on then hiss, so as not to wake the girls: 'Hey, what are you doing in my living room?'

The stranger's eyes open, his hand shielding them as if he is very light-sensitive. He squints at me, then gazes slowly around the room. His dawning awareness of being in a stranger's house is like watching a snow globe settle. Through the window, the night trembles, the moon's face half-turned away. The man continues to stare without speaking. I am conscious of my tight, broccoli-green pyjamas and wish I'd put on my dressing gown.

'Who are you?' he asks in a heavily-accented voice.

'No, who are you?' I demand. 'And what were you doing asleep in my apartment in the middle of the night?'

'Where am I?' he asks, 'can you just tell me that?'

'The Isle of Dogs, East London. Where do you live?'

'I am from Romania. My name is Vladimir – Vlad. I stay in Rayners Lane, North West London, you know it?'

'How did you get into my home, Vlad?'

'I have no knowledge,' he says. 'Too much alcohol to drink perhaps – I went to a nightclub last night with friends. We party until late. I am so sorry. Did I wake you, and your family?'

'How did you know I have a family?'

His gaze lands on the myriad framed photos of the girls; the girls and their dad; our wedding photos.

'Where was the party?' I ask.

Slowly, as if translating the words in his head before speaking them, Vlad describes a party in a Central London club. I nod along as he speaks, like a guard escorting the sentences. It was his friend Gyorgy's thirtieth. He remembers leaving the club, nothing else.

'Gyorgy… Ahh. There's a Gyorgy in the next-door block: top floor. I can see how you might have found the wrong flat. But I don't see how you got in.'

'I must go to Gyorgy's flat,' he says politely. 'I am so sorry for waking you. Do you in fact have my other shoe?'

Does he think I'm holding his trainer to ransom?

'I'll give it to Gyorgy if I find it.'

Vlad limps out of the room. I walk behind him to the front door. It is locked, the key hanging beside it as always. None of this makes sense, but there seems little point in detaining Vlad. He doesn't seem menacing, but I want him out. There is something strange about his story, something that doesn't fit.

I open the door. Vlad moves past me. In the communal hallway, he turns and smiles. His smile makes me shiver.

I lock the door; lean heavily against it. It is then that I realise what was odd: although Vlad claimed to have drunk a lot, he didn't smell of alcohol. At a decent hour, I will call the police. And a locksmith.

As I am climbing the stairs, there is a yell from the twins' bedroom.

'Mum, Jess is bleeding. Her neck is bleeding.'

Phil in Real Life

On the escalator, I recite my mantra: *No big deal, just another date.* My third online meet-up. The other two were easy chats in cosy pubs, quick kisses, the men nice and forgettable. My mum says I'm too picky.

This morning, I'm meeting Phil. We both want children; we both love literature. His linguistic flair attracted me, the ninety-seven words of his profile leaving me longing for more. In his messages, Phil transformed everyday anecdotes into a carnival of words. We clicked 'Yes' a month ago and have written every day since. The caution about meeting was mostly on his side. He didn't want to waste time: he was looking for true love. I want what my mum and dad have: each other forever and the type of house a child would draw.

I push out of the tube station. Phil suggested meeting at the British Museum; the past is another of his passions.

I'm early, but he is there, dwarfed by the columns. *No big deal, just another date.*

It's not easy to talk in a Central London museum. Conversational attempts are shattered by the need to move away from exhibits.

As we plod around, I am smiling so hard my cheeks hurt. My insides are hollow, however. The mantra means nothing: it feels like a big deal that Phil in real life doesn't attract me. Not physically; it's not that he looks entirely different from his profile picture, but he's on the small side of 'five foot nine', and his face is so pale it's as though he's being erased. Most crushingly, his spoken words have none of the sparkle of his written ones. Despite the weight of the disappointment I am lugging around like a rock of raw diamond that can't be turned into a ring, I am too polite to leave. Perhaps Phil is just nervous; we can be friends.

'I'd love to see the Troy exhibition, Tamara,' Phil says. 'I've always wanted to see the "Judgement of Paris", haven't you?'

I have not, but what the hell.

There is a twenty-pound admission fee to get into 'Troy: Myth and Reality'. Phil steers me towards a painting of a gingery, doughy-faced man kneeling before three naked women. Not very Me Too. Phil tells me how Paris had to choose which of the goddesses was the most beautiful; the winner, Aphrodite, gifted him the world's most beautiful woman; Helen's abduction from her husband started the Trojan War.

'Very dramatic,' I say, to fill the ensuing silence. Is Phil expecting applause? An A-star grade? 'No man's fought over me, let alone started a war.'

'I'd fight over you,' Phil says. 'I'd start a war.'

I laugh: he doesn't. When I look at his unlit face, he is staring at me like a painter trying to capture an essence. I don't fill silences after that. Phil comments on what we see as we trudge from ancient sculpture to vase painting to silver vessel, from myth to history to truth.

'Let's find a picnic spot,' Phil says, as if we are in the Lake District. 'Hope you're hungry!'

He has brought lunch, for which I have high hopes. Booze to add a layer of fuzz to the proceedings would be a good start, baguettes and posh crisps too. If he's willing to spend twenty pounds at a free museum, surely he's splashed out on this. But who can tell? Phil is an outline of the person I thought I knew. All those words, squatting inside our screens and phones: what was the point?

The weather has got worse since we were inside the museum, the faded-grey sky thick with clouds. A pathetic fallacy. I suggest going to a café.

'But I've bought food, Tamara.'

Why am I not brave enough to walk away, now it's clear we're never going to see each other again? I envisage my studio flat like a pair of outstretched arms.

Phil and I wander the chilly streets, rain mizzling onto us. At least it doesn't matter if my hair frizzes. Finally, we see an uninhabited green enclave. The single bench is damp, so I sit on my coat. Phil produces packets of food from his rucksack: cold croissants and cold sausage rolls. Diet Cokes.

This could be a funny anecdote, I think.

When I have had a croissant and a sausage roll, I brush crumbs off my best jeans and say: 'I'd better be off, Phil, thanks so much—'

'Shall we go out tonight, Tamara? You've mentioned that pub near you: the Rose and Crown. It gets good reviews on Trip Adviser.'

I stare at the concrete; it is pigeon-coloured and splattered with avian emissions. In my head, Mum murmurs: 'Give him another chance, Tam. You can't afford to be picky at nearly thirty. Your dad and I were married at twenty-three.' Shush, Mum.

'Sorry, I've got a friend coming over tonight,' I lie. 'Gary. We were at university together.'

'Can I see you tomorrow, then? This has been a great date. You're just what I expected, and that's not always the case, is it?'

'I need to go. Thanks for today.'

That evening, my phone doesn't stop. Phil sends texts, voicemails and emails. I craft one message saying it was lovely to meet him, but I don't think we connected, sorry. My phone rings: I don't answer. He keeps on… ringing… texting… emailing. I delete the messages without reading them: block his number and email. Although he doesn't know my address, I double-lock the door.

That night, sleep takes a long time to come. A sound jerks me awake: someone's knocking at the window. I spring up, open the curtains. Branches are raging against the darkened pane. I'll ask the landlord to trim the tree.

Next morning, I am tagged in a Facebook post visible to all. *Brilliant date with Tamara: beautiful as Helen and sexy as Aphrodite. The next will be even more special.* Such hackneyed words; did someone else write his other messages? The fleshy-pink enthused delusion makes me feel sick. Twenty of my friends, two of Phil's, 'like' the post. My best friend Jenna texts to say *Went well then x*

Delete delete: Phil is blocked from my social media. Now he has no way of getting to me.

The next Saturday is my thirtieth birthday party. An area has been reserved in The Rose and Crown, and I've paid for enough Prosecco and food for a small army.

Drink and conversation flow, music is turned up. At ten o'clock, I am squashed on a sofa with Jenna's new housemate Dara. In his lilting Irish accent, he tells me about the park runs he does. Then suggests we go jogging together one weekend. I say I'll meet him for a pint when he's finished running. He laughs, says that sounds good.

As Dara and I are moving closer together, I become aware of someone standing above me.

'Tamara, at last! I've been here every night this week, hoping to bump into you. Have you lost your phone?'

I can't speak.

'Who's this?' Phil points at Dara. 'Are you Gary?'

Well, we are in Spain

'Gloria's looking forward to meeting you.'

'I'm excited to meet her.'

Leanne actually has mixed feelings about meeting Gloria, who Mark refers to as 'my bestie' like a teenage girl. Like Mark, Gloria is originally from Hong Kong; they were in the same halls at Bristol University. The main purpose of their weekend in Madrid is to see her. Mark has promised Leanne they will go out for dinner alone on their second night.

Now they are in the dislocated space of the air, above the clouds. Mark is watching a film and laughing. Leanne is staring at a book, the words whirling. The night before she hadn't been able to sleep, and she can't do it on the plane either. If Mark asks why she's tired she'll say (like a teenage girl) that she's excited about the holiday. Really, it's because the thought of Gloria unnerves her. As soon as Mark had asked Leanne to come on the trip, she Facebook-stalked Gloria. It wasn't hard; she and Mark were tagged in many of the same photos. Pretty and smiley, Gloria is usually surrounded by people. In none of the photos are Gloria and Mark touching. Mark has lots of friends: women as well as men. Still – 'bestie'?

'Would you mind if I had a male best friend?' Leanne asked once, and Mark said: 'Why would I?'

Leanne had thought about adding Gloria as a Facebook friend, but it seemed weird when they hadn't met. She could do that after Madrid.

It is three in the afternoon when they arrive in the city. Leanne is exhausted, and pummelled by the sun. She offers to pay for a taxi, but Mark insists the Metro will be more fun. It is not fun, but when Leanne has dragged her suitcase up the steps she stops in awe. The plaza could be advertising Spain to foreign people: high, cream-coloured buildings with brown shutters and Juliet balconies, a beige-and-white striped boulevard along which tanned people are ambling, bars with cream parasols under which families are eating and drinking. Leanne smiles at Mark and he lifts his fingers and brushes her cheek.

'This is going to be fantastic,' she gushes, just as he says, hefting his rucksack higher on his shoulders: 'Sorry, Leanne, the hotel's a fifteen-minute walk.'

Even that doesn't dim Leanne's pleasure, although by the time they arrive sweat has made her straightened hair stick to her face and her three layers of mascara sting her eyes.

Their hotel's exterior is snow-white, so Leanne is surprised to see the lobby cluttered with colourful ceramics. The dark-eyed receptionist, who is younger than Leanne, smiles at Mark when he tries out his limited Spanish. The hotel doesn't have a porter, a lift or a Juliet balcony. Leanne wonders how much Mark paid for it; if she should offer to pay half. Perhaps she will buy the romantic dinner.

The bedroom door squeals open, and Mark leads Leanne by the hand to the bed that takes up most of the room. The sex is good but quick. Afterwards, as Leanne is snuggling in to Mark, hoping for a quick siesta, he says he's going for a shower.

'We're meeting Gloria in half an hour.'

'Half an hour?' Leanne springs up.

'Don't worry, she's always late.'

'Are we having lunch with her?' Leanne asks.

'She suggested meeting at a market. I guess they'll have food there.'

'Is it a meat market?' Leanne jokes.

'I'm sure they'll have chorizo,' Mark says, not getting Leanne's reference to the sleazy nightclubs of her youth.

Soapy in the shower, Leanne tries to instigate sex again. Mark smiles and says, 'How much energy do you think I have?'

Leanne takes Mark's hand as they approach the wrought-iron-and-glass Mercado de San Miguel. People are everywhere, chattering in Spanish; Leanne cannot recognise more than 'Gracias'. Gloria is studying to be a Spanish translator: she is trilingual.

They are thirty-five minutes late, but Gloria is not there. Leanne wonders if she got tired of waiting and left; Mark laughs at the idea. They browse stalls selling tortilla and tapas, and Leanne's mouth waters.

Another half an hour passes ('Well, we are in Spain,' Mark says). Leanne keeps looking around, as if for a pickpocket. Her heart is bumping.

'Ring her, Mark.'

Although by now Leanne has a heart-lifting hope that Gloria has decided not to come. Why is Mark not bothered that his friend hasn't turned up? She can't think he would be so forgiving of her own tardiness.

'Mak!'

Mark turns. Leanne remembers Mak is his Chinese name; Mark the Westernised version.

'Gloria!'

Gloria launches into an elaborate apology for why she is so late, something implausible about lending her phone to her flatmate. Her smile making her cheeks ache, Leanne absorbs her. Gloria's black hair has midnight-blue ends and she wears a midnight-blue leather jacket – Leanne can't decide if it's obnoxious or the fashion, and isn't she roasting in it? – over a tea dress. Within a minute of meeting her, it is obvious she is what Leanne's mum would call 'A force of nature'.

Watching the circle of warmth enclosing Gloria and Mark, it takes a while for Leanne to realise that there are three girls standing behind Gloria like bodyguards. Their presence should reassure Leanne, three would have been an awkward number, but reminds her of those bitchy-girl films she enjoyed as a teenager: *Grease, Heathers, Mean Girls*. Gloria is Rizzo with her Pink Ladies.

Leanne introduces herself to the girls, who are all Spanish. They are polite, but conversation is effortful as eating king prawns. Eventually, Gloria tears herself from Mark.

'Leanne–,' Gloria's eyes skim her face and body – 'How rude of me not to have said hello before. Great to meet you; I've heard a lot about you from Mak.'

Has she?

'You too, Gloria.' Leanne takes Mark's arm. 'So glad we've got someone to show us Madrid. I love your jacket, by the way.'

They wander the market, perusing displays of oysters, Cava, chocolate, caviar, imitation baby eels and stuffed sea urchins.

'Usually the vendors give samples.' Gloria talks rapidly in Spanish to a young man standing at a stall. He gives them garlic prawns and *banderillas*: cucumbers, olives, pickled onions and peppers on small skewers. Mark says he doesn't like pickled onions and Gloria tells him all food tastes better in Spain. To prove it, she pops a pickled onion on a skewer into his mouth.

'Okay, that is amazing,' Mark laughs. Gloria's friends clap.

Anger spreads through Leanne like a stain. Does Gloria not realise that was inappropriate?

'Mak says you went to Bristol too, Leanne.' Gloria beams. 'Were you there at the same time as us? I wonder if we know the same people.'

'A bit before,' Leanne says, 'so probably not. I'd love to hear about what you're doing in Madrid, Gloria.'

At least it isn't another past-excluding topic. Gloria talks animatedly about her studies at '*la universidad*'; she sounds like someone touched by a guru.

They wander on. Mark and Gloria start chatting about university friends, and round a corner together. Gloria's friends are talking in Spanish in front of a meat stall.

Leanne follows Mark and Gloria. They are at a small-beer stall, two-deep with people waiting to be served. Their backs are to her; she gets closer.

'Serious with this one, Mak?' Gloria asks. 'Must be if you're having weekends away.'

'Well, she kind of invited herself,' Mark says. 'It's early days, but she's very sweet.'

Very sweet? That is how Leanne describes her five-year-old niece (untruthfully). She also didn't think she'd invited herself; surely Mark wanted her to come.

'She seems nice.' Gloria could be talking to a vendor exhorting her to buy a necklace she doesn't like quite enough. 'Hey, I'm coming back for a weekend next month. Shall we get a group together and party in Bristol, if Leanne will give you a pass?'

Holding her dignity like a parasol, Leanne walks back the way she came. She passes a man quartering meat in a bloodstained apron and nausea washes over her.

Leanne finds a bar. It is dimly lit, wood-panelled walls covered with mounted bulls' heads and gold light fittings shaped like bulls' horns, the smell of wine thick in the air. It is the type of place she'd imagined sitting in with Mark, holding hands, before they'd arrived in Madrid.

She texts her boyfriend to say she's giving him and Gloria a chance to catch up. She adds an apology for not saying goodbye. Then she deletes her apology, sends the text and turns the phone off. Perhaps she will see them for dinner; perhaps she won't. Gloria has made a restaurant reservation for nine o'clock; Leanne thinks the name is La Vina.

The barman with the scrub of dark hair and scarred cheek gives Leanne a free glass of wine when she tries out her halting Spanish, to which he replies in fluent English. He tells her he has a sister studying in London and will visit her in the summer. He asks Leanne where her friends are. She says her boyfriend might join her later.

'Might? We do not have these verbs in Espanol,' the barman says. 'We do or do not.'

Leanne takes her wine to a rickety table. A couple nearby are feeding each other chorizo, and she thinks of Gloria's skewer in Mark's mouth. Yet the thought doesn't come with any feeling behind it, as if there has been a power cut inside her heart. She is so tired.

The rioja slips silkily down and Leanne decides to order another. She should get some proper food too, or risk getting very drunk.

What are Gloria and Mark doing, she wonders, staggering slightly as she stands. Is Gloria glad Leanne has gone? Probably. But jealousy has receded like the roar of a jet engine. Mark is the issue: does he care about her? Is she merely a body that opens up to his touch? Perhaps even Mark is not the issue, perhaps it is Leanne herself. The thoughts meander with her to the bar.

Waiting to be served – the barman is chatting with a blonde girl, getting her a free glass of wine; how do they make any money here? – Leanne's thoughts change direction. What is the point of being in Madrid at all? Or, she could get a different hotel and make the most of the weekend. Is she brave enough?

'Leanne,' a voice says, and she looks around in surprise.

Don't Refuse Me

They had to break up. A new start, for a new year.

Poor James, Lucy thought. She hated the fact that she would hurt him. He did love her. She felt him holding her even when they were apart.

Lucy tugged at the cellophane cover of her egg sandwich. It looked and tasted grey. Her mind puckered around the idea of what to do about her boyfriend. As the train left the station, she mulled over his faults.

He doesn't want to live anywhere except London: although he can't afford it.

He doesn't like coming to visit me: he thinks Reading's boring.

Lucy had wished James into being the one, but he wasn't. The magic had melted, like snow turned to slush.

There was a group of teenage girls in Lucy's compartment, screeching with laughter at a video being played at full volume on someone's phone. They were drinking cider, the sharp-sweet smell filling the carriage. Lucy had been their age when she had met James. Cider was their drink then too.

She found a new, quieter seat. Then she sat with her book open on her lap, her mind returning to James.

She would start with a useless, 'I'm sorry'. He would look at her, caught between knowing and not-knowing. He would scratch his eyebrow.

This time tomorrow… she thought. She finished her sandwich, crushing the carton.

James' face was hidden by roses. Pinning on a smile, Lucy wondered if they were a guilt-gift. She had often hinted for him to buy flowers but usually got music by bands that James liked, from the shop in which he worked.

He works in a record shop: even though everyone buys music from Amazon.

He works 'in': when everyone else works 'for'.

She took the flowers. He kissed her. Unfamiliar, peppery aftershave wavered in the air. It mingled with a smell of roasting lamb coming from the kitchen.

'You look very smart,' she said.

James normally wore skinny jeans and T-shirts with ironic slogans. Tonight, he wore a shiny black suit. His wide pink tie was like a fat tongue.

'Happy New Year's Eve, Lucy.' James smiled, too hard. A white vein, delicate as a fishbone, throbbed at his temple. He scratched his eyebrow.

The cluttered, dusty hall felt breathless. Tinsel drooped over the banisters. Sue, a single mum of twin boys, who owned the house in which James rented a room, came down the stairs. Her make-up was a beige wall. She gave Lucy a one-armed hug to protect the roses.

'Don't worry, lovebirds, I'll be out of your hair soon,' Sue said. 'Sure it's still OK to put the boys to bed in an hour? They'll be no trouble for you.'

Thumps came from the floor above.

'Their dad bought them a Nintendo Switch for Christmas,' Sue said. 'James enjoys it as much as they do.'

The list was getting longer.

James took Lucy's hand and pulled her into his room. She sat on the bed, staring at the teetering towers of records. James' name tag was by her feet. She kicked it out of the way.

'I thought we'd stay in tonight,' he said.

'I thought we were going to Fish's party,' she said.

James plucked at the duvet with shaking fingers. She hoped he hadn't taken drugs. She had seen in one New Year's Eve in the A&E department of the Royal Free Hospital, while James had his stomach pumped. The whiskery old man sitting next to her had insisted on a midnight kiss.

'The party will be boring. I'm cooking for you,' he said. 'Surprise!'

'But you never cook.'

He never cooks, or cleans: because he is lazy.

A flicker of annoyance crossed James' face. He pasted a smile over it.

'I love you,' he said. As the front door slammed, he trapped her in his arms. One more time, she thought.

All we have is sex: because we're so different.

The kitchen was dimly lit by two tea-lights, winking between Sue's china cats. It was very hot. The rich smell of the lamb washed over her.

'This is nice, James.' A rope of fear tightened in her chest; it felt worse to dump him after he had made this effort.

'I'll get us a drink.' He was speaking very fast.

She found a vase and placed the flowers in the middle of the pine table; then she sat at it and drew circles inside faded mug rings.

James brought over two Marks & Spencer cans of gin and tonic. She downed half of hers while watching him shove bread into the toaster.

'This is lovely,' she said, quietly.

James flicked out a holly-patterned paper napkin; arranged it on her lap. A plate of pâté on toast was ceremoniously laid before her.

'Your favourite,' he said.

The toast was slathered in pâté. It filled every corner of her mouth. She saw parts of James through the roses, as if he were a Picasso painting. Half a smile: half an eye.

'I wrote something for you, Lucy.' The words fizzed out of him.

James put down his barely-touched toast and ran to his bedroom, bringing back his guitar.

He still thinks he's going to be a rock star: because he was in a band at school.

'Lu-cy. Do you see? What you mean to me?'

He was good at playing and singing, at least. The thuds from upstairs increased, like a discordant drum beat. James' face strained with emotion. She clapped, but it wasn't the end.

When he had stopped singing, he scratched his eyebrow and looked as hopeful as a puppy wanting a walk. The tension stretched like an elastic band.

There was a scream. She ran upstairs, followed by James.

'He snatched mine off me,' Freddie wailed.

He nodded towards Benji, who was holding two games controllers to his chest, his lips pressed into a thin line.

'I don't want to play anymore,' Benji shouted, 'and he won't let me stop.'

Lucy beckoned them over to the shabby sofa in their shared room; made them sit between her. She asked them to tell her, in turn, what had happened, then to say sorry to each other. James stood in the doorway, can in hand. He was always surprised by how Lucy managed to calm the boys. He enjoyed playing with them, but that was all. Would he be the same if he had his own kids?

He says he's too young to have children: because he still thinks he is one.

'Go and finish the dinner, James,' Lucy said gently. 'I'll put these two to bed.'

She came downstairs fifteen minutes later, having read them a story, spinning it out for longer than necessary. James was carving a rack of lamb on the hall table, because a tea-light had died in the kitchen.

'It looks gorgeous,' she said.

'Sue gave me the recipe.'

Again, James hardly ate. As she tried to chew, she felt his eyes on her like heat. She had to do it: now. It was impossible to keep on chewing the dense meat, even if it did taste better than expected. She put down her fork.

'I'm sorry, James.'

'Don't worry,' James interrupted, 'I'm not that hungry either. I'm sure we'll have room for dessert though!'

He stood to clear the plates. Sighing, she helped him. Dessert was frozen sticky toffee pudding, and custard from a carton.

'James, listen....'

'Lucy....' James took a piece of paper from his trousers and peered at it in the dimness. The poem used many of the same words – maybe all of the same words – as the song. 'Lu-cy. You improve me.'

Laughter swelled inside her. As it was about to erupt, the kitchen door opened.

'I just want a drink,' Freddie said, pitifully.

She poured water into a beaker and took him back to bed, holding his hand and stroking his soft forehead; Benji was snoring gently in the top bunk. She thought what a sweet child James must have been. What a sweet child he still was.

Lucy left the kitchen door open to let in the light from the hall. James closed it, saying: 'It's more romantic in the dark, isn't it?'

'I suppose it is,' she said.

'Back to the poem,' James announced, as she sat down. 'Lu-cy. Don't refuse me.'

A cold fear was forming inside Lucy. In the semi-darkness, the fridge freezer glared. She jumped as James's foot rubbed her shin.

'James,' she said, when he'd finished. She said it to his back: he was opening a bottle of Cava. 'James.' The word was the last puff of air leaving a balloon. She tried to pull herself together.

The cork exploded.

'Tell me in a minute, baby. I've got something for you.'

He pulled a carrier bag from under the table.

The big box had been gift-wrapped. There was a teddy bear inside, wearing a leather waistcoat and holding a fabric guitar; a felt heart was on one of its arms.

'Press the heart,' James said excitedly.

She pressed.

'I love you,' the bear said, in James's voice. 'Will you marry me?'

The front door crashed open, followed by the kitchen door. The light from the hall was blinding. Sue stood there, carrying two bottles of Prosecco. Three women teetered behind her.

'You did it!' Sue cried to James; to Lucy, she said: 'Wasn't the bear a brilliant idea? Congratulations, both of you!'

'Congratulations,' echoed the friends.

The Noises

It sounded as if a heavy weight had fallen onto the bedside table. Yet there was no damage. There was no obvious cause of the noise, either. Skin prickling, Sinead laid down the book she had been reading and got up. Her room looked the same as before, as did the landing, the second bedroom, the bathroom, the living room and the kitchen-diner. Had the noise come from outside? It had sounded so close.

You're overworked and exhausted, Sinead, her mother said loudly in her head. *Get to sleep, it's ridiculous that you don't go to bed until one o'clock.*

Sleep did not come. Sinead kept thinking of the noise; so close, so loud. Fear pressed down like a shroud. She turned on the bedside lamp.

The same thing happened on the next two nights. Each time, it sounded as though a weight had dropped onto the bedside table. Each time, nothing looked different. Sinead slept in the living room with the light on.

On the third night, there was a loud noise, again at one o'clock; this time, it seemed to come from the wall.

'What is it?' Sinead shouted. 'What do you want?'

Saturday was stormy, the wind roaring to itself like applause. At ten am, Sinead knocked on her neighbours' front door. Jenna and Felicity had moved in during the first lockdown; Sinead knew their names because she had taken in Amazon deliveries when they were out running. They had had bubble-light interactions, the other women glowing in their shiny Lycra and standing far apart from Jenna, when they claimed them.

She thought it was Jenna who came to the door in a dressing gown, her hair in a braid. Her girlfriend stood behind her in long-sleeved pyjamas.

'Hi,' Sinead said, then had no idea what to say next.

'Hi,' probably-Jenna said.

'I'm sorry to disturb you. I just wondered if – this is going to sound silly, but have you heard any strange noises at night?'

'Noises?' Probably-Felicity scrunched up her face. 'What kind of noises?'

'Loud bangs, late at night.' Sinead looked at the wall behind the women so she didn't have to meet their eyes. She saw a framed photo of skeletal trees, their dark leafless bones reaching for the sky. A strange thing to have prominently displayed in your flat, she thought.

'We haven't heard anything, have we Jenna?' Felicity said.

'We were just saying what a quiet neighbourhood this is,' Jenna agreed. 'We moved from Shoreditch; all you could hear were sirens. Is it kids making the noise, do you think?'

'I think it's in the building,' Sinead said.

'Maybe it's foxes,' suggested Felicity, touching her nose ring. 'You know, knocking over the bins or whatever? Foxes can be really noisy. Or mice?'

'Yes, maybe something like that. Thanks, and sorry for disturbing you.'

'Come over for a coffee one day,' Jenna said as she closed the door.

Sinead watched Netflix until three in the morning but didn't hear any strange noises.

It was another two weeks before the noises started again. When Sinead heard the crash, fear striped through her. She sat up in bed, light on, until she drifted into a thin sleep hours' later and woke with dribble on her pillow.

Perhaps the noises were problems with the pipes, Sinead thought. She called work and said she had to stay in and wait for tradesmen, then googled heating engineers and plumbers. She couldn't find anyone to come out that day unless it was an emergency, so she made appointments for later in the week. Then she called her mum to ask if she could stay. It wasn't convenient because Sinead lived and worked in West London, and her mum was in Kent, plus she would be sleeping on the sofa because her old room was now occupied by a lodger. But she needed to get out of the house and couldn't go to a friend because they all had babies or young children; she would be in the way.

When Sinead got to Kent, she was relieved to find that Ingrid, a young scientist at the local university, was out. She told her mum about the noises. Rosemary was a counsellor, and offered to find her daughter someone to talk to ('Being single in your late thirties and facing childlessness are hard crosses to bear, Sinead. The brain acts out in ways you can't predict'.). Sinead made non-committal noises. Ingrid came home and made dinner, a stew with so much gravy it was almost impossible to find the meat. As they ate, they chatted lightly. Sinead tried to sound normal and to ignore her mother's glances.

Once Rosemary and Ingrid were in bed, Sinead lay down under a duvet on the floral sofa that her mother had had for a decade. The plants in the corners of the room were pale sentries, the television pattered like rain. She had another glass of the wine her mother had opened for her, but it tasted sour in her mouth.

Sinead told Rosemary she would go back to her flat.

'I'm probably imagining things, Mum, like you say.'

'I'll stay the night with you,' Rosemary offered, 'see if I hear anything.'

Sinead knew her mother was humouring her, but she didn't say no. Any company was better than nothing.

Rosemary drove them to the flat after breakfast, as the plumber was coming at nine. The heating engineer had said he would be there at 'lunchtime'. By two o'clock neither had arrived, nor were answering their phones.

'Well, at least we haven't heard any of these noises,' Rosemary said. 'Shall we have another cup of tea?'

'It's at night I hear them,' Sinead said, switching on the kettle.

'You know sleep deprivation creates a propensity for hallucinations, darling. Auditory or otherwise. Plus loneliness, exacerbated by these lockdowns we've had, has caused a lot more people to manifest as mentally disturbed. I've never been so busy.'

'I'm not one of your patients, Mum.'

'No,' her mother said: regretfully, Sinead thought.

The heating engineer arrived as Sinead was making supper. The plumber had texted to say he was stuck on a job and would be there the next day.

Sinead left the carrot-chopping to her mother and told the skinny youth who smelled of marijuana about the noises. Darren frowned and said he'd check the pipes. Half an hour later, he said there was nothing wrong that he could see, but was it an old house? He'd come across unexplained noises in older properties. Sinead said it was built in the sixties.

'No idea then,' Darren said. 'Are you paying cash or bank transfer?'

There were no noises that night, and her mother left after Sinead had promised to find a therapist. Instead, on her lunchbreak, she googled 'paranormal investigators London'. There were over a million results, with some firms looking more reputable than others. She watched the videos on their websites of paranormal activity: lights going on and off, ghostly moans, a white glow reflecting a face. Threads of paranoia dangling in her head as she thought about what her mum and friends would say (she was an accountant, for goodness sake!), she emailed two of the companies. Within half an hour she had a reply from 'West London Investigators': they could send someone over that evening. The price quoted was four times what Darren the engineer had charged.

At seven thirty, the investigator came. Judith was a large Geordie woman with a severe blonde fringe, smartly dressed in a dark coat with an owls-wing sharp collar. She wore a cloying perfume that reminded Sinead of the flowers in her dead grandmother's garden: gardenias, possibly.

Judith strode around the flat like an estate agent, pawing the hardwood floors and inspecting the appliances, as the last ribbons of daylight fluttered outside the windows. She remarked on how paranormal encounters had increased during the pandemic: 'Business has been booming'. Then she asked in a conversational tone whether anyone had died here, and Sinead said not as far as she knew. She asked whether Sinead had heard similar noises before.

'I don't think so,' Sinead turned the thought around in her mind as if inspecting an unusual stone, 'although… it was so long ago—'

'Anything could be relevant.'

'The night my dad died – twenty years' ago this was, in my family home in Kent – I heard a banging on the front door. There was no one there. I'd forgotten all about it, until now.'

Judith nodded. 'Well, there's a precedent, something to go on. For now, let's sit and see what turns up. Presences respond to me, so whatever's here, and I believe you that there is something because I can feel it strongly, should come out soon. How about a coffee or tea while we wait?'

Sinead made coffee and put a plate of biscuits on the glass table between them. The women were making stilted small talk about the one time that Sinead had been to Newcastle when Judith gasped and put down her mug so hard that liquid sloshed onto the glass.

'What is it?' Sinead asked.

'Sorry–,' Judith sounded if she were scraping the word from her throat. 'Have you a cloth?'

'Are you okay?' Sinead mopped up the coffee. Her body felt taut as a rope suspended between trees.

'I felt something very cold go past my legs.'

There was a bang, by the television, as if something had been dropped there. Judith and Sinead both looked to where the noise had come from. Sinead's breathing quickened.

'What is it what's happening why's it happening?' Her words rushed out like water, even though she knew it was pointless to ask the questions.

Another bang: the digibox had crashed down on the TV stand. Sinead and Judith stood motionless for another five minutes, but there were no further noises. Judith sat down again.

'So,' she said, 'whoever this is, is trying to get your attention. You can't think of anyone who has died who had some kind of hold over you?'

'I don't know anyone who's died. Well, my father, as I said, but that was long ago.'

'Could be your father's trying to get a message across.'

'I don't think he'd want to scare me like this. He was a good, loving father.'

Judith shrugged. 'If it makes you feel better, I don't think that whoever this is, is trying to hurt or scare you. They just want to be heard.'

'That doesn't make me feel a whole lot better,' Sinead said.

'No, I don't suppose it does. Just one more question, Sinead – have you ever had a lodger here? I'm asking because this is a spacious flat for one person, and obviously there's two bedrooms.'

'Not a lodger. My boyfriend – ex-boyfriend – Rick and I bought the flat together. We split up years ago, and I bought him out.'

Sinead felt the cold too, then, running like a rat down her back. Judith put her coat on.

'I hope you find out what's going on soon, pet,' she said. 'I have a feeling you will.'

The wind was tearing over the crowns of the oak trees outside Sinead's window. She stood looking out, mug of tea in hand, brain fogged. Sleep had eluded her the night before (and the night before that), even with a fan whirring to block out any noises, until daylight had crept into the room. Today, she would put the flat on the market: property prices were plummeting, but she couldn't stay. Hopefully she would not get followed to her new home by whatever this was.

Barely discernible over the wailing of the storm, Sinead's mobile rang. It was an unknown number. She hesitated. It would probably be a telemarketer, and if she answered they would never stop calling.

A minute later, her mobile bleeped with a voicemail. As the wind beat against the house, Sinead listened to the message.

'Hi, this is a message for Sinead. This is Amy Goodfellow. You don't know me, but I am – I was Rick Johnston's girlfriend.'

The words pressed themselves into Sinead like pins, sharp and hard. She knew something bad was coming.

'I wonder if you could give me a call back on this number?' Amy recited it. 'I have something to tell you – it won't take long. Thanks very much.'

Sinead's hands were shaking so much she almost dropped the phone. She found Amy's number in her phone's 'Recent' list. Amy answered straight away.

'Thanks for calling back, Sinead.' It was a Yorkshire accent, soft as cotton. 'So, I won't beat around the bush... I don't know if you'll know this, but Rick died a few months ago. Well, five months ago, to be precise.'

'Died? Rick?'

'I know: I can't believe it myself some days. He got covid. He shouldn't have died, he was young and fit, went to the gym three times a week, but he'd had asthma badly as a child and....' Amy sounded as if she were crying.

'I'm sorry.' Sinead felt blurred at the edges. She didn't know what to think, what to feel. Her split with Rick had been acrimonious, after she found out he'd cheated on her more than once. She hadn't stayed friends with him or with any of his friends. He had moved to Leeds a few years' ago, which had made it easier. Was Amy calling to invite Sinead to the funeral? But she'd said he died months ago.

'I would have invited you to the funeral, of course.' Amy cleared her throat roughly. 'But I'm afraid I didn't know about you. I knew he'd had a girlfriend when he lived in London, but not your name. I found out when I was going through his stuff. There was a letter to you. I'm afraid I opened and read it. I've just put it in the post, but I wanted to call in advance to prepare you, and to let you know what had happened.'

'That was kind of you. How did you know my number and address?'

'It was in Rick's phone contacts. From reading the letter, it seemed like he always intended to get in touch. I wish he had. I loved him, but I can't say he was the bravest man.'

'Thanks for letting me know what happened.' Sinead wanted to say something more, something nice about Rick, but her mind was blank. 'I can't really believe it. I mean, I do, but – it's so unexpected.'

'I can't believe it either.' Amy sounded as if she were crying. 'I just can't believe that he's not going to walk in the house in his gym gear and ask what's for his tea. It sounds crazy, but I keep watching for signs that he's still here. Of course I don't get any.'

'Amy, I'm sorry, but could I ask you a strange question? What time did Rick – pass away?'

'What time? It was one in the morning.'

'I'm so sorry for your loss, Amy.'

Sinead ripped open the letter in the hallway. It was dated May 2018: four years' ago.

Dear Sinead,

I hope you're okay.

You must be wondering why I'm writing. I don't think I ever wrote you a letter when we were together; I was rubbish even at sending cards. I was rubbish at everything to do with being a boyfriend, really.

I've always felt bad about how I treated you. Although I might not have shown it, I loved you. I thought we'd end up together: marriage, babies, house in the 'burbs. I was complacent and took you for granted.

I'm not asking you to take me back, that ship has sailed: for you too, I'm sure. I'm with a gorgeous girl called Amy, and being with her has made me realise that I owe you an apology. I can't call because you've blocked me, which I deserve. Suppose I could come to London, but I'm not sure you'd let me in the door and Amy wouldn't like it.

I could give a list of excuses about why I wasn't faithful, but that feels lame. I cheated because I thought I could get away with it. It broke my heart when you dumped me, but you were right to. That, and meeting Amy, has made me turn a corner, and I haven't done it since.

I hope you can forgive me.

Rick x

Sinead folded up the letter. She left it on the hall table and went to put bread in the toaster. As she wiped away the tears sliding down her cheeks, she felt the house exhale.

There were footsteps above her and a few seconds later, a knock on the door. In the hallway stood Jenna in her running gear.

'Hi Sinead, I just wanted to tell you that we're finally getting around to having a housewarming party tomorrow night. You're invited.' Jenna stopped, and peered at her. 'Hey, are you okay? You look a bit—'

'I've had a bug,' Sinead said. 'But it's passing, and I'd love to come to the party.'

'Don't bring anything, Fliss has bought up half the Sainsbury's booze aisle and we've loads of food. See you tomorrow.'

Sinead thanked her and went back into the kitchen. As she was eating her toast, tiredness washed over her. She decided to go to bed for a couple of hours. She sensed there would be no inexplicable noises disturbing her rest from now on.

First Love

In her dream, Ally's first love wraps its tentacles around her. She is a winged inchoate Juliet gazing through the fish tank at Romeo glittering in his armour in the 1996 film version, which she and Callum are simultaneously watching in a university city not their own. Afterwards they drink cider and smoke Marlboro Lights in a gungy pub before kissing on and on and on. The happenings twine and twist their vines, and when she wakes, with her alarm, she longs to dream them again.

Being a mother of two children, she can't. Yet as she gets up, the dream hovers over her like a sweaty moon.

Somewhere, a phone is ringing. She thinks: Callum? Madness. Then she thinks of her mother: a second stroke?

Ally searches for the mobile phone, which is still ringing. Why does she not keep it with her at all times? She dashes out of her bedroom. Her daughter Elise has her own phone to her ear. The ringing has stopped.

'A'ight?' Elise is saying, in the brittle London accent she affects with friends.

It is unusual for Elise to have an actual phone call, Ally reflects. Usually, it is the perpetual swiping of the thumb as she messages or Snapchats or whatever the hell she does. Is this a boy on the phone? Elise is giggling.

'Bare good. Naw, I'm with the fam,' Ally hears, and wants to say 'You don't have to talk like a South London gang member, darling; you live in Twickenham.'

But there is no point. Ally feels that a couple of years ago, an evil fairy flew into her daughter's bedroom and replaced her with this version who is either white-hot with fury at her mother or pretends she doesn't exist. 'It's called having a teenager, darling,' says Ally's mother with a smirk. 'Or is it called karma?'

'Who was that?' Ally asks when Elise ends the call, clutching the phone as she had the banana-yellow blanket she carried everywhere as a little child.

'No one,' her daughter answers, staring at the phone screen as if it is water showing her future husband. Or wife? Elise will never talk about matters of the heart.

'Have you done your homework?' Ally asks.

Elise ignores this question. Ally misses the days of her ownership of Elise's burgundy satchel, a bag of hope; the many years of writing preppy little comments in homework diaries, designed to impress upon the teachers that she had a clever daughter but was not a pushy mum and receiving preppy 'Great!'s and 'Wonderful!'s back. Elise now carries a rucksack that she keeps in her bedroom.

'Have we got *Romeo and Juliet*?' Elise speaks in the dead-alive voice of a newsreader.

'The text? You're doing that for English, are you?'

'Like, the book. Have we got the book?'

'Don't the school provide you with textbooks, sweetie?'

'God Mum, have we or not?'

'I don't think so, but I'll buy a copy from Amazon for you, darling.'

Elise sighs; fluffs a hand through dandelion-gold hair. She is wearing a faded Bob Marley T-shirt, perhaps ironically and perhaps not. Ally wonders what Elise would think if she knew that she once spent a whole day with her friend Genevieve lying on the bedroom floor of an older boy they had just met, smoking what he called Gange and listening to Bob Marley.

'Whatevs, Mum, it'll be on the Internet anyway.'

Ally stares after her daughter. Love falls out of her with nowhere to go. If only she had a husband with whom to talk over the problems of teenagers, and she feels a surge of fury at the children's father for leaving them. Then she goes to make the breakfast, remembering Raff has football. At least, given her son is not a teenager, he might talk to her on the way.

That night, another Callum-dream, small as a womb. They are together in a blur of yellow light and rain. Pain and anger circle the wounded land of their love like owls. And then the alarm.

The filigree bones of the dream remain through the day; she holds their wrists.

'Elise is in lurve,' Raff announces through a mouthful of meatballs.

'Shut up,' Elise says. Her lips are clamped like a stapler, but her face is suffused with colour. Elise has never been able to hide her blushes, it's the thing she most dislikes about herself and the thing Ally finds most endearing.

'Why would you kiss him outside the house if you don't want anyone to know?' Raff asks with his unfailing logic, and Ally tries not to smile. 'It was totally foul, I nearly puked.'

'Shut up or I'll punch you.'

'Elise, don't say that. Raff, stop winding her up. You know, you're welcome to have this friend round; he could come for dinner.' Ally tries for calm, as if she's talking about any one of Elise's friends.

'No thanks.' Elise pushes her plate away and leaves the table.

'I made an apple crumble for pudding,' Ally calls after her.

'She's so in lurve she can't eat,' Raff mocks. 'Can I have her meatballs?'

Ally pushes Elise's plate over to him.

'Did you see what the boy looked like, Raff? Was he wearing the St Cuthbert's uniform?'

'Dunno.'

On the way to Waitrose, Ally glances through the window of a café and sees Callum inside. She looks away, then back. It does look like him, but of course it can't be, she last saw him a couple of hundred miles away, twenty years' ago; he has no reason to be here. She walks away, fast. Did he – whoever he was – see her? But it would not have been Callum, so it doesn't matter.

Ally threads along the Green, murmuring hellos to childminders met at stay and plays when the kids were babies, mums from Elise's primary school days, a former neighbour. She passes Raff's primary school, which Elise also used to go to. The children are streaming out for breaktime, rivers of paint in their rainbow-coloured coats and bags. She can't see Raff.

At the high street, she pauses outside Waterstones, looking at the book display. She decides to buy *Romeo and Juliet*. A former literature student now working part-time in a library, Ally believes books should be held in the hand rather than stared at on screen. She goes into the shop. All those ideas, all those love stories, caught and wrapped, trapped in their colourful jackets, the lucky ones turned cover out to maximise sales.

Roaming the shop, she can't stop thinking about Callum, the possible sighting rippling through her body. He and she were tight as the pages of a new book when they were together. Every university holiday, they tore themselves apart. They wrote letters, every day. Light and air pouring into envelopes, flying across the miles. The high point of Ally's days was the rap of the letterbox. Her mother always got to the post first, there was no point trying to pre-empt this. But due to Callum's florid handwriting, he even drew circles and hearts over his 'i's, Verity Mullins took a long time to realise a man was writing to her daughter.

Glass shatters. Ally shrieks. There are shards around her and a large stone rests near her feet. The other customer and the women behind the counter are making noises of horror. A man in a turban rushes in.

'Those bloody chavs on bikes,' he shouts. 'Two of them. Faces covered with balaclavas, of course. Shall I call the police?'

'Are you alright?' The woman behind the counter, in her fifties with a swinging bob, picks her way across to Ally. 'Not cut, are you?'

Ally shakes her head.

'I can't think why they'd do this, but we're the third shop in town to have their window smashed this week.'

'This is Twickenham, not Tower Hamlets, for goodness sake,' chimes in the other assistant, younger with blue-streaked hair and a green cord jacket. 'The police need to do something.'

'It'll be the kids who got expelled from St Cuthbert's.' It's the other customer speaking, a grey-haired woman Ally thinks she has seen in the library. 'Now they've nothing to do but ride around terrorising people.'

'I heard they'd got into the other school, St Richards,' says the man. 'But then of course that's where all the hoodlums go. So my nephew says; he's at St Cuthbert's.'

'My daughter is too,' Ally says in a small voice.

Sirens.

Elise asks to have a sleepover at her best friend Hannah's house. She comes back with grey shadows under her eyes and an unfamiliar silky blue scarf around her neck. She does not take off the scarf, even though it is a mild April day and she almost never wears scarves. Ally wonders if she should phone Hannah's mum to find out whether Elise did have a sleepover there, but she hardly knows her, Hannah had gone to another primary school and now the soft-play whole-class parties and supervised playdate days are over, friendships with other mothers are not formed in the same way. She says nothing, even when her daughter is still wearing the scarf on Monday over her school uniform.

Ally imagines that Elise thinks that she does not know what love bites, or hickeys, or whatever young people call them, are. In fact, she had a phase of vampirically sucking the neck of anyone who let her. She wore her own bites as a necklace of honour. Callum had indulged her by doing it a few times, although he thought it disgusting. She was not allowed to reciprocate, but once she had and he'd touched the red raised skin then left her bed without a word. He wore a grey scarf to his lectures for the next few days.

The app that St Cuthbert's uses to keep in touch with parents bleeps with a message while Ally is daydreaming on her Monday morning library shift; toddler story time is over and the only people in are two old ladies chatting by the Easter display. The message tells Ally that for the first time, St Cuthbert's and St Richard's are putting on an inter-school play, *Romeo and Juliet*, as a three-night run commencing

Thursday 2nd April; tickets are priced at four pounds ninety-nine; booking opens the following Monday at ten am; parents are prohibited from buying more than four tickets each.

'Have you been involved in the production of *Romeo and Juliet*?' she asks her daughter that night, in a casual tone, in case Elise seizes on this as a slight ('Are you saying I have to act now, or do some shitty set design, as well as my studies?').

'I'm acting in it,' Elise says, from inside the cupboard. 'Mum, seriously, how hard is it for you to get that I need low-calorie crisps? Pringles have, like, a zillion.'

'They used to be your favourites.'

'I'll eat them,' says Raff, seizing the tube and pulling out a handful.

'God, you're a gross pig,' Elise snarls, taking out a breadstick. 'No girl is ever going to want you, you get me?'

'So, the play.' Ally tries to keep her voice smooth as the expensive hair serum that Elise has been stealing from her. Not that it ever makes her own hair as smooth as Elise's.

'I'm in the play, like I said.' Elise's eyes bore into her mother's, the breadstick held out like a sword. 'I'm Juliet.'

Raff laughs, and Pringles spray onto the counter. Automatically, Ally scoops them up and puts them in the bin.

'Did you say you're Juliet?' she asks. 'In the school play? Is that true, or is it a joke?'

'Why would it be a joke?' Elise spits. 'Are you saying I shouldn't have got the part? Are you saying I can't act?'

'Of course not, darling. I'm saying I had no idea you were in the play, a play I'd never even heard of before today—'

'Mum, even I've heard of *Romeo and Juliet*,' Raff says. 'Juliet is the main girl's part.'

'Shut up, Raff,' Elise and Ally say in unison.

'I can't wait to see you as Juliet,' Ally continues, 'this is so exciting. What's your Romeo like? Is he a boy from the other school?'

'Enough already, Mum. You are so extra. This is exactly why I didn't tell you. If you want to know about the play, buy a ticket. I'm not saying nothing else.'

After it ended with Callum, Ally wondered whether her mistake had not been what she concealed, but concealing so much. Her mother was always desperate to know what was going on in her life, so avaricious for details: of the boys she was dating, her friends, the texts she was studying. The more questions Ally was asked the less she answered. She saw now that her mother was lonely, her social life having virtually ended with the death of Ally's father, suddenly from colon cancer, aged fifty-five. Her mum had no interests of her own now beyond her garden and Ally. For her daughter, young enough that she thought the songs would never fly out of her, her mother's grip was a noose.

Verity noticed that Ally was getting more letters than usual. She asked if she had a boyfriend: someone from halls, someone from her course?

'No,' Ally snapped, 'mind your own business.'

Perhaps if she had given her mother a feather of truth – admitted to a boyfriend at the university, that would have been enough for her. But she hadn't, and her mother had come into her room when she was out and read a letter that Ally had left on the bed. And then she had read more and more, gorging herself, until Ally had come in and seen her sitting white-faced and surrounded by a forest of paper.

'You're sleeping with your tutor, Alison,' she said.

Ally stared at her: her mother stared back. Pellets of rain fell against the windows.

'If this ever happens again,' Verity hissed, 'if he comes near you again, I am telling the university that they are providing employment to a sexual predator and he will lose his job immediately. You might have to leave the university too. Do you understand, Alison?'

'How about my course, Mum? I'm taking *Shakespeare and Marlowe* with him – with Callum – next term.'

'I will phone the head of English and explain you will be deferring your studies until next year; you can live at home and get a job. Next year you can start again, taking a different module.'

'I hate you.'

'And I'm doing this because I love you.' Her mother gathered up as many letters as she could in her arms. A couple fluttered to the ground as she swept out of the room. Ally picked them up and stuffed them under the mattress: her mother would probably do a check of her room, but by that time she and they would be gone.

The rain cried outside as Ally plotted.

Ally buys three tickets for the first night of *Romeo and Juliet*: for herself, Raff and her mother. She sends Elise and Raff's father the details so he can buy tickets for himself and his girlfriend, if they can find a babysitter for their six-month-old daughter. He says he will come alone, and she is glad it'll be on a different night to herself. They are civil for the children's sake, but her mother will not be if she sees him. She has never forgiven him for leaving Ally with two young children.

Ally tries to engage her daughter in discussions of *Romeo and Juliet*. She tells her she studied the play, can help with any tricky lines. Elise's voice comes down like the heel of one of her chunky boots when she says that they do have teachers at St Cuthbert's, actually. She does permit Ally to drive her to the extra evening and weekend rehearsals, and to pick her up, tired but glowing, hours' later. Ally misses Zumba classes and a book group meeting to do this. She also goes to the Waterstones in Kingston and buys a copy of *Romeo and Juliet*, although Elise's teacher gave her a bound print-out when she got the part. Her throat fills with tears when Elise gives her a hasty one-armed hug as thanks. Then her daughter goes into her bedroom, which still has the fairy lights above the bed that she put up aged nine, to pack a bag for another 'sleepover at Hannah's'. Ally senses that every time she sees her quiet and preoccupied daughter, she carries unseen with her the ampoule containing her star-crossed love. When she comes through the front door, she is moving over a border that only she can see.

When enough light had dumped itself into her bedroom, Ally picked up her suitcase; it contained a few items of clothing and the letters. She had filched twenty pounds from her mother's purse. She would take the train to Callum, phoning him from the station before she left. Callum would know what to do after that. She was not giving him up. If it meant abandoning her degree, she would.

She imagined that her mother would do something like call the police, or lock her in her room, if she knew Ally's plan. She would wait until Verity got up then tell her she was staying the weekend with Genevieve, who lived in Manchester. That would buy her time.

Ally's mother rose at seven every day of the week. Ally's dad had been a police officer, so often worked weekends, and Verity had never wanted him to make his own breakfast. The habit had not died with him. What would her father have done, if he'd found the letters instead of her mother? Ally mused. Would he have understood? Would her mother have behaved more calmly? Ally suspected he would have been the angrier one, her mum seeking understanding. Instead, she hadn't asked Ally one question about Callum. He wasn't a sexual predator, he was only ten years older than her, had just finished his PhD. He was the cleverest and most loving and the best-looking man Ally had ever met. The fact that he was a tutor was a mere accident of fate; they were fortune's fools.

At fifteen minutes past seven, her mother had not left her bedroom and Ally was sweating with the need for action. She would make breakfast to have something to do.

At seven forty-five, there were four slices of toast on the rack, a cafetiere of coffee on the table with two glasses of orange juice, the butter and marmalade laid out along with plates and knives. And still no sound from upstairs. Was her mother so angry that she was waiting for Ally to go out so she didn't have to see her?

At eight, she decided that it was ridiculous and childish behaviour. She hammered on her mother's door, shouting that breakfast was ready. No response. She opened the door.

Her mother lay on the thick white-grey carpet, one side of her face drooping querulously. Next to her was a wide pool of water from a spilled tumbler, inside which lay her reading glasses and a sopping book. On the bedside table, a fort of crumpled tissues.

Ally is making a lamb and apricot tagine, a grandiose endeavour, when the front door bangs.

'Mum.'

'Oh God, what's happened?'

Elise is crying too hard for her words to make sense. Ally turns off the hob. Heartbreak, she recognises. As though she is a damaged baby bird, she edges closer to her daughter, hands stretched out. Elise's sobs gradually subside and, as sunlight falls through next-door's trampoline in red pixels, she talks.

Horror squeezes around Ally like a drawstring bag as she discovers that one of Elise's best friends, Scott, has been stabbed. He is in hospital, and Elise begs Ally, in a way she has not for years, to see him, as if that is a decision she can make. Leaving her daughter with a glass of Coke Zero and the biscuit tin, the best she can do for now, Ally phones the hospital and enquires about visiting hours. She is told that she and Elise can come at five o'clock. She then phones her ex-husband to ask him to pick Raff up, to have him for as long as this will take. He is equally horrified by the story; he too knows Scott, who attends St Richard's but has been a close friend of Elise's from their primary school days.

'Tell her I love her,' Elise's father says, and Ally says she will. Most of the time she feels a milk-sour dislike for him; except when something happens to one of the kids and she sees his love for them.

Ally puts her hammering heart into an ice pack and locks the house. In the car, Elise talks as if fizzy words have been kept in a stoppered-up bottle inside her. Scott and his new boyfriend, Mason, were in a local park, 'Just hanging out,' Elise says, when a group of boys came up close to them and set light to a bin to get high ('What?' Ally is appalled. 'People do that?' 'Yeah, but that's, like, not relevant info,

Mum.'). They then ordered Scott and Mason to buy alcohol for them; they refused, and the boys shouted homophobic abuse. A fight started; Scott was stabbed. The attackers were from St Cuthbert's.

'Year Nine's,' Elise says, 'like me.'

Making soothing noises at Elise, Ally wonders whether she could afford private school fees. Boarding school fees, even. Would her ex and her mother help? It's not possible, it would cost too much for two kids. But how she can cope with another incident like this; what if Elise had been in the park; what if this happens to Raff in a few years?

At the hospital, Ally pays an exorbitant parking fee and they walk to the main entrance in smug unseasonal heat. She takes her daughter's hand and Elise doesn't yank it away. It is so soft, Elise's hand, the skin so unweathered. As a young child, Elise was always wanting to hold hands; it used to irritate Ally sometimes, the sticky hand perpetually clasping hers in ownership.

After roaming a few corridors, they find a sign for the Sunshine Ward. En route, they pass a kiosk staffed by a cheery man purveying confectionary and awful news. Elise wants to get Scott jelly babies because they're his favourites, and although Ally doesn't think he'll be in a condition to eat sweets, she makes the purchase. Then they find the right lift, ascend and walk through double doors into a corridor so yellow it is like being inside Easter. There are children's drawings all over the walls and murals of sunflowers. At the nurses' station, they mention Scott's name and are told to wait in the corridor. A man and a boy are sitting there.

'Mason,' Elise says to the boy, who has a black rose of a bruise on one cheek. He and Elise stumble into a hug. Elise strokes his hair like a mother.

The man with Mason looks up; he stares at Ally. She stares at him. This time she knows that it is Callum.

'Ally, is that you?'

Ally looks at her daughter but Elise, talking to Mason, does not seem to have registered her mother's shock.

Callum stands. He raises his arms, as if he is going to touch her; does not. Inches from each other, they gaze. Ally's tongue is stuck to the roof of her mouth. Callum. There are more lines etched on his forehead and around his eyes than twenty years ago, and she wishes to trace every one of them to the source of whatever made him laugh or frown; belatedly, to share in the pains and pleasures. Apart from that his hair is still buttery-yellow, although there is less of it, his lips are still—

'You live here?' Callum's voice sounds the same. 'In Twickenham, I mean.'

Ally nods. She must speak.

'How about you, Callum?'

'Mason and I were living in the States until recently, I worked at a college there, then got transferred to St Mary's, Twickenham. So yep, this is home now.'

Mason and I: no mention of a wife or girlfriend.

A nurse with dreadlocks tells them Scott can have visitors now, but only two.

'You want me to come with you?' Callum asks Mason. 'Or you two kids can go together.'

Mason and Elise link arms and follow the nurse. Ally sits on the chair next to Callum, heart banging the walls of her chest as though seeking escape.

'Do you know how Scott is?' Ally realises she should have asked this before. This is why there are here: Callum's son's boyfriend has been stabbed. The situation feels like a play.

'He'll be fine physically, it's the emotional impact I'm worried about: on both boys,' Callum is saying. 'I don't know if it was a homophobic attack, or some inter-school feud. I don't know what to say to Mason. What's wrong with these kids, Ally?'

He sounds so angry. Ally wants to say they're just kids, like the ones that Elise sits with in classes and assemblies and in the lunch hall. But surely being a child isn't a feasible excuse for stabbing another child. Scott could have been killed.

'Have the police got them in custody?' she asks.

'For what that's worth. I'm sure Scott's parents will prosecute but I can't see kids of that age being disciplined too severely, not in this country. We'd better get a restraining order against them for Scott and Mason, at the very least.'

Ally wants to touch Callum's arm, in its navy coat, so much that she feels a burning under her skin. She stares at his profile; she had forgotten his beaky nose. Perhaps he never was a man of wax.

'There's a play,' she says hesitantly. '*Romeo and Juliet*; Elise is Juliet. Both secondary schools are performing in it: St Cuthbert's and St Richard's, I mean.'

She falters. She was intending to say: Are you going to it? But it is too unimportant a question for this hospital setting. And why would Callum want to go to a school whose pupil hurt his child? How insensitive she is.

'I first saw you in my Shakespeare seminar, Ally,' Callum says. 'And now here we are.'

And now here they are.

'I never thought I'd see you again.'

Against the sunflowers on the wall, Ally sees their shadow selves. Callum so authorial, so fervent in his desire for her. She so young, so desperate to be loved. She was devastated when her mother's stroke meant she couldn't be with him. She never managed to stuff the right words into a letter, so she never sent one at all. She tore up the letters he wrote, didn't answer the phone, and the love took itself into a sealed tomb: like Juliet, appearing to be dead as it lay dormant.

'My mother found out about us. She read your letters. She went mad, obviously.'

He says nothing.

'I was about to leave home to be with you,' she tells him, 'but she – Mum – had a stroke on that morning. I thought she was dead. It took a long time for her to recover, and there was no one else to help her. I blamed myself, thinking the stress of finding out about us did it to her. Anyway. I took a year out, and then when I went back to university you'd left.'

She doesn't tell him about that year out: when she became her mother, and her mother became a living corpse who drooped on the sofa in the blue-light of the television, speaking in a voice that sounded as if it were locked in a tower. Ally had learned how to clean, how to cook, how to sew, how to nurse, how to collect benefits, how to be as polite as the china mice on the shelf that she dusted each Sunday.

'If only there had been mobiles in the dark ages.' Callum's shoulders are slumped as though he's eating soup. 'I'm really sorry about your mother, I had no idea.'

'Why would you.'

'Years later I tried to track you down, to apologise, but I could never find you on Google.'

'To apologise?'

'I took advantage,' Callum tells her quietly. 'You were my student; I was in a position of responsibility and I abused it. It was indefensible. You or your mother would have been within your rights to have reported me so I was fired for what I did. Now I have a child myself, I can't believe I did it.'

'No,' Ally says, 'I would never have done that. Besides, I wasn't a kid, I was eighteen when we met—'

Not much older than Elise.

'They're coming out,' Callum says.

Their children are holding hands; Mason's eyes are red and Elise is wiping hers.

The teenagers say goodbye, promise to text with updates. Callum and Ally also say goodbye.

'See you at the play,' Elise calls over her shoulder, to Mason. And then she and Ally walk away down the songline of the corridor.

A dream: fishing in water the grey-blue of gunships; a tug at the end of the line and she is reeling in a fish so much bigger than she could have imagined. The fish has her own face. She throws it back, her own face vanishing. She spits, disgorging the hook into her open hand. She wakes, before the alarm, and wonders how it felt like a dream of Callum although he was not in it.

Ally's nerves are knitted so tightly that she has eaten all the popcorn by the second scene. The production has been good, so far: minimal staging and modern dress, the boys in hoodies and jeans, the Prince in a suit. Romeo, a tall dark-haired boy from St Richard's, is charismatic and engaging, making the audience (even Raff) laugh as he windmills his arms and leaps about the stage professing his love for Rosaline. Ally's mother is laughing along too, drinking sour wine from a plastic cup.

'Is the boyfriend as funny in real life?' her mother murmurs, as Romeo reads out the letter about the Capulets' masked ball.

'The boyfriend?'

'Deniz: Romeo. Elise didn't tell you she's going out with her Romeo?'

'Of course she did.'

And then it is Scene 3: Juliet's first scene. Her parents, Lord and Lady Capulet, have morphed into a single person, and her nurse is a boy pretending to be an elderly woman. Ally is not sure what to make of that, but perhaps there is no real significance, merely the two drama departments trying to be different. *You read meaning everywhere; even in the spaces between words* Callum had written in one letter. She has not seen him tonight. What will happen if he is there and her mother realises who he is? Verity has never met him, plus she is in her seventies with poor sight, but she is to scandal as a magpie is to shine.

'There's our girl,' her mother hisses, the wedding and engagement rings she never removes digging in to Ally's skin as she grips her hand.

Juliet is dressed for bed in a onesie and fluffy slippers, long hair in mermaid waves around her face. There are stuffed animals along one wall of the stage.

At first, speaking to her on-stage mother, Elise's voice wobbles. No, Ally thinks, please God, don't let her be bad. This is what she has been afraid of. But then, she realises that the audience is laughing as Elise-as-Juliet lolls on her bed mocking the Nurse, tongue hanging out, eyes rolling, exactly as she does when Ally tells a story she doesn't want to hear. When she tells the Nurse to 'stint' her timing is so perfect that the laughter is the loudest of the night so far. Ally's muscles relax as if she has been carrying the weight of the play.

The balcony scene uses a high black block, Juliet sitting on it in a black chiffon dress embroidered with gold stars and Converse. She dominates the scene, Romeo a puppy gambolling lovingly beneath her. Their desire is so tangible that tears spring to Ally's eyes: part pride and part sadness that she cannot imagine feeling that same amazement in another person, with no idea of their flaws, again. She has never loved another man the way she loved her own first love. Every other was a man she patched onto her heart.

'Elise is not terrible,' Raff says.

Ally smiles at him, but the full-knuckle on-stage love has rendered her silent.

When Juliet says she will not be a Capulet if Romeo will not deny his father and refuse his own name, Ally hears the sadness in each of the words. This is a lovestruck girl, but she is also a daughter who until this point in her young life has never loved any man other than her father. Loss and longing are interconnected. As she speaks, she grows up and away.

Next to her, her mother takes two white embroidered hankies from her handbag. She hands one to Ally and presses another to her eyes.

After the standing ovation, the headteachers come on stage to commend the actors and the heads of drama. Elise's headteacher, Miss Brown, a celery-thin woman with peroxide hair and a singsong Irish accent, then talks gravely about the spate of violence between the schools. The boys responsible for the recent attack on one of the St Richard's pupils have been expelled and the matter is in the hands of the police, she says. The St Richard's headteacher, a man as round as she is thin, so that standing together they resemble the number ten, says they are working in partnership to develop a strategy to ensure this never happens again, that there has always been a friendly and harmonious relationship between the schools before now and there will be again. A strategy is being compiled, details to be disseminated via the relevant school apps. Applause.

Miss Brown smiles and says, 'The bar is open for another hour but before you go: let's have another round of applause for the marvellous actors.'

The actors run back on stage, Juliet and Romeo holding hands and beaming: at the audience and then at each other.

Clapping until her hands ache, Ally sees Callum. All the time, he has been two rows in front. As if he can feel the heat of her stare, he turns and smiles. She smiles back.

'Who's that, dear?' demands her mother.

'Just someone I used to know,' Ally says vaguely.

'Why's he staring at you?' Raff asks.

'I don't think he is. Come on, let's get home. Work and school tomorrow.'

'Oh, there's time for one more drink, Alison,' says her mother.

Everyone Loved Romy

'You wouldn't see me dead at a school reunion,' says Danny's wife Natalie. 'Everyone will be just as annoying, only fatter and with less hair.'

'It might be a laugh.' Danny shrugs.

'If there was anyone you really wanted to be in touch with after twenty-five years, you would be,' she adds.

Danny does keep in touch with Mike, Mark and Michael, who went to St Joseph's Earlsfield at the same time as him. The three Ms are going to the reunion, only Mark as part of a couple as Michael is recently divorced and Mike single. Natalie will be at a seminar for her MA in Counselling. It is so good, they say smugly, that the kids are old enough not to need babysitters. Danny does not say that this also makes him feel old.

Now, he and the others are walking towards St Joseph's, having had a pint beforehand. Danny notices a new green and white building in an architectural style resembling Lego.

The reunion is in the old part of the school. They navigate panelled corridors which still have a musty woody smell, glancing at art displays about climate change and Anti-bullying Week.

In the hall, Danny feels stirred from a long sleep, pulled back to days of tuning out in assemblies and mouthing the words to hymns while staring at classmates. Most of the time, his searchlight gaze was trying to find Romy di Marco.

Danny takes a deep breath and pulls back his shoulders. The room is terribly hot. A blonde woman with winged eyeliner and a yellow scarf bustles over. She has a glass of white wine in one hand and a sheaf of name stickers in the other. She knows who he is without being told, although she calls him 'Daniel', her face tight with pride at knowing the name by which no one, except his mum, calls him.

'Two drinks tickets for each of you,' she says with a wink, picking up a book of raffle tickets from a trestle table and ripping some off. 'Paid bar after that until midnight.'

'Who was that?' Danny mutters.

'Joelle Taylor,' Mike hisses as they move away. 'I used to fancy her.'

'Let's use these tickets,' Danny says.

Danny had got a summer job in a pub as soon as A-levels finished. Paddy's, which had sticky carpets and Irish flags above the bar, although the owner had never lived anywhere but South-west London, was popular with the sixth formers as IDs were rarely checked. Working there gave Danny an unexpected cachet. Even so, he was surprised when on his first night, Romy di Marco came in, walked straight over and smiled at him. She was alone, as she hardly ever was to his knowledge. Danny's breath caught in his throat.

'What can I get you?' he stammered, although he hadn't yet pulled a pint and had no knowledge of many of the spirits in their optics.

Romy flicked her dirty-blonde hair. 'Nothing for a few hours, thanks.'

'Sorry?'

'I work here.'

'Here?' Danny was aware of how idiotic he sounded.

'Started a fortnight ago, Danny.'

'How do you know my name?'

Romy smiled again. Her lips and eyelids were painted gold; her caramel cheekbones shone gold too. 'We went to school together for seven years, Danny... do you not know my name?'

'Of course I do, Romy.'

She took off her coat, and he tried not to stare at her body. Romy slipped behind the bar, then nodded at someone waiting to be served.

'Pint of Carling Premier and a packet of salt and vinegar, Steve?'

Ahh, Danny thought, so she knows everyone's name.

He and Romy circled each other as the pub got busier. Hours collapsed. Romy showed Danny how to tilt a glass to pour a pint; how much gin and tonic to put in a gin and tonic. Their boss Padraig, a fleshy and shifty person, spent a lot of time in the cellar, stock-taking ('Taking the stock,' Romy said) while they worked. By half past ten, Danny couldn't remember feeling so tired.

'Fancy a shot?' Romy asked. 'Tequila?'

'Are we allowed?'

'Paddy won't know. He'll be in the cellar for ages. And Holly and Ivy over there won't care.'

Danny looked at the only customers who remained, two middle-aged ladies. They had their heads together, and one was stroking the other's face.

'Are they really called Holly and Ivy?'

Romy, lining up two shot glasses, laughed. 'Probably not. I like to imagine everyone as a character in a story, though – Holly and Ivy are good names for a couple.'

She poured a generous measure of tequila into each glass, added a rim of salt and handed one to Danny.

'Sláinte,' she said, draining the glass and slamming it on the bar.

Danny didn't know what that meant, but tipped back his head and drank. The liquor burned its way down his throat.

'Well,' Romy said, 'working here just got more fun.'

Danny is trying to have fun at the reunion. He has cheek-kissed, enquired about careers and health, admired children behind glass, commiserated about the deaths of parents remembered from camping trips and sleepovers, laughed about hanging out at the Arndale on Saturdays and Joseph Adamik being caught shoplifting a rubber from the Tate Britain souvenir shop on a school trip. Many people look similar to their younger selves but, as Natalie surmised, fatter with less hair and more lines;

acne-ridden skin was now spot-free but missing its collagen spring, some foreheads were suspiciously smooth. Most are friendly but two of the rugby boys, the type who peed in the street on nights out and drank beer from shoes, stare at Danny when he says hello; he isn't sure if he's broken a cardinal rule that people like them don't talk to people like him or if they can't place him: slightly drunk, he laughs in their faces and turns away.

Yet after spending half an hour beside the buffet eating a soggy egg sandwich and what he thinks is chicken tikka masala, being talked at by Simon Jeffries, whom he'd sat with in GCSE chemistry and whose doggy face and sad eyes make him look like a seal, about the best bike trails in England, Danny wants an escape. Simon has been at the egg sandwiches too, his breath smells sulphuric. Danny says that he's going for a cigarette, and Simon's seal face pinches.

'I didn't know anyone still smoked,' he says.

Danny doesn't smoke, but it's a good excuse. He walks away, past the local band playing The Wannadies' 'You & Me Song' and smiles.

The fire-escape door is ajar and Danny goes through it into splashes of moonlight. In the distance, there is the cry of a train. He takes gulps of air as biting as knives or glass. There is a flight of metal steps, and he descends them. At the bottom is the prayer garden, and on a bench in the prayer garden is Romy di Marco.

On A-level results night, Romy persuaded Padraig to let them have a lock-in. Even better, Padraig left them to it, saying he'd be back to close up. Danny, who had achieved the two As and one B needed to study history at Warwick, mixed snakebite and blacks and chatted to people he never normally talked to as they queued at the bar. He tried not to stare at Romy, who was wearing a soft-looking pink dress with biker boots.

By midnight, people were dancing to Blackstreet's 'No Diggity' and drunkenly divulging crushes (the DT teacher, Mr Akhtar, got the most votes) and grandiose plans – making a million, breaking America as a singer, becoming one of Blair's Babes, not working in the family business. Then Aqua's 'Barbie Girl' came on and extraneous clothes came off. The air was sweaty and filled with potential. Danny felt that he and his schoolmates were standing on balconies overlooking the rest of their lives; no longer children, only nominally adults.

By one o'clock, people were snogging as 'Don't Speak' by No Doubt played. Fiona Mackensie, about to study English at Bristol, was declaiming a poem she had written about not knowing her true self. Claire MacAllister was throwing up in the beer garden. Mike was leaning on the bar shouting at Danny that he didn't want to go to university but it was too late and Danny answered as he cleaned an optic that it wasn't and Mike could be whatever he wanted and Mike slurred that Danny was absolutely fucking right and he would ring Oxford in the morning and say stuff your PPE degree and get a job in the garden centre because he loved plants plus Paz Aggarwal worked there and she'd said he looked like George Clooney. Romy turned the music up, the 'You and Me Song' blasting out.

From a corner table, where Suki Webster was charging for tarot readings, Danny heard shouting. Sian Deacon swing her fist and hit Suki. Tarot cards scattered.

'You only told me to break up with Jamil because you snogged him in Images,' Sian yelled.

'You were on a break.' Suki slapped Sian.

'Oh God,' Romy yelled, 'stop them. If there's blood on the carpet, Paddy will go mental.'

Suki and Sian were a tangle of limbs, like cats fighting to the soundtrack of Hanson's 'MMMBop'. A group formed around the girls; there were cheers and shrieks of distress.

Danny gripped Sian's arms behind her back, like a TV police officer arresting a criminal. She freed herself easily and he felt a blow on his nose. He staggered and hit a stool, which fell.

The music stopped.

'What the devil is going on in here?' yelled Padraig. 'Danny, what have you let happen?'

Blood was running into Danny's mouth; he tasted its iron tang. He fumbled to a chair and tilted his head back. A hand passed him a paper napkin.

'Are you alright, Danny?' Romy sounded admiring.

'Party's over,' Padraig shouted. Someone booed. 'Get out, or I'm calling the cops and then your parents in that order.'

'I don't think he has our parents' numbers,' Romy murmured and Danny gave a small snort of laughter, then winced with pain.

There were sounds of movement.

'Danny and Romy, you're clearing up this mess,' Padraig added.

Gingerly, Danny lowered his head. The napkin was soaked in blood but was only trickling from his nose. Sian muttered an apology at him. He told her, half-truthfully, that it didn't matter. Suki collected her tarot cards.

Soon, the pub was empty of everyone who didn't work there. Livery lips set in a line, Padraig counted the takings while Danny and Romy put chairs in their right places, wiped tables, refilled optics. Danny picked up a tarot card from under a table. A naked man and woman in a garden: The Lovers. He pocketed it.

After half an hour, Padraig told them they could go. He muttered about sacking them, but Danny could tell he didn't mean it. Probably, they would just not be paid for the evening, which would be bad enough. Or he wouldn't be, anyway; Padraig loved Romy.

'Want me to walk you home?' Danny held the door to the pub for Romy. He expected her to say no. She had a boyfriend, a twenty-two-year-old who worked in a bank, who usually collected her after work in his car. He often came into the pub and talked to her; he never spoke to Danny.

'That would be good,' Romy said. 'I'm in Fern Tree Walk, the new estate near the station.'

The two of them walked in silence for a while, bodies occasionally bumping as their paces were incongruent. Danny took a sideways glance at Romy; she appeared as if she had spent the evening looking for something she had not found. He realised he hadn't asked about her A-levels.

'Were you pleased with your results?'

Romy didn't reply.

'Sorry, was that the wrong thing to say?' Danny asked.

'My dad studied medicine, at Cambridge,' Romy said. 'My big brother's there now, also studying medicine. My dad's a surgeon, Mum's a GP. Everyone assumes I'll be a doctor, too.'

'You don't want to be?'

'I want to be a writer; it's all I've ever wanted to be.'

'You can't study English instead?'

'What a waste of time that would be, my parents say. If you want to read books, do it in the bath, do it on holiday. Don't spend three years wasting tax-payers' money and then come away with a worthless degree that won't qualify you for anything.'

'My history degree's not going to qualify me for anything,' Danny said. 'I just want to do something I enjoy.'

'You're pretty cool, Danny.'

'I am?'

She smiled, then gave a shiver. 'Left my coat in the pub. Knowing Padraig, he'll sell it.'

Danny took off his red corduroy jacket and placed it around her shoulders.

'My hero,' she said, and took his arm. They walked on, the only sound the shushing of cars on the distant main road, and Danny could hardly breathe for joy.

They walked quickly through an area with tatty shops and humiliated trees, a street cordoned off by flailing blue tape. They talked about the evening, Paddy's awfulness as a boss, the short story Romy was writing for a competition, the fact that Warwick was in Coventry and not Warwick.

'Come and stay some time, if you want.' Danny was glad his blush wasn't visible in the dark.

'Maybe I will.' Her hand squeezed his arm.

They reached Romy's estate, one which Danny's parents had talked about enviously as it was being built. Only in London would such a nice development be so near nastier ones. In the light from the streetlamps, he saw that these houses were large and detached, with paved driveways and little greenery. He imagined that inside there were cream walls and polished hardwood floors, unlike his own home which was brightly painted and even the bathroom had a carpet. Their bodies ghosted along the deserted paths, until Romy stopped at a house identical to the others. All the lights in the house were off.

'When are you next working?' she asked quietly.

Saturday, Danny said, and Romy smiled and said she would see him then. But she didn't turn to go. He noticed her bright grey eyes; he had assumed they were pale blue, had put the Velvet Underground's 'Pale Blue Eyes' on a mixtape.

Romy held out her arms, and Danny inserted himself into them like a jigsaw piece. She smelled of roses. She touched his bruised nose and he winced; she placed a butterfly kiss on it, then on his lips. Above him, the stars whistled.

'Danny?'

'Romy?'

Romy is wearing a white dress and, despite the cold, no coat. Getting closer to her, Danny feels a residue of feeling like a knot under his skin. Natalie, he thinks, Natalie Natalie Natalie. My wife, Natalie. The mother of my three children, Natalie. Natalie, who is not here.

'Aren't you cold, Romy?' Danny asks. 'Do you want my coat?'

'You always were my hero,' she says, but her smile is weak, as if she's forgotten the mechanics of it. 'I'm fine. Have a seat, Danny.'

Danny sits on the other end of the bench to her, hoping she can't smell egg on his breath. Above, the white moon swings on its cord. He looks at the fish mosaic engraved on the bench and the crosses moving in the trees. The chill in his throat feels like a small bone.

'How are you, Romy?'

She looks as delicate as if she has been cut from paper. Maybe she has had covid; or has long covid. Silence stretches out like a white sheet.

'Do you remember,' Romy says, in a musing tone, 'that Ban the Bomb Assembly we did in Sixth Form? Me, Joelle and Sian. We had to petition Mr Wommel for weeks to do it.'

The three – although Danny had only seen Romy – had stood on stage in the hall twirling their hair while saying how bad nuclear war was. They showed projector slides of Chernobyl and Nagasaki, then handed out small CND badges. Danny had worn one on his puffa jacket for the next three years.

'We were so idealistic,' Romy says, 'really thought we could change the world. I suppose the Labour landslide was a factor. And then look what Blair did with his oil war.'

'What happened with your writing, Romy? Did you get your novel – the one you were talking about when we last saw each other – published?'

Romy gave a small laugh. 'I was sure I was going to be the female Louis de Berniéres.'

'Who?'

'Really, you didn't read *Captain Corelli's Mandolin*? He wrote it in Earlsfield.'

'I think I remember the film.'

'Are you happy, Danny?' Romy asks.

'Yes,' Danny says automatically. 'Are you, Romy? What have you been up to since we last saw each other?'

The last time they saw each other – does Romy remember? – was two days before Christmas, fifteen years' ago.

'That was the time we went clubbing,' Romy says.

So she does remember.

The last time Danny had seen Romy, he had been engaged to Natalie. Christopher had been born the year before, after an unplanned pregnancy. Still in their twenties, Danny and Natalie were the first of their friends to have a child. Although love walked into his eyes every time he saw his boy, Christopher was a bad sleeper and the couple was exhausted by their cacophonous new life. They rarely went out. But then Mike from school had called to say he was having a hook-up with Sian, also from school, did Danny want to come out with them? No, Danny said, I don't want to be a gooseberry. Romy di Marco's coming too, Mike said; she and Sian are still good friends. Bring Natalie, of course. Heart thudding, Danny suggested it; Natalie said no straight away, refusing to waste a babysitting opportunity on Mike and two women she didn't know.

The four met at what had been Paddy's, and was now The Townhouse, a bar sparkly and white as an operating theatre, with pricey drinks. While Mike and Sian huddled up, Danny and Romy shared a bottle of red wine – she still said

'Sláinte'. She looked much the same as she had at school although her hair was platinum and she was thinner, her shoulder blades like the stumps of wings.

They got drunk, and then drunker, as no one wanted food. Mike and Sian began snogging. Romy and Danny laughed at them, and at the other customers, especially at a couple of women ordering melon juice at the bar ('Holly and Ivy would never have done that,' Danny said; 'Paddy used to get Happy Shopper orange juice,' Romy chortled). They talked about Gordon Brown taking over from Tony Blair as Prime Minister, about what could have happened to Madeleine McCann, about Emily getting thrown out of Big Brother for using a racial slur, and about Romy's burgeoning dystopian novel about life after a nuclear catastrophe. She didn't reveal whether she was single, and Danny didn't ask, although he did mention Christopher and showed her a photo. Romy talked more than Danny, and he tried to listen intently but it was like trying to catch the tail end of a kite as it fluttered just above his head. All he could think was that he wanted to kiss her, and must not.

Around eleven, a group of Sian's workmates broke up the Sian and Mike snogathon and suggested going to a club. Mike Googled Images; found it was still there. What a laugh to go again, Sian said. Danny hadn't been to a club for years, disliking dance music and the impossibility of holding a proper conversation over the noise of it even more, but when Romy said she would go he said he would too. Mike wiggled his eyebrows at Danny, who looked away.

Leaving the pub, they passed what had been Mr Wong's, where Danny had eaten many pieces of fish puffed out with batter and sweaty chips, which was now Amaranth Thai and Noodle Bar. Romy said how sad it was that nothing stayed the same.

At the club, Danny found he was drunk enough to go on the dance floor. Romy danced very close to him, and he put his arms around her waist. She still smelled of roses.

At the end of the night, he walked her home, remembering what had happened the last time he did that. Again, she took his arm. They passed a café with a dark grey exterior, where Romy said she worked and wrote. Danny wondered how her family of doctors felt about that.

Outside her home, now a downstairs flat in an Edwardian terrace with plants on the window ledges, they held each other. Romy lifted up her face and they kissed. She asked if he would come inside. Almost weeping, he told her he was sorry, he couldn't do that to Natalie, and she smiled and said not to worry. He found a taxi on the high street and went home to his sleeping wife and baby. Christopher woke at five am; as Danny sang 'Baa baa black sheep', a fir tree tapping on the window and mist a bandage in the sky, he cried into his son's soft downy scalp.

'What happened, Romy?' Danny asks.

He is shivering from the cold. She is not.

'When?' Romy asks.

To us, he wants to say, but despite his paper-cloud hopes there had never been an 'us'. They were an almost-us. He looks up at a looming tower block that hadn't been there twenty-five years ago, because he can no longer look into her face.

'What happened in your life?' he asks, trying for cheerfulness.

'I married Andrew,' she says. 'South African: into tennis.'

'Congratulations. Is he here tonight?'

She shakes her head, and Danny hopes he doesn't look as relieved as he feels. Perhaps she is no longer with Andrew – 'I married' is not 'I'm married'.

'Kids?' he asks.

Another head-shake.

'Hey, did you know Paddy's is Café Viva now?' he asks. 'It's all so gentrified around here; well, I guess you know – unless you moved away? Remember those clothes shops that sold checked shirts for a fiver? All gone, replaced by champagne bars and Vietnamese restaurants. People travel here from Clapham for a night out these days.'

He is rambling.

'We had fun at Paddy's, didn't we?' Romy's eyes are hard pits of the past. 'We were so young; everything was possible. Cool Britannia.'

'You're not old now, Romy. You've still got time to become a bestselling author and tour the world, like you said you would. Did you publish your dystopian novel?'

Are there tears in her eyes?

'I hope your life's been happy,' Romy says. 'I hope it is happy.'

A bang: Danny's eyes fly to the fire door. Mike is there. Mike, who only stayed with Romy's friend Sian for a month after the clubbing night. Would it have been different if they had married and had kids? Would that have changed things for Danny and Romy?

'Are you alright, mate? What are you doing out here freezing your balls off? Come on in, there's a pint with your name on it. Do you remember Carlo, the one all the girls called the Italian Stud Muffin? He's eaten all the muffins; you need to see.'

'In a minute,' Danny says.

He looks at Romy to give her an apologetic glance – is Mike ignoring her because of Sian? – but the other end of the bench is empty.

'Did Romy just go past you?' he asks Mike.

'Romy di Marco? Didn't know she was here.'

Where did Romy go? It's an enclosed space. Did she nip up the stairs and into the hall when Mike opened the door? But he would have seen her.

There is nothing Danny can do: he follows Mike inside. As he takes the pint his friend has bought for him, he looks around. He sees Suki Webster, and remembers he has her tarot card. He does not see Romy.

'Danny.' It's Sian, looking much the same as she did fifteen years ago. 'How are you doing?'

'Oh, hi. Can I get you a drink, Sian?' He tries not to look for Romy over her shoulder. The conversation in the prayer garden feels unfinished.

Sian says she will have a gin and tonic; he orders it.

'Sláinte.' As she clinks her glass against his pint, he sees a ring on her fourth finger.

Mike and Michael, standing in a group with Joelle and a woman Danny doesn't recognise, glance over. Mike looks from Danny to Sian.

'Sláinte. That's what Romy used to say,' Danny says.

He imagines that Sian will smile, perhaps launch into a memory of Paddy's or Images, but her face seems to freeze. 'That was so sad.'

Danny's heart thuds against the prison walls of his chest.

'Sad?' he asks.

'Yes, what happened to Romy.' A slight touch of impatience in Sian's voice.

'Sian, I'm not sure what you're talking about.' The conversation is like boning a fish, and doing it when drunk to boot. 'What happened to Romy?'

'You don't know?' Impatience has become accusation.

'No. Sian, please can you tell me what happened to Romy?'

Sian sucks in air through her teeth.

'Oh, God. It was five years' ago. She had an eating disorder, and it developed into full-blown anorexia. She was about to be admitted to a clinic as an in-patient, her parents were terrified and she'd admitted she needed help, when she had a heart attack; they thought it was caused by the anorexia. She died straight away. I'm so sorry you didn't know, Danny. I thought you were friends; I thought you'd know.'

Her words have pinned Danny to the ground by the throat.

'We'd lost touch,' he says. What a strange expression – lost touch. How can you lose touch, the way you lose the sense of taste or smell? He had lost both with covid. Why is he thinking about covid? Romy is dead. Romy is dead.

'To be honest, there weren't that many people at the funeral,' Sian says. 'She'd got divorced a couple of years' before; even her ex, Andrew, didn't come; well, I think he was back in South Africa. It was so sad, she was so popular at school – well, of course you know that. I think she alienated a lot of people in the year or two before it happened, though. I tried my best, but she didn't want to socialise, and I didn't see her much at the end. I feel terrible now, but she was so secretive, I had no idea how ill she was.'

'I saw her,' Danny says.

'You saw her? Just before she died, you mean?'

There is a tingling sensation in Danny's palms and feet.

'I saw her tonight. In the prayer garden: she was sitting on a bench. I spoke to her, Sian. I know it sounds mad, but I really did. Then Mike came out and she wasn't there anymore, I thought she'd come in here without me noticing.'

Sian reaches out and touches his arm. Touch, with anyone other than a family member, is so rare in 2022 that reflexively he pulls away.

'Grief can do funny things, Danny.'

'Come out with me; I'll show you where it was. Please.'

She frowns, but follows him.

'Don't do anything I wouldn't do, son,' Mark shouts. 'We won't tell Natalie.'

There is laughter, but Danny ignores it. He is walking so fast that Sian half-runs to keep up. He shoves open the fire escape door; cold blasts into him.

Sian goes ahead of him down the steps, heels clinking on the metal, into the prayer garden. There are cigarette stubs to indicate that people have been there, but there is no one now.

'It was that bench,' Danny says, pointing. 'She was wearing a white dress.'

His throat is thick with tears, and he swallows hard.

'Really, a white dress?' Sian asks.

'Yes; why?'

'At her funeral, there was a photo of Romy on the coffin. She was wearing a white dress.'

Danny cannot speak.

'Poor Romy, she had so much potential. Of all of us in our school year, I thought she was the one who'd be famous: be remembered, you know? I told her mum, at the wake, how much everyone loved Romy.' Sian carries on talking, but the words are a muted monotone. Pain has put a thick glass box around Danny.

After a while, Sian lightly touches his back. 'Let's go in, Danny, it's so cold out here. I'll get you another pint, you look as though you could do with it.'

'Thanks.' Danny makes an effort to focus. 'Thanks, Sian. But I need to go home now.'

'Well, maybe see you at the thirty-year reunion, then, Danny,' she says with a small smile. 'I'll buy you that pint then.'

'Yes,' Danny says, knowing this is the last reunion he will attend.

Apple Crumble Baked by A Ghost

Charlie stares at herself. She has foundation the colour and texture of cement, over-excited eyelashes and purple lips; the make-up artist claimed the effect would be toned down in the photos. Her hair has been both straightened and waved. The spirit-white lace dress makes her stomach and breasts appear flattened.

Her mum is in the room. 'You look beautiful, Charlotte. You are sure, though?'

'The only thing I'm unsure of is whether Neil's going to turn up. He's so forgetful, I can imagine him not remembering we're getting married today.'

'Marrying your father was the best thing I ever did. Neil loves you, I do know that.'

Her mum disappears.

Charlie hears her phone buzz; before she gets to it, it has gone to voicemail. 'Neil', says the caller display. Is it bad luck to talk to the groom before seeing him on the wedding day?

The doorbell rings: it will be her dad. She puts her phone away, knowing that whatever Neil wants to say can't be urgent.

The Grade II-listed registry office building is rampant with police: on the steps, on the pavement, even in the road. There are more officers than Charlie has seen outside of *Line of Duty*. There is an ambulance and many, many bystanders taking photos and videos – of what, Charlie is not sure.

In the Rolls Royce, Charlie and her dad stare at the scene – at each other – at the scene.

'Something's going on,' remarks the driver.

'Well, obviously,' Charlie says. Anxiety seeps in; an insidious stain.

Her dad lays a hand on her arm.

'Stay here, I'll find out what's going on. Drive round the block a couple of times, mate,' he tells the driver, who grunts.

Charlie turns in her seat as the car moves away. There are more police arriving, like brightly coloured bees swarming.

As they encounter the same scene again after driving slowly around the block ('Seen that film *Groundhog Day*?' the driver says), Charlie's phone rings: it's her dad.

'Love, don't be scared, but there was a bomb threat. The police had an anonymous call; said it would go off in forty-five minutes. There's no evidence of a device, so it may be a hoax.'

'How long am I meant to go round in circles?' the driver asks.

Charlie phones Neil. He sounds on the verge of tears.

'I'm sorry, Charlie,' he says. 'This was meant to be the happiest day of your life.'

'It's not your fault, Neil. It was meant to be the happiest day of your life too.'

She notices a group of people outside the registry office, heads down as if prospecting for gold. Bomb disposal experts, perhaps. For the first time, underneath the adrenalin, she experiences ripples of fear.

'I'm so sorry, darling,' Neil says.

'It doesn't matter about the wedding, we can do it another time. Imagine if there really is a bomb, we could have been blown up if we'd been inside. You don't think we were the targets?'

Who could want to kill them? Charlie can't think of anyone who hates her.

'There wasn't a bomb. It was a hoax, Charlie.'

'It was? You've spoken to the police, then? Did they say we can get in to the venue?'

'I'm so sorry, Charlie.'

'You don't have to keep saying that. What could you have done?'

'I've never quite trusted him, Charlie,' says her mum. She is wearing a loose-fitting white blouse; not traditional mother-of-the-bride attire, but then she is not a traditional mother-of-the-bride.

Down the phoneline come hoarse, racking sobs.

'What is it, Neil?' Charlie asks.

'We can't get married today. We've lost our space.'

'I'll talk to them,' she says. 'They'll have to fit us in later.'

'They were adamant, I spoke to them for ages. We'll have to do it another day. But what about the reception, do you want to go ahead with that?'

Charlie feels everything falling away like beads on a string. First the wedding, then the reception. She has been so looking forward to the honeymoon, which her father paid for: five nights in Crete.

'Let's do the reception, Neil,' she says. 'We can do it in reverse: reception, honeymoon and then wedding.'

There is a weak 'Hooray' when Charlie and Neil enter the converted barn that has been hired for the reception. Charlie has changed into a cream silk evening dress, leaving her hair and make-up as it was. They circulate among their guests, holding glasses of Cava. Neil's breath whispers on Charlie's neck. He stays pinned to her like a badge, even in a group of her school friends whom he has only met once or twice.

'He hasn't got many of his own friends here, has he,' Charlie's mum murmurs. 'When your dad and I got married, we had so many friends we could hardly find a venue big enough. But you're so popular, darling.'

Charlie chats on to her friends, mostly speculation about the bomb hoax, while Neil munches on mini tacos. These are the sole canapes, chosen in honour of the fact that Neil and Charlie met in a Mexican restaurant; he there for an interview with the manager, for the local paper he works for as a journalist, she to meet her friend Vicky, who stood her up due to a work emergency. The manager had been too busy to talk to Neil, but he sat alone hoping and waiting. Charlie and he looked at each other awkwardly for a while, before Neil asked if she wanted to share tacos and beer. Then they had gone to a wine bar. Charlie had been so drunk she had been sick in a gutter, and Neil helped her home. She hadn't expected him to call the next day, couldn't remember giving him her number, but he had. He had quickly become a fixture.

Six months after that, Charlie's mother was killed in a car accident while driving home from work. Neil was there when Charlie got the news. He supported her and her dad, arranging what needed to be arranged when they had been too broken to do so.

A year later, he proposed. Now here they are, Neil's hand sweating in hers, her mother a ghostly presence alternately carping and cheerleading.

Looking up from cutting a giant cupcake, Charlie sees a police officer walk into the barn. The officer, a round-faced middle-aged man, introduces himself as Police Constable Winter and requests that Charlie and Neil go outside with him for 'a few words, please'. Charlie avoids the anxious eye of her dad and leads the men out into a murky-black night. There is a yard with a broken-ribbed bench, cigarette ends littered around it and a smell of marijuana. Charlie hopes the police officer won't comment on the smell: he doesn't. He has a proper crime to discuss.

'There are fewer than ten thousand phone boxes in the United Kingdom now,' PC Winter states, in the voice of a portentous TV police officer. 'One of the few remaining is on John Street. That is the street next to the one on which you both live.'

Charlie cannot remember seeing a phone box. Then she realises what the officer means, and her skin freezes.

'The call to the police about the bomb, which we now know was a hoax, was made from this phone box. This could, of course, be a coincidence. But I need to ask whether either of you know anything about it?'

'Absolutely nothing,' Neil says, and Charlie knows by the way he speaks too fast that he is lying. 'Why would we do that? It meant we couldn't get married.'

'I'm aware that you didn't get married,' PC Winter says. 'However, it seems that you would not have been able to get married today anyway.'

'What?' Charlie looks into PC Winter's hazel eyes. 'Of course we were going to get married. It was all booked in with the registry office.'

'You booked it yourself, Miss Starr?'

'No, Neil booked it,' she murmurs. 'I booked this reception.'

'Mr Hilland?'

Neil says nothing.

'There was no record of a booking for your wedding at the registry office,' the police officer says. 'We contacted them in relation to all the weddings taking place today. The next one was due to occur at two-thirty; it had, of course, to be postponed due to the bomb hoax.'

'I didn't book the venue,' Neil says to Charlie. 'I thought I had, I really did, I sent them an email, and then today I rang to check everything was okay and they said they had no record of a booking being made. They said the email might not have been read because they had fewer staff working due to covid last year, or it might have gone astray. They said I should phone, next time.'

Charlie feels as though white wax is lodged in her throat.

'Told you he couldn't be trusted,' her mother says, and Charlie would kick her if she could.

'Did you make the phone call stating that you believed there was an unexploded bomb at Low Fell Registry Office, Mr Hilland?' PC Winter asks, in a voice that knows the answer.

'I didn't want you to be angry with me, Charlie,' Neil says. 'The wedding was all you talked about. I called before I knew you'd be leaving for the registry office, but you didn't answer. I was going to tell you.'

Through the windows of the venue, Charlie sees guests taking selfies with the party props she had ordered.

'Mr Hilland?' PC Winter repeats. 'Did you make the phone call?'

Neil's mouth is in an O shape, like an infant's. A soft gurgling comes out.

Charlie's dad goes to the sentencing, not wanting Charlie to hear what happens from anyone else. She has refused to go herself.

'Twelve months in jail, a hundred and fifty pounds of court costs for communicating false information with intent,' he tells her afterwards. They are in Charlie and Neil's garden; she is picking apples from the sagging tree.

'The judge said the hoax was irresponsible and would have terrified everyone concerned,' continues her dad. 'With luck, Neil will only serve six months. He said how ashamed and embarrassed he was, and he certainly sounded it. Probably be the end of his career at the paper, it was front page news at the *North East Times*, they didn't mention he was one of their journalists, funnily enough. They didn't mention you either, love: not by name. Don't know where Neil found his barrister, he didn't help much, said it had the markings of a comedy: not sure that went down too well with the judge.'

Charlie is reminded of a time when, as a student, she went jogging and was stung by a bee. She had floundered about trying to close the wild eye of the sting, furious to have been taken by surprise like that, to have had her run interrupted.

'I thought he'd get a suspended sentence,' she says. 'Not go to prison.'

'I can help you with the apples later, love, why don't you sit down?'

Charlie doesn't, but she stands still, a pale-green and rose-pink apple in her hand.

'He'll be in Hatfield,' says her dad, 'it's not too far. I can drive you when you get a visiting order, if you like. It's an open prison, shouldn't be too bad for him. As good as prisons ever are.'

'Have you been in a prison, Dad?' Charlie pulls down another apple but sees it's rotten and throws it on the ground. Her phone rings: Vicky. She will have found out what has happened: all her friends will have. She can't bear to hear commiserations.

'Once, love,' her dad says, and Charlie doesn't know what he's talking about before remembering her question about prison. 'Let's not talk about that now. Let's go for lunch: my treat.'

'I'm not hungry, Dad.'

An insect lands on Charlie's hand and she crushes it with her nail. Her dad picks up the bucket of apples she has picked. A red-eyed sunset has appeared in the sky.

'Your mum used to make lovely crumbles, you remember? I'm not taking no for an answer; you need feeding up.'

'Charlie, I'd love to be able to go out for lunch with your dad.' Her mum is not there this time, just a voice.

'Do you ever – see – or hear – Mum?' Charlie asks.

'What?'

'Don't worry.'

'I'd give anything to see her. You'll think I'm a ridiculous old man, but I even contacted a spiritual medium I found online. Nothing. I'm hoping that means she's at peace.'

'I'm sure she is, Dad.'

They go into the house. Charlie's dad puts the bucket of apples on a kitchen work surface.

'Dad, can I ask another question? Did I talk about the wedding all the time? It was what Neil said, just before he was arrested.'

'You talked about it,' her dad says slowly. 'But not all the time. Your mum talked about our wedding incessantly, I was glad when the day came around so she'd stop carping on about flowers and food and fripperies.'

'What would have happened if you'd forgotten to book the registry office?'

'That would never have happened. Principally, because she would never have trusted me to do it. Her own mother, God rest her soul, made all the arrangements.'

'Should I forgive him, Dad?'

'All I can tell you is what I think. Neil made a mistake. It was absolute stupidity, but no one was hurt. He did it because he didn't want you to be upset. He loves you.'

'I'm not sure you feel the same, though,' her mum adds.

Charlie's mum has taken to visiting in nightly dreams. In these, they are sometimes together in Charlie and Neil's garden, her mother wearing the printed green and pink dress that was her favourite. In the good dreams they garden in comfortable silence, pinching dead leaves from trees and collecting apples. If the dream becomes a nightmare, lightning strikes the tree and splits it in half and Charlie's mum screams a scream that turns into wailing sirens.

A month passes, and Charlie does not visit Neil. Her dad stops volunteering to drive her. She returns the wedding presents that arrive in a van from John Lewis, Vicky helping her. Vicky doesn't think Charlie should have anything more to do with Neil; she is an estate agent, wants Charlie to sell the house for 'a great price' so she can get a 'lovely, bijou, city centre flat', the kind that Vicky herself lives in.

Charlie tries multiple things to take her mind off her non-wedding; off Neil. These include meditation, yoga, pilates, life-drawing, even tree carving with an artist with long mahogany hair who wears free-flowing tops and big hoop earrings and cuts pictures of dancers into her bark: Charlie cuts an apple with a gargoyle grimace into hers ('Wonderful,' the free-flowing woman says, slightly sceptically Charlie thinks). Charlie wants her mum to turn up to the tree carving session and laugh, as surely she would have done in real life, but she doesn't, and when she tells Vicky about it over artisan coffee her friend nods and turns the conversation back to house prices ('It's a seller's market, Char.') She doesn't tell her dad, because her frenetic flurry of activities would worry him. It shouldn't, really, because Charlie knows she is okay. This isn't the same as the shambling grief for her mother, which always had a stain on its shoulder, unkempt hair and holes in its clothes; this is sharper, more up-tempo, a running away from thoughts clad in Lycra.

Charlie does feel bad about Neil, who probably cannot carve on trees to help free his negative energy. She knows he wants to see her, receives his visiting requests and letters regularly. All go unopened into a drawer. Charlie knows she should feel guilty about this but there is usually only a vague sadness, apart from the times that she sees something of Neil's – a sock at the bottom of the wash basket, the salt and vinegar crisps he loves at the back of a cupboard, an airline boarding pass from when they went to Malta acting as a bookmark – and is destabilised.

She spends a lot of time in her garden, staring up at the dead and living stars and wondering if her mother is watching, if up there is where heaven is. She wishes her mother was as alive as Charlie's grief, and she wonders whether Neil gets to see stars.

'Why are you so angry with him?' her dad asks, reclining on Charlie's new metal garden furniture with an aperol spritz.

'He lied,' Charlie says to the apple tree. 'And he caused mayhem.'

'It's not because you didn't manage to get married?'

'That was probably for the best.'

'I wonder,' says her dad, 'whether it was because he turned out not to know you after all. Or at least, not as well as you thought. Not as well as a parent would. Because you know, no lover will ever know you as well as a parent would.'

'I don't know what you mean,' Charlie says, although she knows exactly what he means. And he is right. 'Will you tell me about the time you were in prison, Dad?'

'It wasn't me who was in prison, I was visiting Sylvia.'

'No way – Mum? She was in prison? For what?'

'Oh, nothing bad. She was in a CND demo – a protest. Ban the Bomb. You know how she was, always supporting some cause. She and her friends wanted to get arrested, so they could raise the profile of their case. She spent a week in prison.'

'How do I not remember that?' Charlie asks.

'You were only eight at the time. I didn't take you to visit her, she didn't want you to see her there. I remember when she came out, she slept almost all weekend. It was impossible to sleep in gaol, she said. Too much screaming and crying.'

'I had no idea.'

'You would have been upset, or scared. You were such a sensitive little girl. So imaginative, always having nightmares and night terrors, but creative with it.'

'I would have been proud of Mum, if I'd known. Did she not want to tell me later?'

'I don't know, love.'

'Dad,' Charlie says, 'I've never asked before, but – have you visited Neil?'

Her dad looks away.

'It's alright, if you have. I'd like to know he's having visitors, strange as that sounds.'

'His own family haven't forgiven him,' her dad says. 'They're embarrassed, I suppose. I just don't want him to be alone there. He was so good when Sylvia died. And he really does feel so bad about what he did, love.'

Charlie looks away from his blinding gaze.

'I don't want to tell you what to do, Charlie,' her dad says. 'But Neil needs to know, at some point, whether it's over for good. I think you do as well.'

The wind clenches its fingers around the doors and windows and the apple tree shakes. There is a nebulous sense of impending rain. Charlie eats one of her apples, which she has been storing. It is meaty and aromatic, the flesh snowy white. She considers making something with the apples, but she never bakes. That was her mother's domain. Neil liked cakes, but always shop-bought them. What would she do with whatever she baked, eat it all herself? She could invite someone over to share it, her dad or Vicky, but her dad has high cholesterol and isn't meant to eat cake and Vicky is always slimming. Still, Charlie flicks through the recipe books that were her mother's, the pages stuck together and stained, 'Sylvia Smith' scrawled on the flyleafs.

Charlie can't decide what to bake, whether to bake. It feels like an insurmountable problem. She goes to the fridge, takes out a bottle of wine and pours herself a large glass.

Soon, the air is brittle and fragrant with apples and wine and Charlie, who has only eaten toast and soup all day, is feeling hazy.

The doorbell rings, then rings again. Charlie peers out and sees little kids, dressed as ghouls and witches and Harry Potter, holding buckets. She had forgotten about Halloween. She was sure that people weren't supposed to come trick or treating anymore unless the house had been decorated to show this was welcome. Then she remembered what happened last year: the child next-door put a lit pumpkin in her living room window and, due to it being a terrace, people mistook her house for Charlie and Neil's; Neil ran to the Co-op and bought bags of chocolates to hand out.

Charlie has nothing to give but apples, and doesn't want to go to the Co-op. She ignores the doorbell and takes the wine to the living room. By ten o'clock, she has got through a series of *Lucifer* and one-and-a-half bottles of Sauvignon Blanc.

'You shouldn't drink so much on your own, sweetheart.'

Her mum stands in the doorway, wearing the printed dress. Her skin is moon-white.

'Yes, Mum. I'm going up to sleep it off now.'

'I never went to bed without doing the washing-up,' her mum says reprovingly.

'Ah, it was always Neil's job,' Charlie says. 'Sometimes I forget he's not here. I'll do it in the morning, anyway.'

'Get to bed,' her mum tells her. 'I'll sort it out.'

'Ghosts can wash-up?'

'I'm Mum first, ghost second.'

'What was prison like, Mum?'

'The worst thing was being away from you and your dad. Now, get your beauty sleep.'

Late the next morning Charlie, head heavy on her neck and mouth furred, draws apart her curtains. It looks as though it is a warm day, the clouds cuddled in the arms of the sky.

She remembers the night before. Surely her mother can't have done the washing-up. There are ghosts, and there is madness. Her dad would say she needs therapy, after what she has gone through, and she does.

Taking a deep breath, Charlie puts on her dressing gown, wraps it tight around herself, and descends the stairs.

The kitchen smells of sugar and apples. It is spotless, with no sign of the dirty pots that Charlie left beside and in the sink. Everything is in its correct place, including the empty wine bottle in the outside green glass-recycling box.

'Oh, Mum.'

Tears spring to Charlie's eyes. She thinks of what her dad – Vicky – anyone – would say: you were drunk; you would have done the washing-up before you went to bed and forgot about it.

Then she notices something else. A serving dish with a clean, white-as-milk tea towel covering it. Charlie takes off the cloth. Beneath lies an apple crumble.

She leans against the counter; she weeps.

'Charlie, how lovely,' says her could-have-been-mother-in-law. Norma has dyed ash-blonde hair and seems to wear all her jewellery at once.

For a moment, Charlie doesn't know what to say. She should have planned this better. She has never been alone with Norma for longer than ten minutes.

'I'm afraid I was just going out,' Norma says. 'Is there something I can do for you?'

'I brought you an apple crumble, Norma. It's home-made, the apples are from the tree in my – in our – garden.'

Norma looks surprised, unsurprisingly. Charlie hands over the dish.

'How kind, Charlie. I didn't know you baked.'

Charlie is tempted to say that the dessert was made by her dead mother, but doesn't want Norma to think she's insane, especially as she's wondering this herself. She had driven the two miles to the house with the crumble a silent passenger next to her, looking over to check that it hadn't dematerialised at every red light.

'I thought I'd give it a try,' Charlie says. 'It turned out quite well. Also, I wanted a quick word, but I can come back.'

Norma puts down the crumble as if she is laying down a baby.

'I can be ten minutes late. Just off to a coffee morning – Amnesty.'

'Right,' Charlie says, knowing nothing about what Norma does in her spare time. Neil hadn't talked about his parents often. She assumes Amnesty is Amnesty International, and the thought of *Daily Mail*-reading Norma being involved in humanitarian work is so unlikely she smiles.

'Come into the drawing room,' Norma says.

The smell of lavender air freshener wraps silkily around Charlie as she follows Norma into a normal-sized sitting room. There are bay windows stuffed with framed photos of Neil's siblings' children, white pillar candles and white fake flowers, a fireplace filled with pine cones. No books. Charlie has sat in the room a few times before, the last time being when she and Neil had told his parents about their engagement. They had all sat very upright and drank small glasses of sweet wine. The conversation had been stilted. On leaving, Charlie felt her soul exhaling.

'I'm here to talk about Neil,' Charlie says, sat on the white leather sofa facing the window.

'Yes, I thought you might be. How is he?'

'I haven't seen him, Norma. I think you haven't either?'

There is a silence.

'It's difficult to forgive him, Charlie,' says Norma at last. 'It was so mortifying, what he did, and then the court case – we paid for his lawyer, and that meant we couldn't afford a summer holiday. And now everyone knows he's in jail....'

'Sure, I get that it's embarrassing, but... he's your son. He needs you.'

'He's your fiancée,' Norma snaps, 'but you don't see Peter and me coming to your house to lecture you on your duty.'

'You're absolutely right,' Charlie says, although she doesn't believe this. If she is ever a mother, she will never abandon her child. Who cares what Norma's snobbish friends think?

'But I am going to see him, Norma. And when I do, I'm going to tell him our relationship is over. I should have done that long ago; we weren't right for each other and I should have ended it before. He deserves someone who loves him as much as he loves them. He's a forgetful, impetuous, frankly rather stupid man but he's got a good heart.'

Norma is staring.

'What I'm asking, Norma, is whether you'll visit him so that he knows there is someone who loves him. Unconditionally loves him.'

'Well, I don't know that he'd want to see me.' Norma's voice is quiet. 'He must feel that his father and I have let him down.'

Charlie rises, the leather giving a soft whuft: a noise of approval, she fancies.

'Oh, he will want to see you,' she says.

Inaccrochable

April 2020

Confettied by cherry blossom, I wait for his call. He would laugh at the self-created romantic picture, I think. How I miss that laugh.

Every evening for the past month, my lover has rung between six and ten past six. I save my once-permitted daily exercise for this time. He is always finishing a run, panting when he says hello.

For the past half an hour, I have stared at my mute phone. How much longer? It was hot when I left, this spring's weather matching the hyperbole of global events, but the sky is chilling. No-one has passed by for a while. I should go home. I should, yet it seems like a bad omen to do so.

October 2019

The road stretches on, naked as paper. The mountains are behind, the village ahead. I hope I have the energy to reach it.

A man is coming towards me, carrying a newspaper. Joe: a writer of historical novels, short stories and poems. He is on the retreat too. At the embarrassing introductions, going round in a circle, Joe said he had won first prize in the short story competition in which I had come second; our prizes were places on the retreat. When he sat at my dinner table, I felt shy of him: the 'real' author.

Then I noticed his twinkling eyes and how he listened intently, as if he really cared about what people said. He made everyone laugh, too, in that over-the-top way of recent acquaintance combined with alcohol. Even when he was silent, my eyes strayed to his face, as if to a TV in a waiting room; they also strayed to his fourth finger: bare.

Now, I stand still as Joe moves towards me. He isn't conventionally attractive: too thin, nose too long, chin jutting, but his dark eyes are beautiful. When he sees me, there is a flash of recognition followed by the instant light of his smile. He says he has been to the village to get the papers. I ask what the village is like. My head is filled with thatched, wisteria-coated cottages and mock-Tudor pubs with horse brasses hanging from low, dark-wood ceiling beams. Joe laughs and says he saw a mock-Tudor McDonalds, a Spar where he got the papers and a posh hotel with Gothic windows. I scrabble around for something else to ask, but he beats me to it.

'Are you enjoying the retreat, Juliette?'

'Of course, I'm so lucky to be here.'

It's true and it's not true. I am lucky to be here, at this highly-regarded retreat centre where a week's stay would normally be more than I could afford. The tutors are knowledgeable and enthusiastic; most of the other writers are interesting and friendly. The Grade Two-listed building we're staying in has the perfectly symmetrical pale face of a nineteenth century heroine. There are views of Snowdonia from the windows. It is a place to write sonnets and ghazals in. Yet it hasn't ignited my creativity. Weaving together a story has been as impossible as weaving together a rainbow. I haven't created even one phrase that glows, and tomorrow is the last day.

'You know what Ernest Hemingway said?' Joe says. '"If I started to write elaborately, I would cut that scrollwork or ornament out and throw it away and start with the first true declarative sentence I had written." You've probably written some great stuff; you just may not realise it.'

'Hemingway also said, "You shouldn't write if you can't write."'

I laugh, self-deprecatingly; Joe doesn't. He can write: properly, professionally, not one fluke story. There is a silence, and I smile in preparation for us moving in our separate directions.

'Have you been to North Wales before?' Joe sounds as if he really wants to know.

I tell the story of a family holiday to Gwynedd, when I was ten. In the days before TripAdvisor, my parents were told about a farm BnB; we spent seven hours driving there, including the hour of being lost; it was so filthy my parents refused to stay; they went to accost the owner, who was hiding in the pig sheds; we got our money back; found a village pub that rented rooms; it was too noisy to sleep; we drove back in the morning; our next holiday was three years' later. In my memory, it isn't really a funny story. Joe transforms it, throwing his head back as he laughs.

'I booked a holiday in Berlin, once – always wanted to go,' he says. 'But I accidentally chose a youth hostel; sharing a room with four Swedish backpackers.

My wife didn't speak to me until day four. Years later, she loves telling that story about her dumb husband.'

Why did I think that because he wasn't wearing a ring, he wasn't married? Not all men did; my ex-husband hadn't.

'Couldn't you find somewhere else to stay?' My smile strains my cheeks.

'Waste of money,' he says brusquely.

Have I displeased him? Did I sound too much like a wife; like his wife? I try to rectify the situation. 'Do you have kids, Joe?'

Joe beams. Olivia and Kirsty are nineteen and sixteen. Olivia is at Cambridge studying English; Kirsty is at a college in Manchester, where they live, taking GCSEs this year. I say that my own daughter is seventeen, in the first year of her A-level studies; we live in London. Joe asks my daughter's name.

'Safie,' I say, 'after....'

'After the woman in *Frankenstein* who makes the monster want to read books. That's a brilliant name.'

No-one has guessed why I called Safie that before. I had tried to tell Stephen, her father, but he hadn't been interested.

'Maria chose our daughters' names – she said she'd done the hard work, it was only fair.'

Joe has mentioned his wife twice now. Maria: surely a Spanish senorita, flowing dark hair, Mediterranean complexion. Very different to me, with my lily-white skin and dyed blonde hair; an English daisy rather than a rose.

'Fancy finding a bench and reading these papers together, Juliette?'

We won't be missed at the centre; when workshops aren't on, the writers scurry away with tablets, notepads and pens, scribbling as if under timed conditions. I envy their ability to whisk together words. 'Write a thousand words a day,' one of the workshop tutors prescribed: full of daily good intentions, I take up my flowery notebook, find solitude, fail to concoct a story and snooze in the flat August sunshine.

Joe and I sit on a nearby bench. On my right is Snowdonia with its centuries of secrets; on my left a man I want to know more about. It's so peaceful, just us and the birds writing invisible stories across the sky.

'Which section would you like, Juliette?' Joe asks.

It is *The Sunday Times*, a paper I haven't read since Stephen moved out. My preference would be *Style*, but I don't want to appear vain and vapid.

'*Culture*, please.'

'Great, then I can have *Style*.' Joe grins.

This man will always surprise me. Always? The only time I will see him again after the retreat will be in print.

That evening, I walk into the deep silence of the centre's library and Joe is there with his laptop. We smile. I look down at my notepad. The nothing on the pages no longer seems like an absence. It is potential. By the end of the day, I have created a romantic short story. Tomorrow, it may feel superficial and inadequate: at the moment, it is lit pink with promise.

One week later

The silence is split by a message notification. Probably Safie. She likes to text from upstairs to request her mother-slave gets something, makes something, does something. For Safie, all my creations are for her. I try to remember selfishness is normal; she is more sensible and less easily led than me as a teenager.

I don't look at the message straight away; I am editing a journal article for an academic in Taiwan. Seven thousand words about emoticons in retail marketing. The concept, as well as the tortuous syntax, makes me wish I had charged more. Although my freelance work pays little, I am financially stable as Stephen paid off the mortgage and gives me plenty of money for Safie. Considering how he hurt her, she deserves all of it and more. I work so that I can get her things with my money, and so I can fill my time.

An hour later, I remember the message. I don't recognise the number.

Juliette, hi! Am coming to London next Tuesday, fancy a coffee? Joe x

My heart pounds: stupid, it's just a message from a nice man. A nice, talented, beautiful-eyed man. A man who typed a kiss in the message, a cross marking my place in his mind. All the writers swapped numbers at the end of the retreat but I hadn't expected to hear from anyone. Although I am thrilled to get Joe's text, I know I 'should not go there' as Safie would say. Married men are off-limits. I have been the cheated-upon myself.

And yet, my head spins with *Joe x*. Men don't ask women out for coffee with no agenda. Or do they? Despite my romantic short stories – 'write about what you want' rather than 'what you know' could be my motto – I know little about erotic love; Stephen and I were childhood sweethearts who lasted nearly thirty years before he left me for a woman at work. I tried online dating, as friends advised, met pleasant men who bored me, insincere men who pursued me, and one attractive man who announced over steak and chips that he believed in polygamy.

It seems rude not to reply to Joe. Fifteen minutes later, I have twisted words into place with the same effort used to turn Safie's rebelliously curly hair into neat French plaits when she was at primary school.

Joe, how lovely to hear from you. Afraid I'm busy on Tuesday, but hope to see you another time. Juliette x

The single grey tick doubles and becomes bright blue, like a science experiment. He has read it straight away. I keep watching for 'Joe is typing' to appear. It doesn't. Have I misunderstood? Perhaps coffee did mean a beverage and not 'coffee' with its languorous vowels stuffed with desire. How arrogant to assume that he fancies – a silly, puff-pastry word – me. He's forty-seven; a professional writer. I am fifty; an amateur. He has a gorgeous, passionate wife and two clever children. My own child would be appalled if I became involved with a married man. Or so I assume, it's not like I can ask.

A jaunty beep from my phone. Safie wants a cup of tea.

I spend the evening googling Joe, and reading his work online. His style is a bit like Hemingway's: broad brushstrokes, a lot of action and few decorative flourishes, full of delightful twists and turns. I order his books from Amazon and read every review. When I have devoured everything, I get wearily up from the sofa and head for bed. By the time I turn my phone off at midnight, there has been no message from him. But in the morning there is a reply. *Definitely another time. Joe x*

November 2019

My heart in the gap between excitement and fear, I take another slug of wine. I have already got through half a glass.

    A hand on my back: I turn. Joe looks handsomer than I remembered, in a shirt the vibrant green of samphire. He kisses my cheek.

    'It's great to see you again, Juliette.'

    I can't stop smiling, joy has lodged in my veins.

    'How was your friend?' Joe asks, once he has ordered a flashing-red bottle of rioja. I prefer white wine, but don't mention it.

    'Annabelle's feeling better,' I say. 'She was very glad I could visit. I haven't seen her in so long, it was lovely to catch up.' Like all liars, I am giving too much information. I stop, slug more wine. The alcohol has gone to my head.

    'Have you eaten, Juliette? I can order bar snacks. The Hot Wings and mini-burgers are good.'

I had assumed he was vegan. The retreat only served vegan food and he'd been full of praise for the meals, requesting that Tim the chef email recipes. Unwise to assume where Joe is concerned: I think of his story about the hostel in Germany.

We order bar snacks; drink more wine. Joe's dark eyes sparkle. He asks questions about my writing, listening attentively to the answers. I tell him about coming third in another competition, with the story I started on the retreat. His praise and interest are flattering; my family and friends ask few questions about my writing.

I say no more about Annabelle with the broken leg. It is true that she seemed glad I had visited; it had been nice to catch up. But her skiing accident had not been the motivating factor for my trip north. After I had turned down Joe's coffee, the knowledge that I done the right thing vied with disappointment: disappointment won. I had to see him once more, to get these feelings out of my system. One meeting. I just had to engineer it.

And then, browsing Facebook, I saw a photo of Annabelle with her leg in a cast. She and I had lived together in London in our early twenties; she then married a quantity surveyor and moved to Whaley Bridge, and I married Stephen. I sent a message oozing sympathy for her accident and said that I would be in Manchester for a client meeting, would she like it if I visited? Yes please, she replied. I texted Joe: a good friend had sent an SOS call, did he fancy that coffee? Yes; or a drink (wink face) in Piccadilly before I caught my train home?

Now, the conversation and the alcohol are flowing, the non-vegan bar snacks have been eaten. I ask about Joe's writing. He's meant to be working on a novel but only wants to write poems. He is wondering what his agent will say if he gives up with the book.

'Maybe go on another retreat for inspiration?' I ask.

'I did bugger all on the last one,' Joe says. 'Couldn't concentrate.'

We look at each other, and the moment stretches. A new chapter has begun in our intimacy. He does fancy me, I realise, and of course I fancy him.

Then it is time to catch my train. I wonder, for a second, if Joe will ask me to stay: ridiculous.

The pub is above the station concourse; as we descend, I wobble slightly from the wine. The train's platform has not flashed-up on the departure board. Chivalrously, Joe waits until it does. I thank him for meeting me; stretch out my hand. He puts his arms around my back, and we are knotted together. There will be no way out of this for me, I understand. He has brought my body back to life.

December 2019

After Manchester, Joe and I fall into a routine of daily contact. He sends a long email at lunchtimes; evening is punctuated by his texts: both quickly become very personal. He describes his parents' messy divorce when he was a child, and how writing helped him to express how he felt about it; he sends drafts of the poems he is working on, which I praise fulsomely; and he writes about his children, including photos. I say how attractive they are, trying to work out how Maria looks from their faces and bodies. Sometimes she is fitted into a story – he and Kirsty were confined upstairs for a weekend while Maria was sanding the downstairs floorboards; at a dinner party, one of the guests gave Joe a tarot reading but Maria wouldn't have one. When I discover that Maria is Italian and a paediatric nurse, the myth I had created crumbles. She does seem passionate, but primarily about her job; 'It's everything to her', Joe writes: I can't discern his tone but assume he feels neglected. I wonder if she reads drafts of his poems; if she feels neglected herself. These jagged words I keep inside me. In my messages, I tell him about my writing, I'm trying to assemble a collection of stories; about Safie (I don't send photos); about nights out with friends; about articles I have edited. I am creating a portrait of a cultured and popular woman, someone who doesn't need anyone else in her life. I am aware this is simultaneously to attract him and to protect myself.

    Thoughts of sex with Joe circle in my mind like bats. It doesn't seem possible that it will happen; it doesn't seem possible that it won't, after being held in that way in Manchester. The fact that I have to keep him to myself grieves me, but I could confess to no-one. Safie has noticed I'm glued to my phone: I say I'm in regular contact with a group of writers from the retreat.

    And then Joe wins first prize in a poetry contest run by a London writing magazine. *Want to come to the prize-giving, Juliette?* I go straight online to buy a dress.

Alone in a draughty hall, I watch Joe leaning against a lectern and reading his award-winning villanelle. He does so rigidly, and I wonder if he is nervous or just not a good public reader. I want to give him a cuddle. At the end there is polite clapping and he looks relieved, sitting on a chair while the second-prize winner gets up for his turn. I loiter, glass of pricey cheap-tasting wine in hand.

When all the poems have been read, and the competition organiser has given a short speech about this year's exceptionally high standard of entries from thirty-one countries, all there is to do is drink and eat canapes. I am getting another glass of wine when Joe strides over to me.

'Oh Joe, congratulations—,'

'Come back to my hotel, Juliette.' He takes the wine glass out of my hand, puts it on a table.

I am longing to; I am terrified to. 'Shouldn't we get another drink here? Shouldn't you talk to a few more people?'

'I only invited you. And I don't want to talk to anyone else.'

I don't want to talk to anyone else – I want to live inside those words. We slip away, no-one seeming to notice. Outside, Joe grabs my hand and pulls me around a corner. My body is on fire. We stare at each other and then we are kissing, hungrily, desperately, like teenagers, on and on.

February 2020

Feeling like a teenager has its upsides and downsides. Life is bright-red, thrilling. Life is painful. The longing for Joe creates an unpleasant tugging in my chest, and has destroyed my sleep. I stop writing romances, possessing no language that will either fence in my own feelings or set them free. I take on fewer editing jobs. Instead I spend hours creating emails to Joe that are erudite, witty, original, sexy, and yet innocuous in case his wife happens upon them. Re-reading one, I recall Gertrude Stein's words to Hemingway: 'It's good... That's not the question at all. But it is *inaccrochable*. That means it is like a picture that a painter paints and then he cannot hang it when he has a show and nobody will buy it because they cannot hang it either.' All those words, skulking in email inboxes: *inaccrochable*.

Joe emails frequently: not always every day; he is busy, his agent pestering him for the novel. We speak often, when he is out of the house. We meet twice more: in a hotel in Manchester, in a hotel in London. The sex is good, but it is the intimacy that has hooked me; our words that are the tie. And then we part again and my heart aches more every time. How long this can go on, I don't know; surely it must change as all things do. Will his wife find out? If she is suspicious, Joe doesn't mention it. I feel sorry for her, but not enough to stop this.

Then one weekend, the stars are on our side. Safie stays for two nights at her dad's house; Maria takes the kids to her family in Rome. Joe comes to me from Friday until Sunday. He brings red lilies. I cook a lavish meal, and we drink two bottles of red wine. We tear off each other's clothes on the living room carpet, watched by the fragile lilies. Afterwards, as I am starting to unmoor into sleep, I feel a shifting and open my eyes to see Joe staring at me.

'I want to be with you, Juliette. All the time.'

'Joe, don't say things like that—'

'I mean it.'

I stand and move to the window, which has become a dark mirror. It is a windy evening, the trees sounding enraged.

'If we were together… how about the kids?'

I can't imagine Joe would want to upset his kids, and I don't want to be a wicked stepmother. I am in an easier position than him, being divorced, but I can't bear for my daughter to be hurt again. Safie could be happy for us, but what message does it send her if my relationship breaks up a marriage? I deliberately don't think about Maria.

'Our families will understand in time; people are resilient. But I'm not saying it has to happen now. Kirsty will have left home in two years, we can be together then.'

Perhaps it would work. Certainly, I adore Joe. Certainly, I will be lonely when Safie is at university, even though she has been blooming out of reach for the past few years. Then I realise that he hasn't mentioned coming to London; perhaps he is imagining me moving to Manchester. These are mere details, though; our love story is the most important thing.

March 2020

All of a sudden, a hole has been rent in the fabric of the world. The virus, the virus, all the news is the virus. Words shoved together for the first time – lockdown, self-isolation, the new normal – become omnipresent and omnipotent.

'I can't bear the thought of not seeing you for twelve weeks, Joe,' I tell him mournfully over the phone. I'm in the garden; he is in his garden office. I wonder how long we can go without being found out in what is repeatedly called an unprecedented time, but don't want to say that in case he suggests cooling it.

'It's a nightmare. Maria is so stressed,' he says. 'Scared we're all going to get the virus; scared the economy will collapse. She sees it first-hand at work, I get it, but it's driving me and the kids mad.'

I sympathise with Maria, who has been pulled over to work in the ICU at Manchester Royal Infirmary. But I don't want to be drawn into talking about her.

'How about us?' I say plaintively, childishly. 'Everything's changing.'

'Juliette, we'll speak every day,' Joe says, with a touch of impatience. 'You'll see: things will stay the same.'

But things have already changed. My body has a gravity it didn't before, I am more aware of its vulnerabilities. My dreams are vivid colours, and I am drinking more heavily than I have ever done. Everyone's life is at a standstill and this is bringing out the best and the worst in people. There are leaflets from people I have never met, offering to shop for anyone in the local area who is unable to get out. But my usually polite, considerate middle-aged neighbours are regularly shouting at each other; I hear them through the wall and over the fence. Safie is always in her bedroom, on Zoom; when she emerges, we frequently shout at each other too.

'Juliette, did you hear what I said?' Joe asks.

'Sorry, darling, the people next door are yelling, I'll go in a different room.'

'I'll go running every evening at six, I'll call you then. Nothing has to change.'

April 2020

It is seven in the evening, and I am still beneath the cherry blossom tree, listening to silence. Surely there is no need to worry, I keep telling myself; Joe will have lost or broken his phone, and it will not be an easy task to get it repaired or to acquire a new one. Perhaps it was stolen on his run.

Or, he has the virus. Or Maria is ill, and he is looking after her; or one of his daughters has come down with it. In every phone call, he says how hard it is at home. Maria is stressed; Olivia and Kirsty are unhappy they cannot take the exams they have worked so hard for, or see friends. Joe says how glad he is that I am not being neurotic.

Ten past seven. There are two other possibilities, I consider. Maria knows about us and has demanded Joe end the affair, or he has decided to finish it.

I feel like a half-erased book. If there is nothing left of us, I have to know. I have to know if I have created the idea of his love, if this has been my fiction. But how can I find out? Joe told me not to call or text during lockdown, the virus making Maria paranoid about everything. But in that case, he should have contacted me.

Hi Joe, how are you? Just checking in to make sure you're well and safe. Juliette.

No-one could be suspicious of something that anodyne. The tick doubles, stays grey. I walk slowly home.

Dinner is made, dinner is eaten. Everything tastes of dust. Safie stares at her tablet during the meal, and I am glad not to have to speak. Afterwards, she goes to her room and I sit at my PC and open my latest story. Yesterday, I was full of enthusiasm for it, keen to talk about it with Joe. Now, the characters seem rigid and lifeless. I close the screen; stare into space. Remember my first conversation with Joe. I have read all of Hemingway's thoughts on writing since; what comes to mind is how he would omit a piece's real ending to make the reader feel something more than they understand. Is this what Joe is doing? Will I never understand our ending, just feel the pain of it?

No: we have written this story together. I have to believe it will have an end, its lines emerging from nothing, its lovers leaping back to life.

The Cleaner

Carys attacks the master bedroom with a Henry hoover, tucks the sheets – 'hospital corners', her mother whispers from beyond the grave – and changes the pillowcases, one of which is streaked with what appears to be spray-tan. She also picks up a pair of frilly knickers and worries a stain on the carpet until two pairs of latex gloves are ruined. Then she takes two white towels from the ensuite and folds them into swans to go on the bed; she saw it done in a film about Japan and regards it as her special touch. It eats into her limited time but makes her clients feel special.

The kitchen is next. Deflating helium balloons bob, including an '18'. It must be for the daughter, Isla. She was 13 when Carys first came here. Carys was employed by an agency called Mrs Mop then.

Carys is blitzing the work-surfaces as the client, Morgana, appears. It's the first time she's seen her today: Carys was given a key after two years' weekly service. Morgana is wearing purple Lycra and carrying her iPhone in its glittery purple case. She looks tired, yellow skin under her eyes.

'I'm making coffee if you'd like one?' she asks.

Carys has a rule not to accept hot drinks from clients, so declines as she always does. Morgana turns on the coffee machine. Carys brushes away food scraps, takes the plastic and glass recycling to the bins outside, sweeps and bleaches the floor. Morgana drinks her cappuccino and talks about Isla's party at the weekend. Carys makes appropriate noises in response. Morgana is one of only a few clients who talk to her while she's working; she suspects the others hide, or pretend to be very busy at their laptops; but she has seen games of solitaire on the screens. Once, at the end of a shift, she passed a café and saw the client whose house she had been cleaning on their laptop.

Kitchen finished, Carys takes her cleaning supplies to the family bathroom. Morgana follows to the threshold.

'Hey,' she says, 'you're married?'

Carys starts; had she talked about her husband? She had a dream about him the night before and its cobwebs have clung to her all day. Then she follows Morgana's gaze to her ring finger; her hands are usually concealed by latex gloves but she'd just run out.

'Yes,' Carys says, 'married for fifteen years.'

Morgana doesn't need to know that her husband died three years ago, after the black tentacles of cancer latched onto him.

'Ahh, quite the stretch.'

Morgana wants to hear more; Carys doesn't want to say more.

After a pause, Morgana starts talking about her husband. Now that the lockdown rules have been lifted, he is in the office almost every day and out a lot in the evenings.

'It's like he doesn't want to spend time with us,' Morgana moans. 'I'm sure people aren't meant to go back to work full-time in offices even now.'

'I'm sure he's very busy,' Carys says meaninglessly.

She removes the plastic bag from the bin, stuffing the tissues that were on the floor into it. Her hands brush against a plastic stick. She shouldn't look, but she does. There are two pink lines on the stick. It could be a Covid test, but they usually have C and T on them. Morgana is looking at her phone, so hasn't noticed. Carys wonders whether to tell her about what might be a pregnancy test, but what if it is Morgana's rather than Isla's? Despite the amount of time she has spent listening to her client, she doesn't know how old she is: anywhere between thirty-five and forty-five.

Carys ties the handles of the bag and places it outside the bathroom. She washes her hands for twenty seconds, singing 'Happy Birthday' twice in her head. Then she sweeps up the hair on the floor, sluices water, scrubs sink-grime and tackles shower-mould. Morgana's phone rings, and she walks away to answer it.

In the hall, Carys feather-dusts photos of Isla at various ages. She sprays glass cleaner on the wedding photo of Morgana and her husband Al. In the photo, Morgana is wearing a surgical-white gown with a sweetheart neckline, which Carys knows was handmade in London, and clutches a bouquet of deep-red roses; Al wears a matching red tie and button-hole rose. Carys and her husband don't look like that in their one wedding photo. They married on a trip to Scotland, witnessed by two registry office staff, one of whom had taken the photo. She wore a pale blue dress, her husband a checked shirt. Their daughter was born nine months to the day later. Has she ever told Morgana she has a daughter? Clemmie is the same age as Isla; Carys cannot imagine her daughter with a baby.

Carys's final task is the living room. They have a cat the colour of Morgana's wedding dress, and Carys lint-rolls its hair off the sofa. She feels a pang of pain as she does it – her fingers are a bit arthritic now.

The four hours (plus ten minutes, which she won't be paid for) are up. Carys calls to Morgana that she is leaving; Morgana shouts goodbye from upstairs. The cat gives a sad-sounding *miaow*.

Carys wipes her sweaty face with a piece of kitchen roll, lugs her bucket and brushes to her car, and drives away. One more client to go, and then she can clean her own home.

As she drives down Morgana's road, she passes a car parked at the far end. She recognises the man on the driver's side from the wedding photo she has just dusted, but not the woman. They do not see her.

The Second Therapy Session

'Why are you in this relationship?' asks Julianne. For our second session, she is wearing a pink cardigan with her hair in a tight swollen bun, like the peonies about to burst into bloom in the yard outside. Around her neck is a crucifix on a thin chain.

'Lauren?' Julianne smiles. 'Why are you in this relationship with Paul?'

'Well, we have a cat and a flat.' I laugh at the rhyme, the only one who does.

'Is there anything else you'd like to add?' Julianne asks, as if I am on the witness stand. I suppose I am, but in comfier surroundings and with a smaller judge and jury.

'Did you ever hear about that tree that grew around a bike?' I ask. 'The bike was left beside a tree in 1914. Maybe by a soldier who went off to war. Over time, the tree treated it like a wound, scarring and scabbing its way around it until the bike was seven feet off the ground.'

Paul is staring at me.

'Are you the bike or the tree in this analogy, Lauren?' Julianne leans forward.

'It's just a metaphor for every long-term relationship. You grow around each other and become something different until you're mutually interdependent. I'm with Paul because I can't imagine not being with Paul.'

'I'm the bike,' Paul says.

'Can you tell Paul how you feel about him right now, Lauren?' Julianne asks. 'And Paul, I'd like you to listen until she has finished, maintaining eye contact. Lauren, remember we talked last week about not blaming or shaming, and working from the 'I' perspective.'

Paul and I had ignored that advice. In the first session, emotions flew and landed like small grenades. Neither of us had let the other talk uninterrupted, and at the end Julianne suggested this might be a central issue in our relationship. I hadn't needed to pay fifty pounds to hear that.

'I feel like he's going through the motions,' I say. 'Like he's only here because I blackmailed him into it. Also, he doesn't want sex any more—'

'You feel like he doesn't want sex any more—'

'He doesn't even want a conversation any more—'

'This is just bullshit, Lauren.' Paul cups his neck as if it's stuffed with the feelings I've been expelling.

'Paul, please listen to Lauren. You can have your say when she's finished.'

'If she ever is,' Paul mutters.

'He goes out with his mates every weekend, never makes a meal, never feeds the cat, doesn't remember our anniversary. I'm presuming you get the picture, Julianne.' Anger clings to me.

'You feel he's going through the motions.'

'He is going through the motions.'

'This is just bullshit, Lauren,' Paul says, as if this is a TV drama and the rewind button has been pressed.

'Whatever,' I say, like a child.

No one says anything. Time curls in on itself.

'Paul,' Julianne says, 'I'd be interested to hear from you. Why are you in this relationship, and how do you feel about Lauren right now?'

'That's two questions.'

Julianne does not respond. I stare at the vase of gentians on the table between us and her; the flowers smell of pain-relief medicine.

'Lauren's a great storyteller,' Paul says.

'I am?'

'You don't know that?'

'You've never said that.'

Paul sighs, as if my mendacity is a heavy rucksack strapped to his back. He looks at Julianne.

'Lauren has the ability to turn any mundane experience into a great story. Like, she'll be on the bus and a drunk person will sit next to her, and she'll tell me about it at home and it'll be the funniest thing ever rather than just an unpleasant experience. Then she'll go to the supermarket and forget her purse, and when she tells me about it later, I cry laughing.'

'That last one was actually traumatic,' I say, but I'm smiling. Then something occurs to me. 'Wait, is this a nice way of saying that I manipulate facts with language? So everything I'm saying here is a manipulation?'

'You're manipulating my words right now,' Paul says, and his rage scalds me. 'You could never take a compliment, could you?'

'How would you know; you so rarely pay me any.'

'We have to end there for today,' Julianne says hastily, 'but I'll see you next week. Until then, I'll set you homework. Every day, do something nice for the other. Just one small act: set the table if you normally let the other do it, for instance.'

'Thank you,' I say, standing up. Paul walks out of the room, biting his lower lip.

I open the curtains to an icing-sugar world; the cars and trees are Christmas-cake decorations.

'Snow!' I shriek. Paul opens his eyes and curses: 'It's the middle of the night, Lauren.'

'It's seven. Come on, Paul, let's go outside. You love the snow.'

When Paul looks at me, I see the truth, shining hard and white as ice. We are breaking up. Have already broken up; are just two people living in the same apartment. At least it'll save on therapy bills.

'Well, I'm going out,' I say.

After putting down food for the cat, curled-up tight in sleep, I wrap up in what Paul calls my duvet coat, slide into Ugg boots and gloves and open the front door. Breathtaking cold blows in. There is no one else in the street.

The snow is moist and packable, achingly cold even through gloves. I make three snowballs: one small, one medium and one large, rolling them one way and then the other as my dad taught me. A carrot for a nose, forks for arms, figs for coat buttons. My dad always added a scarf, the most colourful he could find. I don't have a colourful scarf.

Suddenly, tears flood my cheeks.

'Lauren.'

Paul is in the doorway, holding his bright-yellow scarf.

They Sang

Now

Lexi hears the singing as she is walking down the corridor. Gracie is in the lounge, alone. She is singing at full power, upper body and dangly pearl earrings in metronomic sway. Lexi recognises 'Ain't Gonna Let Nobody Turn Me Round' by the Dixie Hummingbirds.

'You've got a wonderful voice, Gracie,' Lexi says, clapping when the song has finished. 'You could have been a professional singer.'

Then she thinks: maybe Gracie was a professional singer, why not? She doesn't know much about the woman, who is relatively new to the care home, apart from that she is originally from the American South. How she ended up in Stratford, Lexi has no idea.

'Did you ever sing in public?' she asks.

Gracie raises her arms and starts 'Strange Fruit' by Billy Holliday. Her red cardigan slips down her waving arms. Lexi recalls nail varnish, 'Starlet', the same red as the cardigan. She wonders what happened to it; she hasn't worn nail varnish in years.

Another member of the group, Genevieve, who wears picture-postcard blue and smells of lavender water, enters pushing a walker. Gracie does not stop singing or acknowledge Genevieve, as she has not acknowledged Lexi.

Lexi helps Genevieve into a chair and asks how she is.

'I'm well, thank you, Alexia. How are you and your family?' As she speaks, Genevieve runs a hand along her hair, thinning with a slight curl at the end. She holds a white embroidered hankie in her other hand. The hankie reminds Lexi of her mum, who abhorred tissues.

Lexi tells Genevieve that she and her family are very well, thank you, and Genevieve smiles a regal smile.

'How are you, Alexia?' Genevieve asks again, blowing her nose with the hankie. 'And your family? I believe you have a husband and three daughters: quite a lot of mouths to feed.'

'It certainly is. We're all well, thank you.'

'I'm well, too.' Genevieve smiles again. 'Apart from a slight head cold. You know, my husband and my eldest daughter Sylvia are visiting today. Sylvia lives in Newcastle, works as a general practitioner. I'm hoping she can slip me something for this cold!'

Lexi knows Genevieve's husband and daughter are dead—Genevieve, aged ninety-two, is the last remaining member of her family. Lexi's husband is also dead, and two of her girls have flown the nest, leaving Kirsten at home, although she will soon be leaving for university.

'I hope you're not going to keep me too long here,' Genevieve adds. 'I have a lot of catching up to do with Ron and Sylvia. Catching up is what you young people say, isn't it?'

'It'll just be the usual half an hour session,' Lexi says, smiling.

A care home assistant, Clare, a blonde with a pink dip dye, brings in two patients, Alan and Alice. Now they are all here, the session can start. Lexi puts on one of the CDs she keeps at the home; they will listen to classical music, today: Bach first.

Alan nods off, the hat he always wears sliding to the angle of Chesterfield's crooked spire. He comes to, feet doing a nervous dance, then sinks back into slumber. Clare meets Lexi's eyes and gives a small smile, but Lexi does not return it. It's natural to find humour in such situations, necessary perhaps, but she wants Alan and the other elderly people to have their dignity.

'I don't want to listen to this boring old white man stuff,' Gracie announces. 'I want to sing, I'm gonna sing.'

Gracie sings 'Ain't Gonna Let Nobody Turn Me Round' again, drowning out Bach: 'I keep on a-walkin', keep on a-talkin', Marching on to freedom land.' She rocks from side to side in her armchair, hands moving as if combing the sounds.

'Gracie.' Clare is frowning, but Lexi shakes her head. This isn't a concert she's putting on, it's music therapy. She turns off Bach.

As Gracie launches into the next verse, Lexi notices Alice looking at her. Alice, the youngest of the group at seventy, always looks glamorous; today she's wearing a pale pink cinched-at-the-waist tea dress. Her eyes sparkle; she has chandelier eyes.

'Okay, Alice?' Lexi asks.

Alice opens and closes her mouth. No words come out. Lexi has never heard her speak: apparently, she has not done so for years.

It's clear that this will be a singing session. Lexi asks everyone, although she really means Gracie, to sing 'Bridge Over Troubled Water' if they know it.

'Ooh, I like that one,' Genevieve says.

Lexi lets Gracie lead the singing, keeping her own voice soft. Alice sways.

'Hello,' Alan says loudly, to the room at large.

Alice stretches out her hand and Lexi moves to take it. It is so soft and powdery it feels like dust, and there are blue road-maps of veins. Alice's diamond eyes bore into hers, as if she's trying to tell her something.

'She wants help standing, I think,' Clare says. 'Let's get you up, Alice, my love.'

Clare holds one hand and Lexi the other. Alice is fairy cake-light. Leaning close, Lexi thinks she hears her sing 'la la'.

'When you're down and out—' It's a baritone, Alan's. Genevieve is singing too, her 'water' long as hope. It is as if the door to a loft has been opened and the room inside is visible. The light changes from diaphanous grey to rose.

They sing the song once more, and then it's time to end the session.

'That was wonderful, all of you,' Lexi says, 'and thank you especially to Gracie for transforming the session.'

Gracie flops into a chair and closes her eyes. Perhaps she has understood what Lexi said, perhaps not.

Alice is still holding Lexi's hand. She says: 'You.'

'You? You like to sing?' Lexi hears herself elongating the syllables of the words; dislikes herself for talking to Alice as though she is a child. She has always sworn she will not do that.

Alice makes no response.

'You still do like singing, I think.' Lexi smiles at the woman. 'Do you have any requests for next week? I can play the piano or the guitar as well as sing, as you know.'

Alice's tongue works the inside of her cheek. The moment hangs by a thread: breaks.

After Clare has led Alice away, Lexi wonders if she was trying to say 'Thank you'.

Then

Three-part harmony fills the air. Gracie and her daughter Aliyah are singing with friends and strangers who now feel like friends; like family, even. They are doing it on the road outside the segregated school, sitting on mattresses brought from their houses, under a dreamy blue sky. Gracie had suggested the mattresses, concerned about Aliyah being tired. She had not wanted her to come on this protest, but she insisted.

'No one else to keep you in check, Mom,' she'd said.

Gracie knows that Aliyah is worried her mother will be the police's main target, for although she has not organised the event she is the songleader. She starts the songs, the people located within the music raise them into life. Gracie is a well-known singer locally; has recently done a concert with Mahalia Jackson. Aliyah is proud of her, and her father would have been, too, if he'd lived.

The group has been singing for two hours by the time the school tips out its children, who stare as they pass. Some of the mothers tug their children's hands to make them go faster, some join in the singing until they are out of sight. Teachers come out to watch.

As the sunset is dodging across Aliyah's hair, and they are singing 'This Little Light of Mine', the police come. They stomp their way into the protestors' voices, but do not stop the singing.

'Shut up or we take the mattresses,' a police officer calls.

Gracie grips Aliyah's wrist and sings: 'You can take my mattress you can take my mattress.'

After a few moments, her daughter joins in: 'Oh yeah, you can take my mattress you can take my mattress', and then they are all singing: 'You can take my mattress I'll keep my freedom, oh yeah...', a concert spiritual transfigured into an arranged concert spiritual.

'Disperse,' another officer, fingering his gun, shouts.

Gracie starts 'I Wish I Knew How It Would Feel to Be Free'.

'Stop that, or you're all going to the slammer,' yells another policeman.

Harriet, the event organiser, stands from her mattress; there is a beat from the arch of her foot. Gracie stands, candy-coloured skirt billowing outwards, and Aliyah stands next to her. Another person gets up and another and another and another. They link arms, beads threaded onto one string. They sing 'Ain't Gonna Let Nobody Turn Me Round'.

'Oh, I, keep on a-walkin', keep on a-talkin',' Gracie yells, gripping her daughter's hand. Aliyah is roaring out the words.

Gracie doesn't see what happens next, having closed her eyes as the music takes her to another place, but they snap open when Aliyah gasps. Harriet is on the ground, being beaten by a policeman. The singers try to tear the officer away from her, but he is too strong, too vicious.

And then Gracie hears 'We Shall Overcome', sung by Harriet as blows rain on her. They all join in, even as their voices shake, as Aliyah sobs; they sing louder and louder, and Gracie watches the policeman's fist bunch in mid-air and then drop away.

'You're all going to the jailhouse,' another officer says.

They sing as the police grip their shoulders; the brutality not able to move through the melodies. They sing in their cells, night dropping in fistfuls, and the men in another wing join in. They sing when their throats are parched from being denied water. The veery thrushes insist they carry on, and so they sing when, battered and bruised, they are finally freed.

Now

Carrying the good things that happened in the session in front of her, the way she carried her babies in a sling, Lexi sets off for the tube. The sun beats down, and she walks slowly and luxuriously, Gracie's strong voice playing on a loop in her mind.

Outside the station, a man plays a crumpled accordion; he gives a red-faced smile as Lexi puts coins into his hat. A police officer walks down the road towards them; Lexi wants to tell him not to move on the accordion player, but knows he won't listen.

She descends into the hot bowels of the earth and gives a pound to the busker sitting on the floor, who nods to thank her, not pausing in his acoustic rendition of No Doubt's 'Don't Speak', which Lexi remembers from her university days.

The Central Line westbound platform is a growing mass of bodies. Lexi weaves through the crowd, passing a couple locked in an embrace, stopping near young men whose talk is an indistinguishable roar. The tube takes six minutes to come, and there are no seats free. Lexi squashes in beside a man with music emitting tinnily from air pods, taking off her denim jacket. A woman coughs repeatedly.

There is an exodus at Oxford Circus, and Lexi helps a woman with a baby in a pushchair to get off. The baby looks at her, eyes decades older than them both.

By the time Lexi reaches home, there is a stick of sweat binding her clothes to her back. The front door has swollen in the heat and it takes a while to open it. It is not locked, so presumably Kirsten is home, she is meant to be on A-level study leave. She is probably not studying, being young enough to think she owns her days.

The stairs creak like a pair of lungs as Lexi climbs. Kirsten's door is shut. In her own room, she changes her clothes, looks in the mirror at her shiny face and smooths down hair that is more grey than ash-blonde these days. She gathers an armful of washing from the laundry basket, remembering when it was a daily chore, before Steve died and when all the children were at home. It seemed like a thankless task, at the time; now she misses that unrelenting busyness.

As the washing machine babbles and rumbles, and the kettle hisses for the cup of tea she always has when she gets home, and a motorbike buzzes somewhere, Lexi gets the leftovers from the fridge. While the microwave hums, she finds 'Ain't Gonna Let Nobody Turn Me Round' on Spotify.

The double doors clunk open.

'What's that music, Mum?' Kirsten pokes her head around the door.

Lexi tells her that a client sang it in a session today.

'It had such good results with all of them; I couldn't believe it.'

Lexi's heart hums as she watches Kirsten sucking up the music like a flower sucking up rain.

'Play it again,' her daughter says, and they sing together, getting louder and louder, not stopping even when their neighbour bangs on the wall.

Sam Szanto lives in Durham, England. Almost 50 of her stories and poems have been published/ listed in competitions. As well as her many published stories, in April 2022 she won the Shooter Flash Fiction Contest, was placed second in the 2022 Writer's Mastermind Short Story Contest, third in the 2021 Erewash Open Competition, second in the 2019 Doris Gooderson Competition and was also a winner in the 2020 Literary Taxidermy Competition. Her short story collection 'Courage' was a finalist in the 2021 St Lawrence Book Awards ('If No One Speaks' is a revised version of this). She won the 2020 Charroux Prize for Poetry and the First Writers International Poetry Prize, and her poetry has appeared in a number of international literary journals including 'The North'. When she's not writing, she looks after her young children and aged cat, hikes and practices her Tarot skills. Twitter: @sam_szanto

Acknowledgements

'If No One Speaks' was published by Writer's Mastermind in 2022
https://letsgetpublished.com/if-no-one-speaks-sam-szanto/

'Quiet Love' was published by Erewash Writers in 2021
https://erewashwriterscompetition.weebly.com/winning-entries-to-open-short-story-competition-2021.html

'125' was originally published in the 2020 Literary Taxidermy Short Story Competition Anthology by Regulus Press

'Letting Go' was published in the 2019 Wrekin Writers' anthology Chairman's Challenges

'A Good Boy' was published in 2022 by Fresher Press in Dark Circles

'The Yellow Circle' was published in 2021 online by Storgy https://storgy.com/tag/the-yellow-circle/ and in print in the 2021 Personal Bests Journal 3

'Making Memories' was published by Michael Terence Press in 2019 in The Forgotten

'The Thought of Death Sits Easy on the Man' was published by the Writer's Workout in 2022 in WayWords, Issue 5

'Phil in Real Life' was published in 2021 in Secret Attic #6

'Don't Refuse Me' was published in the Parracombe Prize Anthology 2020

'Inaccrochable' was published in 2020 by Storgy:
https://storgy.com/2020/12/16/inaccrochable-by-sam-szanto/

'The Cleaner' was published in 2022 by Shooter https://shooterlitmag.com/2022/04/11/the-cleaner/

Printed in Great Britain
by Amazon